Sounds Like Fun

About the author

Bryan Moriarty lives in London, where he moved from
Dublin to train as an actor. In addition to performing and
teaching, he has written and produced short films, plays
and a web series. *Sounds Like Fun* is his first novel.

Sounds Like Fun

BRYAN MORIARTY

HODDER

First published in Great Britain in 2023 by Hodder & Stoughton
An Hachette UK company

This paperback edition published in 2023

1

A CIP catalogue record for this title is available from the British Library

Paperback ISBN 978 1 529 39348 4
eBook ISBN 978 1 529 39349 1

Typeset in Plantin Light by Manipal Technologies Limited

Printed and bound in Great Britain by Clays Ltd, Elcograf S.p.A.

Hodder & Stoughton policy is to use papers that are natural, renewable
and recyclable products and made from wood grown in sustainable forests.
The logging and manufacturing processes are expected to conform to the
environmental regulations of the country of origin.

Hodder & Stoughton Ltd
Carmelite House
50 Victoria Embankment
London EC4Y 0DZ

www.hodder.co.uk

Sounds Like Fun

Chapter One

By the time I spotted the pothole, it was too late to change direction or pull on the brakes, so as the front wheel of my bike buckled and I was catapulted over the handlebars, all I could do was shut my eyes and hope the impact wouldn't be too bad.

Strangely, I heard myself hitting the footpath more than I felt it. There was a dull *whump* as I landed on my right arm, followed by the hiss of my helmet scraping across the concrete, and my own strangled moan as I came to a stop and rolled onto my back.

I lay there for a few seconds, breathing through the pain in the shoulder I had landed on and cursing myself for not paying attention to the road. I had been craning my neck to read a street sign, trying to remember my way to the pub where I was meeting Rich and his friends, and hadn't noticed the small, vicious hollow lurking in the shadow of the kerb.

I heard the blast of a car horn and looked up, dazed, to see a man gesturing violently to my bike, which was blocking his way. As I sat up, a jogger skipped over my outstretched legs and sprinted away, clearly determined not to let this whimpering heap affect their average speed.

Typical London, I thought.

I raised one hand to the driver and mouthed, 'Sorry,' but that seemed only to aggravate him further. He began flailing his arms around with such force that I worried he'd put a fist through his own windscreen. I hauled myself to my feet and dragged the bike towards the kerb. The driver scooted around me, lowered the window long enough to snarl something about keeping the fucking roads clear, and zoomed off in the direction of the traffic lights at the end of the road.

I propped the bike against a wall and pulled out my phone to call Rich. I felt guilty to be ringing with such a mood killer, especially since I was already running late and had only recently resolved to make more of an effort when seeing Rich's friends. Rich and I had been together for nearly six years, and it had started to bother me that I wasn't closer to the other people in his life.

'I'm after coming off the bike,' I told him, when he answered.

'Oh, shit! You okay?' he asked. I couldn't help feeling comforted by the concern in his voice.

'I'm grand,' I said, slowly rotating my shoulder to see if I could feel any damage. 'It was just a bit of a shock. And the bike's fucked.'

'Did you get doored again?' Rich asked.

This was an innocent question, but I prickled at his use of the word 'again'. Yes, I'd previously been knocked off my bike by a family of tourists getting out of a taxi, but that had been years ago, and it wasn't as if I went roaming the streets of London in search of car doors to collide with. In fact, considering how dangerous this city could be for cyclists, I thought it was impressive I hadn't come a cropper more often.

'It was a pothole,' I said.

'Big one?'

I looked over at the offending crater, which was about the size of a cereal bowl. 'Enormous,' I said.

'How far away are you?' Rich asked.

'Probably less than ten minutes on foot,' I said. 'I'll just need to figure out how to get the bike there, is the only thing.'

I waited for him to offer some help. He usually did. 'Any chance you could give me a hand?' I asked eventually, when it became clear he hadn't taken the hint.

'Oh, of course,' he said, his voice surprised but enthusiastic, as if I'd suggested a detour past an ice-cream shop on a long car journey. 'I'll come and find you … Eoin's fallen off his bike,' I heard him say to someone else, who made a sound of vague concern in response.

'Sorry,' I said to him. 'Thanks.'

'No worries, I'm on my way.'

I sent Rich my location, and turned to examine the bike. The shape of the front wheel made me nauseous. It reminded me of when, on a family holiday in Mayo, my elder sister Ciara had broken her arm so spectacularly, while showing me how to jump off a sand dune, that by the time our parents found us, she had passed out and I was throwing up at the sight of her mangled wrist.

Clearly the front wheel wasn't going to roll with a dent like that, so I lifted the bike by the handlebars and plodded off, the back wheel ticking softly as I went. I felt awful for damaging it so badly, betraying the faithful machine I used every day. I'd cycled everywhere I could in London ever since, six months after arriving, I had realised that doing so would be the best way to avoid the money-sapping torture of travelling on the Tube. My friend Jax had taken me to Brick Lane market, and haggled on my behalf for so long that the dealer eventually agreed to sell me a second-hand, almost-definitely-stolen bike for half the asking price if we would only piss off and leave him alone. The cycle home through central London, which Jax worried would be the last thing I ever did, felt like the first day of the rest of my life. Buying my current bike three years later had been a moment of pride that I imagined others must experience at the birth of a child, if your new child was twice as fast as the previous one and a gorgeous shade of pale green. I hated to see it so messed up by my own carelessness, and I almost welcomed it when, as penance for my sin, one of the pedals spun round and banged into my shin.

I reached the corner of the road and spotted Rich walking my way, the concern on his face contrasting with his generally relaxed appearance. He had let his hair grow out over the school holidays and, in the evening sunshine, the grey streaks in it looked like blond highlights. He was trim and weathered from all the time he'd spent swimming outdoors over the break, and it struck me for maybe the millionth time what a stumpy oddball I must seem beside him. He caught sight of me and picked up speed, his expression changing to one of suppressed amusement.

'What are you smiling at?' I asked, when he came within hearing distance, though as usual, I found his smirk infectious. Just the sight of him was enough to make me relax, and my injured shoulder spasmed as the tension left the muscles around it.

'You just look terribly hard done by,' Rich said. 'Like you're carrying the weight of the world on your shoulders.'

'Not quite,' I said. 'Just this stupid broken bike.'

I lowered the front wheel to the ground, and accepted Rich's kiss.

'So,' he said, checking his watch, 'there's a bike shop down the road. We could see if it's still open.'

He picked up the bike, which looked a lot lighter in his hands, and rested the crossbar on one shoulder.

'Careful of the oil,' I said. 'Your shirt, I mean.'

As always, Rich was dressed immaculately, in a white button-up that was just the right thread count for a summer's evening, sleeves folded carefully to just below his elbows.

'I'll keep an eye out,' he said. 'Come on.'

A car beeped, and I looked around, wondering if the driver I'd blocked had come back to yell at me again. But Rich was raising his free hand.

'Hello, Sandra!' he called to the flame-haired woman waving in our direction from her car. Sandra glanced at the traffic lights, which had just turned green, and mouthed, 'How's your mum?' as she released the handbrake. Rich gave a thumbs-up, and Sandra responded with a delighted toss of her head as she accelerated away.

It was something I could never get used to. Walking around this area of north London with Rich, the city somehow felt like a village, where every second person was ready to greet him.

'Who was that?' I asked.

'Oh, she used to run a yoga studio,' Rich said, 'back when they were still relatively rare. I worked there as a receptionist over the summer holidays one year.'

He made it sound so normal, this chance encounter and the sense of connection to the city that came with it, that I decided not to draw attention to how odd it felt to me.

Instead, I returned to my misfortune with the pothole, which grew in diameter and depth as I described it, emphasising that I'd been distracted by my eagerness to join Rich and his gang. I then moved on to my favourite rant: the state of London's cycle lanes, most of which, I argued, were purpose-built to eradicate as many cyclists as possible, and which left me searching health websites for the phrase 'bruised perineum' roughly once a year. Rich winced and laughed in all the right places, and I could feel my mood lifting the further we walked.

'I mean, it's not like Dublin was perfect for cyclists,' I said, as the bike shop came into view, 'but there, it felt more like neglect than design, you know?'

Rich didn't answer. He was waving to the bike mechanic, who was wheeling in some of the models he had out on display.

'Room for one more?' Rich called.

'Always.'

'Great.' Rich put down the bike and turned to me. 'Do you mind dealing with this? I'm going to run back to the pub.'

'Sure,' I said, 'but it won't take long.'

'No, but Danni and Shanice are leaving early, and I haven't seen them properly in ages.'

I was sure he'd seen his whole uni gang in the past month or so, which hardly counted as ages, but I thought it would be a bit petty to say as much. 'Of course,' I said instead. 'Sorry. I'll be there in a few minutes.'

Rich gave me a peck on the cheek and jogged up the road in the direction of the pub. I squinted against the evening sun and watched him go, another Londoner in a rush.

'Fuckin' hell, mate,' said the mechanic, who had caught sight of the front wheel. 'What did it ever do to you?'

I got to the pub about twenty minutes later, having dutifully nodded and sighed as I listened to all the ways I had been neglecting and mistreating my bike, and how it was really just as well I had wrecked the front wheel because the whole bloody thing was on the verge of falling apart, thanks to my feckless joyriding. I turned down the offer of a full-body service that would have cost me a month's rent and escaped with the promise of a new front wheel in a few days' time.

Rich and his group of friends (whom I had privately named the 'Member-Whens due to their insatiable appetite for anecdotes from their uni days) were gathered around a table by the front window of the pub. They were sitting in a shaft of evening sunlight so strong that Kev and Olga were obliged to shield their eyes with one hand to look at Shanice and Danni, who had their backs to the window. Rich's friend Andrew was at the head of the table, slumped in the high-backed armchair he always chose when we met at this pub.

He was the first to spot me and beckoned me over with a regal flick of the wrist.

Despite Rich's suggestion that they'd be leaving early, Danni and Shanice seemed in no rush. They were telling a story in their usual style, Danni prompting and annotating Shanice's narrative as she went. They had been friends since they were three, and had lived together since they were eighteen, so each of them was the world's leading expert on the other.

'And it wasn't just the fancy stuff he did,' Shanice was saying, as I dropped my backpack and squeezed Rich's shoulder to see if he wanted a drink. 'I mean, you know me, I prefer plain food, simple things.'

'Dry chicken and rice,' Danni reminded the table, and I wondered if I saw Olga glance at Kev, recalling that Shanice had brought her own meal to their wedding reception.

'But he also remembered *everything*,' Shanice continued. 'Like I mentioned that the clock in our kitchen was stopped.'

'We never really look at it,' Danni said. 'I just check my phone for the time.'

'And next time he came over, he'd brought me fresh batteries.'

'I saw them,' Danni added, just in case anyone claimed that such generosity was beyond belief.

'And then,' Shanice said, 'he goes AWOL for two weeks. I'm thinking, is his phone dead? Is *he* dead? So I—'

'He has a wife,' said Andrew, who had clearly had enough set-up and was ready for the twist.

'No, he does not,' said Danni, while Shanice reached for her goblet of gin and tonic.

'He has a husband,' said Olga.

Kev snorted into his drink.

I left them guessing and went to order. While waiting for the barman to notice me, I watched the group in a faded mirror hanging behind the bottles of spirits. Danni was still fielding guesses, while Shanice adjusted her glasses, preparing herself for the story's punchline. The rest of the table was leaning towards them. Only Rich was looking elsewhere, his head turned towards the bar. I waved at him through the mirror, but he seemed not to be looking at me.

When I returned to the table, the group was engaged in another guessing game.

'Three?' asked Olga.

Shanice shook her head.

'Not three,' said Danni.

'Twenty?' said Kev.

'Oh, come on,' snapped Shanice, with the annoyance of someone whose extraordinary answer has been spoiled.

'Six,' I said, pulling over a stool from the next table, unsure of what we were guessing.

There was a short pause as everyone looked at me properly for the first time.

'That's exactly right,' Danni said, with the understated panache of a daytime-quiz host.

I was delighted to have been able to contribute something to the conversation, and so soon after arriving. Between the age gap (Rich and his friends were all five or six years older than me) and my lack of insight into the experiences that bonded them together, I often found that when I was with them half an hour could pass without me saying anything. As a consequence, I would start to drink quicker than the rest of them, and the fear of blurting out something stupid in my drunkenness would make me even quieter.

'Six, including you?' Andrew asked Shanice.

'Six women, including me.'

'And did the rest of them know he was sleeping with five other women?' Olga asked.

'Two of them were living together,' Shanice said, 'so …' She shrugged and took a sip of her drink, while Danni tutted.

'Are you still seeing him?' Rich asked.

The table laughed, while Shanice placed one hand on her chest and winced.

'I'll take that as a no,' Rich said.

'Even if he hadn't *lied*,' Shanice said, 'which, by the way, he had been doing for nearly four months, I have no intention of being in someone's harem.'

'Well, polyamory is way more popular now,' Andrew said.

'Not with me,' Shanice said. 'It sounds like getting stuck in a house share for the rest of your life.'

Danni nodded, seeming relaxed enough about her own lifelong house share.

'Well, I wouldn't mind living in a house like that,' Andrew said, looking around the table with an 'Am I right, fellas?' expression. Rich caught my eye and grinned, perceiving, I guessed, my internal eye-roll.

'And on that enlightened note,' Shanice said, 'we'd better be going.'

She pushed away her drink, Danni knocked back hers, and the two wiggled out from behind the table.

'Sorry to miss you, Eoin,' Danni said, tapping me on the shoulder as she passed. 'Did you get your bike sorted?'

I opened my mouth to reply, but the pair were already waving goodbye to the rest of the group. In the brief pause that followed their exit, I noticed Kev giving Olga a swift kiss on the cheek, as if to reassure her that he didn't have any other wives he'd neglected to mention. I looked back to Rich, hoping for another private smile, but he was staring off towards the bar again. I turned to check that there wasn't a match on that I hadn't noticed, but there weren't any screens behind the bar, just a couple of staff members bobbing in and out of sight as they restocked the fridge.

Because I had arrived late, my drinking was out of sync with the rest of the group's, so when Andrew drained the last of his IPA and announced that he'd have to go, I still had two-thirds of a pint in front of me. Rich said he'd get one last drink to keep me company. I felt like I'd won a prize in a raffle. In return for seeing Rich's friends, I was being rewarded with a bonus mini-date, just me and Rich. I'd have to be up early to open the café – even earlier than usual, I remembered, because I wouldn't be cycling – but it would be worth it, I thought. Time with Rich was always worth it. He ruffled the hair on the back of my head as he returned to the table, and I smiled up at him.

'Were you here for Shanice's story?' he asked, as he sat down. I could hear the hint of a slur in his words.

'I caught the ending,' I said. 'Bit of a bombshell after seeing him for that long.'

'Well,' Rich said, clinking his glass against mine, 'I suppose you and I were seeing each other casually for a long while before we committed.'

'Sure,' I said, though I felt he was skipping a lot of our courtship in summing it up like that, 'but at the end of it, we were committing to one relationship each.'

The corners of Rich's mouth slid downwards into the expression of an unhappy clown, the face he always made when he disagreed with something but wasn't sure if he could be bothered arguing.

'By the way,' I said, leaning in, 'do you reckon Olga's pregnant?'

'What?'

'She was drinking tonic with no gin for the evening.'

'And?'

'And,' I said, 'when Kev went to the bar, I noticed he poured it into her glass while he was up there, which I think means she wanted to hide it.'

Rich laughed. 'Perhaps you're reading a little much into it. But, yeah,' he said, 'the Shanice thing, I take your point. That guy really was a bit two-faced about it all. I mean, I don't know if you were here for the bit when he suggested they go on holiday together?'

I shook my head. Rich and the others had picked over the story at length already, so why was he insisting on circling back to it?

'And I see what you mean,' he went on. 'If he had been honest and made sure everyone was aware of the situation, then maybe they'd all be happy with it.'

I didn't think I had made the point Rich was now agreeing with. Somewhere at the back of my head, muffled by the haze that descends after two and a half pints, an alarm bell began to ring. 'Maybe,' I said, 'although that's quite a big "if".'

'And,' Rich said, his gaze drifting into the middle distance, 'I suppose that polyamory, which was what he was suggesting, is one thing, but there are degrees as well.'

'Degrees,' I repeated. The alarm was growing louder, and I wanted to steer the conversation away from this subject but had no idea how. I looked at the glass in my hand, and briefly considered dropping it.

'Well,' Rich went on, 'for instance, one could have a relationship that was open, say, sexually, but was otherwise a loving, monogamous unit.'

Rich tended to adopt this abstract way of formulating sentences whenever he wanted to bring up something awkward, or something that was bothering him. If I suggested seeing a slasher movie he didn't fancy, he would start to muse aloud about the morality of the horror genre until I took the hint and suggested something else.

'Sure,' I said. 'One … *could* have that kind of relationship.'

Rich picked up his sunglasses from where they'd been resting on the table and began polishing them with a stray napkin. From the way he fumbled with the lenses, I could see that he was a bit drunk. I loved Rich in summer mode, when the careful, methodical side of him took a step back and was replaced by something a little more carefree, less controlled. He left the glasses on the table and looked at me from under his brow.

'Is it something you've ever done?' he asked.

'What?'

'An open relationship.'

I laughed. 'What do you think?' I asked.

Rich knew pretty much my entire romantic history and, given how brief it was, I felt it was obvious that I'd have mentioned something like an open relationship before.

'Is it something you'd be interested in?' he asked.

The alarm in my head stopped ringing, replaced by a deep, dark roar. I put down my glass and rested my hands on the table, attempting to tether myself to something solid and unbreakable.

'I've … I've literally never thought about it,' I said. 'Is it … Do you think it's something you'd be interested in?'

As soon as the words were out of my mouth, I realised they sounded more like an invitation than a question. Unlike Rich, I was no good at speaking in the abstract. Rich smiled in response, and with his mussed-up hair, his face shaded by the day's beard growth, he looked suddenly wolflike, almost dangerous. Despite the roaring in my ears, I felt a sudden urge to rip that beautiful, pristine shirt off him.

'I might be interested,' he said, his smile growing. 'It could be fun, I suppose.'

I didn't say anything, assuming the confusion and panic I felt would show on my face. I waited for Rich to laugh, to say he was only joking. I didn't particularly care whether or not he'd be telling the truth, I just wanted to hear him say it. But instead he trailed his hand across the table towards mine, and gently ran his middle finger across my knuckles. 'Maybe it's something we could try,' he said.

For the second time that evening, I felt as if the ground had opened up beneath me, and that I had been launched forward through space. I wondered if the landing would be as painful this time round.

Chapter Two

It was just after four, and the café was quiet enough for me to hide behind the coffee machine and message Jax. *Don't suppose you're free in a bit?* I wrote. *Could do with a chat.*

She rang me back three minutes later. Between us, sending the message 'Could do with a chat' was akin to scrawling 'EMERGENCY' in red paint on the other's bedroom window. The last time Jax told me she 'could do with a chat', she was convinced she had a tick bite on her leg and was in the latter stages of Lyme disease. It turned out to be an ingrown hair and trapped wind.

I ducked under the counter to answer her call. I noticed that some of the shelves down there were in serious need of a clean.

'What's wrong?' Jax asked. 'Are you okay?'

'I'm fine.' I traced my finger through a layer of dust and coffee grounds on the bottom shelf, and attempted to sound casual. 'It's just Rich.'

'Oh, no. Is he sick?'

'No, no, nothing like that.'

'You guys haven't …' Jax trailed off.

I felt a tiny sting of tears but blinked them away. 'Listen, I'm still at work,' I said. 'But I was wondering if you'd be around in a couple of hours.'

'I'm heading out at seven, but all I'm doing between now and then is whittling.'

Jax adopted a new craft roughly once a month, discarding it just as she was on the brink of mastery. I could arrive at her house expecting to view a new etching, and instead find her peering into the oven as a piece of pottery collapsed into a semi-solid lump.

'Well, I don't want to interrupt your work,' I said.

'I can listen while I whittle,' Jax reassured me.

I heard a soft cough, and looked up to see a bespectacled woman peering down at me, her eyebrows raised in an expression that said, 'I don't make scenes, but ...'

'Better run,' I said to Jax, and sprang from my hiding place.

'What can I get you?' I asked.

'Understaffed, are we?' the woman with the glasses replied, eyebrows still raised. I wondered if she was a teacher. If she was, she had the look nailed.

'Oh, understaffed, understocked, under-slept,' I said, as I moved to the tablet we used as a till and cleared the last order off the screen. I looked back at the customer and smiled, hoping I was coming across as weary yet cheerful, rather than bitter and arsey.

'A cappuccino, very dry, extra hot,' she said. 'And I found this on the way in.'

She handed me a card. I glanced at it while I tapped in her order. It was a gym pass, belonging to someone called James Howard, who was giving the camera a suspicious look and tilting his head slightly, as if the receptionist taking the photo had just made a lewd remark.

'Thanks for that,' I said, leaving it on a shelf under the till.

I rinsed my favourite jug and measured out the milk I'd need. During the morning rush, I found it hard to make a dry cappuccino that didn't resemble a milkshake after a child had blown bubbles into it. Now, though, I could concentrate on introducing air in sips and hisses just long enough to keep the milk looking like high-gloss paint.

'Oh, my,' said the teacher, when I brought the coffee over to her, giving me a twinkle that made me feel I'd got ten out of ten for my long-division homework. 'That's just lovely.'

It would be an hour before I could reasonably start to kick people out, so I decided to tackle a few of the grimy shelves under the counter. Rebecca, who owned the Quarter Turn Café, was due back from holiday that evening, and I wanted a head-start on the deep clean she would inevitably demand in the morning. I was also hoping that busying myself would keep my mind off Rich's proposition. I hadn't slept much the night before, and had compensated for that with an extra shot of coffee at lunchtime, in the hope it would perk me up. If anything, though, the caffeine had left me feeling even more exhausted, only now my muscles were twitchy, my shoulder was aching from yesterday's fall, and my elbows were knocking into every sharp corner and stray object they could find.

At half four, Hugo shuffled out from the back room we ambitiously referred to as the kitchen, equipped as it was with two microwaves, a panini grill and a single-ring hotplate. With this set-up, Hugo produced the café's limited menu, all the while shaking his head and muttering under his breath at the absurdity of it all.

'Finished,' he declared, and went to write his hours into the staffing book we kept beneath the till. This was how Hugo always ended his shift: at an hour of his own choosing, announced with a finality that dared you to contradict him.

I almost asked him to make sure the kitchen was clean for Rebecca's return, but as usual I lost my nerve and instead asked if he had any plans for the evening.

'Nah, man,' he said, with a leonine yawn. 'Gonna totally chill out tonight. It was a crazy service today, fucking ridiculous if you ask me.'

Hugo had made a total of four toasties at lunchtime. Two had been ordered at the same time, which had made him fling a tea-towel against the wall of his little kitchen, raging at the cruelty of a world in which a man had to produce such vast quantities of food for a gluttonous and unfeeling populace.

'Yeah, you should try to unwind,' I said. I was on my knees, wiping down the shelf where we kept takeaway boxes for the rare occasions when someone ordered a panini to go, a request that had previously left Hugo slumped in the emergency exit with his head in his hands.

'Hey,' he said, and nudged me with his foot. I looked up, and he smirked. 'Wanna see who's messaging me?'

'Not really,' I said.

'Look what she sent me last night,' he said, crouching next to me, bringing with him a powerful waft of body odour and cigarette breath.

I couldn't be sure why, but no matter how often I referenced my boyfriend in conversation, Hugo still seemed convinced that I was up for seeing nudes he had been sent by the women in his life. I couldn't fathom what it was about my uninterested reactions that made him keep doing it. Nor could I fathom what it was about this pudgy, volatile man that attracted such an endless parade of women to him. Perhaps, harrowing though I found it to picture this, he was great in bed, but how did he entice them there in the first place?

'What do you think?' he said. I looked briefly at the photo, then turned back to the shelf, at the back of which there was a pile of what looked worryingly like mouse droppings. I swept them out quickly, choosing not to think too deeply about what they were.

'You like?' he asked.

'Not really my thing, Hugo.'

'Sure, sure. She's coming over later, I think.'

He laughed and put his phone back into his pocket. I often envied people who could make themselves laugh so easily.

It must be like living in a cheap sitcom, with canned laughter punctuating every sentence.

'See you tomorrow, man,' he said, and left, still chuckling.

I closed the coffee machine early, not wanting to risk getting an order of four mochas at three minutes to five. This was exactly the kind of skiving Rebecca hated to see happening, but I'd been in since seven that morning, and I wanted more than anything to get to Jax's house. While I waited for the remaining punters to finish the dregs of their coffees and hit the road, I went to fold up the outdoor furniture, exchanging a wave with one of the staff in the chicken shop opposite as I stepped outside.

The Quarter Turn sat on the corner of an arterial road and a residential street lined with birch trees, which, as Rebecca liked to explain to anyone who would listen, was why all surfaces in the café were made of birch. I looked back inside as I folded a chair, trying to spot any disorder she might complain about on her return. She wouldn't be happy with the stray fingerprints on the windows, but otherwise the place looked fine.

Just before five, I flipped the sign on the door to Closed and turned to Trevor, our oldest customer, who was asleep by the window. His fourth cappuccino of the day sat, half drunk, in front of him.

'Will I put that in a takeaway cup for you, Trevor?' I said, loud enough to wake him.

'Yes, please, Eoin,' he said, without a moment's hesitation, as if he had been reading the paper instead of snoring softly. 'I'll take it home with me.'

I poured the sad, milky remains of his drink into a paper cup and brought it back to him, while he folded up his magazine and donned a purple fedora. Everything about Trevor was odd, from his wardrobe to his prodigious caffeine intake to his sporadic naps, which Rebecca complained made the café look like an opium den. But he was polite when he ordered, chatted with us when we were quiet, and left us alone when we were busy. For me, he was the perfect customer.

'What do you think your chances are tomorrow?' he asked, as I handed him his coffee, and my heart sank. In much the same way that Hugo was convinced I enjoyed inspecting his various girlfriends' breasts, Trevor held an unshakeable belief that I shared his passion for sport. He would often commiserate with me when 'my' team lost, never giving me quite enough information to figure out who my team were. The commiserations I could usually handle, but it was harder when he asked me for a prediction.

'Oh, I wouldn't be massively optimistic,' I ventured, adopting what I assumed was the pained expression of a long-suffering fan. Trevor nodded sagely and gathered up his things.

'I think you're right,' he said. 'Will you get the chance to watch the match?'

'Depends what it's like in here,' I replied, wondering if he'd at least drop a hint as to what sport we were discussing.

'Well, I hope you catch the highlights anyway,' he said.

'If you could even call them *highlights*,' I said, feeling proud when he chuckled at this. I idly wondered if Trevor had long since realised my ignorance and was now inventing sporting fixtures just to watch me squirm.

I locked the door behind him. Now that the café was empty, with only a playlist of acoustic covers filling the silence, I was faced once again with the image of Rich grinning as he trailed his finger across the back of my hand. I tried to put all my concentration into the cash-up, holding back any emotion until I got to Jax's house.

I heard a rap on the door, and looked up to see Al standing there, in his usual summer outfit of short-sleeved shirt, cargo shorts and sandals. He waved his keys and pointed to the lock, in which I'd left my own set. While Rebecca was away, Uncle Al (who might or might not have been Rebecca's uncle: I had never got to the bottom of their relationship) had been dropping in now and then to see that everything was in order. I could never tell what he was inspecting, but it didn't really matter. Al had a way of looking around a room, in total silence, then turning to me, still in total silence, which always made me feel that he must suspect me of a terrible crime. I called this look 'The Dad', or at least I did until I realised that not everyone's father fixed them with such an intimidating glare when asking how they were.

I opened the door and stood back as Al strolled past me, jangling his keys. The folds in his neck hung low and bounced gently off the top of his chest as he walked. The few grey hairs that remained on his head were greased and arranged in a swirl, while the darker, thicker tufts emerging from his ears and the collar of his shirt had been left to grow wild. My eyes watered from the scent of TCP that he left in his wake, and I snatched a gulp of fresh air as I locked the door behind him.

Al paused in the middle of the room, squinted at the ceiling and began cleaning out his ear with one of his keys. He nodded towards a lamp. 'Cobwebs,' he said. Sure enough, a fine gauze was wrapped around the exposed bulb. It looked quite pretty in its way.

'Well spotted,' I said, trying my best not to be intimidated by this inspection. I folded my arms and peered up at the ceiling. 'There's another one in the corner,' I said.

'Details,' said Al. I waited for more, but Al just wiped the waxy key on his shorts and got to work on his other ear. I returned to the counter and pulled up the end-of-day report on the tablet while Al continued to peer around the room. I began counting out the notes from the cash drawer. The card machine had packed it in earlier in the week, so we were only accepting cash until Rebecca could order another. Al sniffed loudly.

'How's the hay fever?' I asked.

'All right, son, not so bad this time of year.'

For a minute we were silent. I managed to get all the twenties and tens counted before he said: 'It's all about the details, y'know? The little things. Not saying you're slouching or anything. But ...' He took a sniff and continued: 'If I see a cobweb, then it stands to reason that a customer, he's going to see it, and unless he's easygoing like me, that might be enough to put him right off the place, yeah?'

I finished counting the stack of fives and wrote down the total for the notes. I used to engage with Al's rambling, but now I tended just to let him at it, making only the occasional affirmative noise, as if I was attending an interesting lecture series entitled 'Life Explained for Gobshites Like Eoin'.

'So you need to be looking round every day with fresh eyes,' Al said.

'True.'

'Fresh peepers.'

'Yeah.'

'What do you see?'

I didn't answer him. I had lost count of the pound coins and was starting again.

'What do you see,' Al repeated, 'when you walk in the door and look round? I'm asking.'

I resisted the urge to sigh. If Rebecca had to endure tedious thought experiments like this regularly, it was no surprise that she had taken off on an unexpected holiday for the past couple of weeks. Certainly, in the month leading up to her departure, I had noticed that she was increasingly agitated by Al, and once, in the middle of a morning rush, she had yelled at him to fuck off and stop skulking by the door. Everyone in the queue had gone quiet, no doubt as shocked as I was to see Rebecca, who was usually so self-possessed, lose the head like this. She had clearly needed a break. I just wished she had explained to Al that I didn't need any mentoring while she was gone. He was still waiting for my answer, and I decided that admitting defeat would be the quickest way through it.

'Sure that's just it, Al,' I said. 'I probably wouldn't see anything out of order. I don't notice details like you do.' Al didn't smile, but he gave a slight nod, liking what he heard, so I pressed on. 'I'd probably be looking at something else.'

'Or you'd be looking at your phone, no?' Al took his own phone from his pocket and mimed lots of swiping and texting. He was enjoying himself now.

'Exactly,' I said.

'Oh, yeah, everyone's on their phones, day in, day out.'

'Desperate.' I shook my head, happy that we'd finished dwelling on my inability to see cobwebs. I had only the silver coins to get through, and then I'd be done.

'How's Billy doing?' Al asked.

I counted the fifty-pence pieces into stacks of ten while contemplating my answer.

Billy, a baby-faced twenty-one-year-old, had been working at the café for three months and still didn't know what a flat white was, much less how to make one. He tended to stare vacantly out the window during service, humming softly to himself, while customers waved desperately at him to get his attention. He saved crumbs from wiping down the tables and fed them to pigeons on his break. He laughed merrily and shrugged his shoulders whenever a customer asked about allergens, often adding, 'What doesn't kill you only makes you stronger, eh?' He danced along with whatever music we had playing, even when that music was *The Best of Einaudi*. He dropped things, broke things and added, on average, forty-five minutes' labour to my day, every day he worked. What was more, Billy had left just before three today, with no notice and for reasons he would only describe to me as 'strictly business'.

But Billy was very sweet, and genuinely sorry when he made a mistake. And, crucially, he was a cousin of Rebecca's, and therefore (perhaps) a relation of Al's.

'Billy's doing well,' I said.

'Good, good,' said Al. He unfolded one of the chairs I had brought inside, pulled a pair of reading glasses from his shirt pocket and began texting, breathing deeply as his stubby thumbs tapped away at the screen.

'Can I get you anything, Al?' I asked.

'Nah, mate, we're all right.'

'I should be done in a minute.'

'Good, yeah.'

This was new. Usually Al's visits, though conducted at a glacial pace, had some momentum to them, as if he had somewhere better to be. Now, though, he looked as if he was settling in for the evening. The time I could spend at Jax's house before she had to leave was diminishing, so I concentrated on finishing the cash-up. There was a fifty-pence difference between the end-of-day report and the actual takings, but I decided it would do. I took the money and the tablet downstairs to the storage area, which was equipped with a desk, a safe, and a subterranean staff toilet so grim that we almost never used it. In contrast to the sparkling, minimalist café upstairs, the storage area was a chaotic mess that we just never seemed able to put in order.

I knelt to open the safe, then became aware of Al hovering behind me.

'All correct?' he asked.

'Fifty pence over,' I said.

'Details, innit?'

'I'll check with Billy tomorrow, he may remember how it happened,' I said. Billy had a better chance of reciting the Qur'an than he had of remembering such a thing, but Al seemed satisfied with that. Then, just as I opened the door to the safe, he said, 'Take a twenty for yourself, son. You've had a long day.'

There was something different about him now, the boring uncle buttonholing someone at a wedding replaced by someone more watchful and vaguely menacing. It brought to my mind a morning near the start of my time in the café, when I looked out the window to see Al grabbing another man by the front of his shirt, snarling in his face, and shoving him out of sight.

I paused, the bag of cash in my hand, then said, 'Ah, no, thanks, Al, but actually I got a few quid in tips today, so I'm grand for the moment.'

'You sure?' he asked. This was definitely a test.

'Ah, yeah,' I said. 'Sure, listen, the last thing Rebecca needs on her first day back is a float she can't make head nor tail of.' I was doing what I often did when I felt intimidated, making my accent stronger, hiding behind the Irish lilt in the hope that my nation's reputation for being sound, likeable people would protect me.

It must have worked, because Al smiled. 'Fair enough, son.'

I jumped to my feet and said, 'Right, all done. I'll lock up unless you want to.' I climbed back up the stairs, where my jacket was hanging on a hat-stand near the door. I grabbed it, trying to get out as fast as possible without breaking into an actual run.

Al emerged from downstairs. 'I'll lock up, son,' he said. 'You look like you're in a hurry.'

'Cheers, Al. I'm just heading over to a mate's house.'

'Well, have a pleasant evening, young man. Anything I need to do before I lock the door?'

'Just flick off the lights. Oh, and then the shutters outside. Do you want me to do that?'

'No, no, you've done plenty, on you go, son.'

I yanked open the door and scampered off in the direction of the bus stop. I glanced over my shoulder as I went. Through the window, I could see Al standing with his hands flat against the door frame, his head bowed. As I watched, he sighed heavily, and I momentarily worried that he was about to come after me to complain about another cobweb he'd spotted. But then he pushed himself away from the door and strode back into the gloom of the empty café.

Chapter Three

'At last,' said Jax, as she opened the door. 'I was beginning to think you'd fallen off the bike.'

'That was yesterday,' I said. 'Thanks for having me over.'

'Don't be ridiculous,' she said. 'Come in.'

Jax was one of five people I'd shared a house with when I first came to London. It was a crusty old heap of a place with lino floors curling up in the corners, but the fact that so many of us lived together meant there was always someone around, a relief in a city as massive and unwelcoming as London had seemed to me when I first moved over. In the evenings, Jax and I would sit at the kitchen table (the living room of the house was occupied by Tony, a failed Australian rugby player) and bond over a shared love of *Murder, She Wrote* and agony-aunt columns. The first time I actually felt happy in London was when Jax and I spent several hours composing a reply to a question in the paper about how someone should tell her new husband that she no longer loved him. Jax had been so sure of her answer, so pragmatic in her outlook – 'She needs to tell him now, because he's not going to thank her for stringing it out' – that she soon became the first person I would turn to for advice. She seemed supremely worldly to me, and brought a weary familiarity to even the oddest questions of love and life. 'Oh, yeah,' she'd say, nodding sagely when I told her a rumour I'd heard about a former colleague being breastfed until he was eighteen. 'That's more common than you'd think.'

'What kept you?' she asked now, leading me into the living room, where, I noticed, the tapestry that hung on one wall had grown since my last visit.

'I got cornered by Uncle Al,' I said. Al was a familiar character in my tales of the café, so Jax groaned sympathetically.

'I honestly think I'd kick off,' she said.

I thought she would too. This was why I had never suggested Jax work in the café whenever she was looking for a job. Jax was a freelance fashion writer, so there were times when she needed to top up her earnings through bar work and the like. She had actually got me my first job in London, in a sports bar near Kentish Town. She'd also prevented me from being immediately fired when, on my first night, a beer tap somehow acquired the water pressure of a fire hydrant as I was pulling a pint. The beer hit the bottom of the glass I was holding and shot directly back up, drenching me and many of the punters in the five-deep scrum pressing against the bar. Amid the howling that followed, Jax had the presence of mind to lift the tap as I tried to stem the flow with my hands.

'I don't know why you don't get a better job,' she said. 'You shouldn't have to put up with that interfering old geezer.'

This was easy for Jax to say, of course. It seemed to me that she could walk into any interview and convince the employer at least to let her take a stab at the job. I couldn't imagine myself fooling anyone like that. Besides, I liked the rhythm and the rituals of the Quarter Turn, the morning rush and the afternoon slump as regular as the tide. And I felt in control there – in any other job, I suspected I'd be outed as the same eejit I'd been at the sports bar, standing over broken glass and trying to collect beer in my outstretched hands.

'What are you working on?' I asked Jax, keen not to dwell on my career prospects.

'A christening present for Claudia's niece,' Jax said, picking up a small embroidery hoop with the outline of the words 'Bad Ass' stitched into the fabric.

Claudia was Jax's flatmate: she'd moved in with her when our house share came to an end, following the mysterious imprisonment of our landlord. Their flat was the polar opposite of the warren we'd had in Oval: bright and clean, with brilliant white walls perfect for hanging canvases and posters. It felt like an adult's home, while my house, which I'd found not far away, was closer to a student's first digs, complete with industrial carpets, peeling paint and floorboards in the bathroom that sagged gently beneath your feet as you walked across them. I lived there with Tony the Australian and a reclusive data analyst named Polly, and the best thing I could say about it was that at least it was near Jax.

'Looking good,' I said, as Jax held up the hoop for inspection. 'I'm sure the baby will appreciate it when she's old enough to read. What happened to your whittling?'

'This felt more pressing. And I snapped the spoon I was working on in half.'

'Where are you going this evening?'

'It's someone's leaving drinks at the paper.'

To my knowledge, Jax had only done a handful of days at the paper since she was brought in for their quarterly fashion supplement. I couldn't imagine why she'd want to go to a leaving party.

'I thought it would be a good chance to mix,' she added.

'Mix with who?'

'Eoin, I only have an hour till I have to go. What's wrong with you?'

I looked at Jax's sewing basket, at the threads and needles and the cuddly rhino that was acting as a pin cushion, and my eyes misted over.

'You said it was something to do with Rich,' Jax said. She continued stitching, seemingly absorbed by her work, though I knew she'd put it down if I let the tears flow. I took a breath and tried to find a way of putting it that didn't sound blunt and slightly absurd. There wasn't one.

'He wants an open relationship.'

Jax looked up, one hand on the wooden frame and the other raised, string taut. '*Rich* wants an open relationship?'

'Yeah.'

'Right.' She blinked, seeming genuinely confused. 'I didn't think he had it in him.'

'What do you mean?' I asked.

'Well, Rich just seems quite career-y, quite, um …'

'Boring?'

'Sorry.' She put down the hoop. 'I'm really fucking this up.'

I wondered, for the first time in years, what Jax actually thought of Rich. They probably saw each other just a handful of times a year, for events like my birthday, but I'd always assumed she shared my opinion of how wonderful he was.

'How are you feeling?' she asked.

I fiddled with the drawers of an upcycled apothecary cabinet while I tried to think of an answer, but found I couldn't, or didn't want to, describe to Jax the thoughts I was having. They seemed too personal to share even with her. Rich wanted to kiss other guys, touch other guys, fuck other guys. He wanted to have sex, but not with me. After five years together, he wanted more than our relationship gave him.

'I feel like a bit of a failure,' I said eventually. 'It feels a lot like this is a sign that I'm a failure as a boyfriend and a partner.' Jax was shaking her head, but I went on: 'Like, if I was enough, he wouldn't want my permission to go off with someone else.'

'If your relationship was a failure,' Jax said, 'he'd have gone off with someone else already. I mean,' she added quickly, spotting that I looked ready to throw up, 'I'm sure he hasn't, Eoin. I mean, he didn't say he had, did he?'

'I didn't ask.' I was feeling a bit dizzy. I flopped into an armchair covered with a handmade throw, which doubled as a banner at climate marches.

'When did he bring it up?' she asked.

I recounted the story about the polyamorous man and Rich's reaction.

'By the way,' I said, 'do you think that was a coincidence? That it just happened to come up in conversation?'

This detail had been bothering me all day. The timing of Danni and Shanice's story, followed by the group's early exit, made them feel like Rich's accomplices, just waiting for his signal to attack our relationship.

'I think that's a wee bit paranoid, hon,' said Jax. 'His friends will have better things to talk about than how he should suggest a lifestyle change for the two of you.'

I thought the accusation of paranoia was a bit rich coming from a woman convinced that her friends held an annual reunion to which her entire school year, minus herself, was invited.

'Fine,' I said, 'but either way, that's how it came up.'

'And it's not something you've considered?'

'No,' I said truthfully. 'And I'm not knocking it. Tony had something like that on the go with his girlfriend, the one back in Adelaide, remember?'

'I'm not sure Tony's girlfriend was up to speed on that arrangement,' said Jax.

'Sure,' I said, 'but nevertheless, I'm happy that open relationships exist, I just …'

'You just don't want one.'

'I just don't want anyone touching my boyfriend.'

Jax nodded.

'What did you say when he brought it up?' she asked.

'Well, at first I assumed he was joking.'

'Okay.' Jax picked up the embroidery hoop again, and examined it thoughtfully.

'And then,' I continued, 'he said I should consider it, that it might be fun.' I looked at Jax, expecting a snort of derision. When none was forthcoming, I repeated the word. 'Fun!' Still nothing. 'It was as if he was suggesting that we go snorkelling or something. *Fun?*'

'Well,' said Jax, 'it could be.'

I wondered if I had fallen through a wormhole, or whether everyone around me had taken to sniffing glue. 'What part of my boyfriend going off and fucking a bunch of random strangers is fun?' I asked, hearing my tone of voice change from heartbroken hero to stroppy teen.

'Has it occurred to you that an open relationship applies to both parties?' asked Jax.

It hadn't.

'Of course it has,' I said, 'I'm just not interested in that. Anyway, last night, the longer we talked, the more it felt like an ultimatum.'

'Did Rich say it was an ultimatum?'

'No.' I wanted Jax to stop being reasonable and join me in saying how simply awful this was. But, no, here she sat, the devil's advocate in all her finery.

'He didn't say it in so many words,' I went on, 'but it was as good as him saying he isn't happy and wants something to change. And if we don't change as a couple, he'll just go and change himself.'

'But he didn't *say* that,' Jax insisted. 'Did he?'

I had a sudden urge to throw her Bad Ass embroidery project out the window, but instead I shook my head, and sat watching her for a minute or so. Eventually she put down her work and took a sip of water from a hand-decorated glass.

'I'm sorry, pal,' she said. 'That sounds shit.'

I nodded. 'I know it's not the end of the world, no one is ill ' – Jax tapped the coffee-table – 'but it just feels like something's ending, I suppose, and I quite liked what I had.'

'Do you want some advice,' she asked, 'or do you want to get anything else off your chest first?'

The question was a strangely calming one. I took a breath and let it out slowly. 'Advice, please,' I said.

'How did you leave it?'

'I said I was tired and had to get up early – which was true,' I added, spotting Jax's almost imperceptible eye-roll. 'I was opening the café this morning. And I said I'd think about it.'

'Well,' she said, 'the first thing you should do is consider yourself. Remember, this is your choice. Is it something *you*'d enjoy? Having the freedom to try things?'

I stared at her. It was like she was suggesting that being shoved out of an aeroplane would give me the freedom to fly.

'I mean,' she continued, 'you've only ever been with Rich.'

'That's not true,' I reminded her. 'There were a few guys back in Dublin.'

'Fine,' she said, waving her arms as if to dispel the ghosts of the men I'd kissed at Mother all those years ago. 'But Rich has been your one big life-defining relationship and maybe, before you get too settled into it and turn thirty and move in together –' she held up one hand to stop me interrupting '– *maybe* it's worth trying something new.'

I was silent. Jax was clearly insane, but I wasn't going to win an argument when she was doing such a good job at making her insanity sound like common sense.

'Don't you ever fancy guys on the street?' she asked. 'Or in the café?'

'Sure.'

'Well, now you can flirt with them without feeling guilty.'

'I don't avoid flirting with attractive men because I'm in a relationship. I avoid flirting with them because they won't fancy me.'

'You don't know that.'

'And I never even know whether a guy is gay or not.'

'Well, that just tells me your gaydar is rusty.'

'My gaydar is non-existent.'

'It's *dormant*. And now, if you want, you can wake it up.'

I stayed silent, but I really wasn't buying Jax's promise of legions of handsome gay men waiting for me to seduce them.

'And the other thing you should do,' she said, getting into her stride, 'is come up with a timetable.'

'What – like which days of the week we can go bang other men?'

'No – well, you could do that too – but what I meant was, have a three-month review or something. A probation period. See how you both feel at the end of it. And this way you have some control over it all. I'm a bit peckish,' she said, getting up. 'Do you want some toast?'

'Actually,' I said, producing a crumpled brown bag from my backpack, 'we had a croissant left over, do you want to toast that?'

'Ooh, yeah, I'll warm that bad boy up.' Jax grabbed the bag and made for the kitchen. I felt that the life advice was concluded for the day. I wasn't sure I'd got the answer I wanted, but it was good to have some fresh thoughts in my mind. It took the washing machine in my brain off Spin and into a more sluggish setting – Woollens and Delicates, or something like that.

'Who did you say is leaving the office?' I asked, as Jax took out a bread knife and sliced the croissant in half.

'Michelle,' said Jax. She stuck the two halves into the toaster. 'I haven't spoken to her yet, but I think she works in IT and she's moving to Canada.'

'Good for Michelle,' I said. 'Shaking things up.'

'Oh, that's classic Michelle. She's always had that wander-lust.'

'And do you know anyone else going to Michelle's drinks,' I asked, as Jax rooted about in the fridge, 'or is it just going to be the pair of you?'

'Well, if you must know,' she said, with a bubble of joy in her throat, 'I may be hoping to run into someone else. I've been sharing a lift with this guy at the paper.'

It was unusual to hear Jax speaking like this. To my knowledge, she had been in just one relationship since I'd known her, and I wasn't even sure if she would label it as such. Abi, whom Jax knew from uni in Edinburgh, would visit the house in Oval once or twice a year. She and Jax would be insepa-rable for the duration of her stay, and then she'd be gone, leaving Jax with a new tattoo and a week-long bout of wistful detachment. The visits seemed to stop after a few years, and if I ever mentioned Abi now, Jax tended to shut down the conversation. So the fact that she was volunteering informa-tion about an office crush was an event, and not one I was used to dealing with.

'Sharing a lift?' I said. 'Jesus. Have you met his parents?'

'Eoin, it's happened five times, and each time it's been just the two of us in there and there's an awful lot of smiling going on.'

'That sounds awkward.'

'It's not.'

'I'd take the stairs.'

The croissant halves popped up, and she grabbed them.

'Yesterday there was a talk at lunchtime, something to do with protecting whistleblowers, which is obviously com-pletely irrelevant to what I'm doing – here, have that,' she said, handing me half the croissant topped with a generous slather of spread. 'I can't have this much butter at once or I'll have a heart attack.'

I took it, and realized I hadn't eaten since I'd had a banana at midday.

'And, anyway, we were sitting in a semicircle,' said Jax, 'and he was sitting on the other side, and I *could not* stop looking at him. He's tall and brawny, but you can tell he takes care of himself. I'd say he's no stranger to a charcoal face mask, you know?'

'Sure.'

'And I was trying to undress him with my eyes while taking notes on what to do the next time Edward Snowden calls the fashion desk, when I noticed that every time I snuck a look, he was looking back.'

'That's happened to me in the past.'

'Oh, me too, but usually it's horrible and awkward and you wonder if the other person is going to report you to the police, this was just quite funny. I could tell he was struggling to keep a straight face.'

Jax took a bite of the croissant, sighed deeply and twirled on one leg.

'You look like a giddy schoolgirl.'

'And I make no apologies,' she said.

'Has he told you his name in between all of this erotic smiling?'

'His name's Aaron, but I found that out by other means.'

'Have you spoken?'

'We have not.' She took another bite. 'This is delicious.'

'So is he going to the drinks tonight?'

'I fucking hope so, or else I'm going to an IT nerd's farewell bash for no reason.'

'It sounds like love,' I said. 'I'd better leave you to get ready and put fresh sheets on the bed.'

'I'm not that kind of girl,' Jax said, and swallowed the last of the croissant.

'Hey, listen, apparently I'm in an open relationship now,' I said. 'Anything goes as far as I'm concerned.'

Jax saw me out. 'Give me a call when you've spoken to Rich,' she said, 'I want to know how it goes.'

'Will do. Oh, wait,' I said, just as Jax was closing the door. 'Answer me this: last night, a friend of Rich's wasn't boozing, and it looked like she and her husband were concealing it. Why?'

'She's pregnant,' Jax said. 'And they don't want any questions while they wait for the twelve-week scan.'

'That's what I thought! Thank you.'

Jax nodded and closed the door. The light was beginning to fade, and I decided that I'd walk home while I absorbed Jax's advice. Despite what she'd said, I wasn't convinced I had much of a choice. I could either share Rich or lose him, and while the idea of sharing him was painful to imagine, the idea of losing him altogether was simply unimaginable.

I leaned against a traffic light and watched a man cross the road on the other side of the junction. He was wearing a football kit with a suit jacket over the jersey, clearly on the way home from a kick-about. His calves bulged, and I wondered whether the rest of his body was as muscular, whether the thick hair on his legs indicated a similarly hairy chest. He looked my way, and I gave him a smile. He pointed somewhere over my head, and I looked up to see that the green man was illuminated. I stepped onto the road, head down.

Chapter Four

The only thing left on my shelf of the fridge was a hardened block of Cheddar, so dinner was a cheese sandwich with butter borrowed from Tony, eaten alone in the front room. The house was still, though I could hear the tinny noise of music playing from a laptop in someone's room. I decided to message Rich.

Good luck with the interview tomorrow, I wrote. *Hope all the prep went well.*

Rich was on the look-out for a deputy principal job. He had grown frustrated with the small private school where he taught, and how limited he was in what he could do there.

He replied a few minutes later with a photo showing his fresh haircut. It looked good, though I was sad to see the summer mop go.

Thanks, he wrote, *will let you know how it goes. x*

This was such a normal exchange of messages that I considered simply ignoring yesterday evening's suggestion until it went away. In the agony-aunt columns Jax and I used to read together, we would occasionally come across stories of partners who adopted this head-in-the-sand tactic. They were invariably the villains of the piece, though, fantasists who had to be yanked back into the real world and forced to confront their problems. Besides, I knew myself well enough to accept that I wouldn't be able to live like that. No, I had to follow Jax's advice and grab the bull by the horns.

But, for now, I avoided taking any such action by going onto Rich's Instagram and then his Facebook page, looking for evidence that he had been getting itchy feet over the past few months. I didn't know what I was looking for – maybe a shot of him salivating as he stared at another man – but the search proved unfruitful. Most of the photos were group shots with the different sets of friends he bounced between: in addition to the 'Member-Whens, there were the poker boys, the D&D group, the football team and the seemingly endless parade of individual friends I might have met once or twice, but whom Rich described as old and loyal pals.

Eventually I went to my own profile, and started retreating back through the years, comparing recent photos of the two of us with those taken in the past, searching Rich's face for signs of discontent or fading happiness.

Rich and I had met in Dublin while I was still at UCD. I was on a night out with Terrence, a loud, camp, big-man-on-campus I had met at an Irish-language debate. Terrence and I had only spoken a few times, but a fortnight after I started telling friends I was gay, he texted me out of the blue. *Welcome to the club*, he wrote. *Night out Friday?*

I was in the smoking area out the back of the George when I first saw Rich, laughing with a friend and looking handsome and bright and strikingly crisp. That was the word: crisp, like a shirt that had been starched and ironed so thoroughly it could almost stand up on its own. Even leaning against a wall, his posture was excellent, the result, I learned later, of ballet lessons as a child. He had deep-set eyes, which glimmered from under a heavy brow. His light brown hair had the tousled look that comes from diligent but unfussy application of product. If this all sounds quite square and mainstream, well, it is, but at the time, surrounded as I was by other students, smelling clothes that had been air-dried in damp flats, the sight of someone so clearly together and at ease and, yes, *crisp* was enough to stop me in my tracks.

As I half listened to the story Terrence was telling our group, I kept looking over at Rich, whose eyes eventually flicked my way. Without missing a beat, he raised a hand, in the kind of salute you give someone you've always known, a friend from school you see on the other side of a crowded train carriage or at a gig, the kind of wave that says you'll catch them in a minute, no rush. I nodded at him. He turned to his friend and resumed his conversation.

Emboldened by this familiarity, as well as the bottle of wine I'd drunk on the Luas into town, I walked up to Rich a few minutes later with a confidence I hadn't known I had.

'What brings you here?' I asked.

'We had to escape, didn't we, Max?' said Rich to his friend. Funny to think that, at the time, his English accent was a novelty to me, making him stand out all the more.

'*You* had to escape, mate,' said Max, in a voice altogether plummier than Rich's, the kind they adopted in DramSoc whenever they put on *The Importance of Being Earnest*.

'Where have you escaped from?' I asked, holding eye contact with Rich as if Max hadn't spoken.

'From an out-of-control stag,' said Rich, and I felt my heart sink a little, as I wondered if I was talking to two straight tourists who had stumbled into the George by accident.

'I've never actually been to a gay bar before,' Max said, seeming to confirm my suspicion. He looked around with an appraising eye. 'Mind you, the smoking area doesn't seem so different.'

'We don't always paint them neon pink,' said Rich.

I hoped my delight at Rich's use of *we* wasn't too obvious. I suddenly felt a warm glow of fondness for Max, who had really helped clear matters up. It didn't occur to me until later that he might be playing the role of wingman to Rich. But, like any decent wingman, he went to make himself scarce, asking Rich if he'd like another drink.

'Please,' said Rich. 'I'll wait here.'

Max turned to me. 'Would you like one …'

'Eoin,' I said. 'No, thanks, I'm fine for now.' I gestured to my pint glass, then saw there was nothing but dregs in it.

'Get him another, Max,' Rich said. 'On me.' He handed Max a note and turned back to me. 'Eoin,' he said. 'How do you spell that?'

I had been studying English for two years at that point, and in all my reading I had not yet encountered a great romance that began with a spelling test. But so began ours. We talked about the various ways of spelling Eoin/Owen/Eoghan, Irish names in general, the Irish language, Rich's Scottish mother, learning Irish at school, and how, after realising that working in the City wasn't for him, Rich was now retraining as a teacher, by which time Max was back with the drinks. Curiously, he had ordered only a half-pint for himself, which he finished pretty quickly. Terrence, meanwhile, had disappeared back inside with the rest of the group, blowing me a kiss as he left.

'I might see if the other boys have landed back at the hostel,' Max said.

'I'll stay and finish this,' said Rich, indicating his drink. 'You'll keep me company, though, won't you, Eoin?'

I shrugged and nodded, not wanting to seem like an over-eager student in front of the two of them, who were both definitely in their late twenties.

After Max left, Rich and I talked for what felt like ages, though I honestly couldn't say what it was all about. It was talking for the sake of it, for the sake of locking eyes as long as possible, for the sake of one of us interrupting the other so he could say, 'Sorry, go on,' while laying a hand on the other's arm. It was saying things in a secretive tone so that you could lean in and say them softly, sharing the same air. But mainly it was about talking until the conversation reached a natural pause, and the silence that hung between us seemed to scream, 'Kiss him!' and Rich finally leaned in.

As we kissed, I felt Rich setting down his pint glass on the window-ledge beside us and, without breaking away from me, taking mine and placing it next to his. There was something thoughtful and sleek and gentle about this gesture, which would always make me smile when I remembered it.

We continued kissing as the smoking area emptied out, until a bouncer told us the bar was closed. We took our plastic glasses out onto George's Street and started kissing again.

Then came the tedious admin. I was still living at home: bringing anyone back for the night would be out of the question, never mind a man. Rich thought it would be a bit much to invite me back to the hostel where he was staying with the rest of the stag. We spent another half-hour kissing, groping and periodically breaking off to lament the lack of anywhere to go.

Eventually, it started to rain, and Rich decided we had better call it a night. We exchanged numbers, though he said he was off go-karting the next day before flying back to London in the evening, and that he probably wouldn't be able to get away from it all.

'Well, next time you're in Dublin,' I said, 'make sure you book a single room.' He promised he would, and hailed a taxi. It was a Friday night, and I managed to get the last Nitelink home. On the bus I texted him: *Hope you got back safe. Good luck on the racetrack tomorrow.*

I was disappointed when, after half an hour of checking my phone, it became clear that he wasn't going to reply. The elation I'd felt when we said goodbye dissolved amid the drunken squeals and arguments on the top deck of the bus.

I looked out the window and felt very romantic and melancholic.

The next morning, however, I woke up feeling very stupid and fearful. As I replayed the night in my head, what had seemed witty and charming banter revealed itself to be witless squawking from me, and polite tolerance from Rich. I slumped in front of a reality TV show, staring at gorgeous Californian men attending a pool party while thinking longingly of Rich.

It was about midday when he texted me. Just the sight of his name was enough to make me leap to my feet, which was a terrible idea on a hangover: I almost blacked out from the massive head rush I got and had to wait until my vision cleared before I could read his message. Apparently there had been an argument over breakfast about his sudden disappearance the night before, and he had been uninvited to the rest of the stag. He now had about six hours to kill before he needed to head to the airport. He had taken the liberty of looking up a hotel, and he could book a room there if I happened to be free. When could I be in town?

I replied to say I'd be there in an hour, dropped my phone and charged up the stairs to shower. As I grabbed a towel, I called downstairs to my sister Ciara to see if she'd give me a lift into town. When she asked who I was meeting, I closed the door to the bathroom and let the sound of the shower drown out my vague explanation of a friend who was visiting. Ciara and I no longer wound each other up the way we had when we were teenagers, but I still wasn't sure either of us was ready for me to tell the full truth about going for a hook-up with an English tourist.

The hotel was a new building on the docklands. Ciara dropped me on the south side of the East Link ('I'm not spending a fiver to drive you over a feckin' bridge!') and I crossed the Liffey feeling as if I was about to sit an exam, praying I wouldn't go completely to pieces when it started.

Rich was drinking coffee in the reception area, dressed in more casual, softer clothes than the night before.

'Hi,' I said, hovering awkwardly, unsure whether to join him on the sofa or to sit in the high-backed, winged armchair to his left. He saved me the bother by knocking back the rest of his coffee and standing up, a smile on his face.

'Come on, then,' he said, and walked off in the direction of the lift. I could have sworn I saw one of the receptionists smirk as I followed him, but figured they must see this kind of thing all the time.

'So,' I said, grasping for something to say as the lift doors closed, 'feeling hung-over?'

'Yup,' Rich said, then pulled me into him and kissed me.

By the time we reached his floor my pre-exam nerves had been replaced by an adrenalin rush. All I wanted was to get this guy's clothes off and take things from there.

What followed was, to say the least, passionate, and I did wonder at times whether we would be interrupted by the smirking receptionist telling us there had been some complaints about the noise. But it was surprisingly tender as well: probably for the first time since I'd come out, kissing was enjoyed for its own sake, rather than merely as a prelude to humping. In the years to come, Rich and I would learn more about what each other liked, and what we liked about each other, but in that shiny, sterile, underused room in that heavily indebted hotel, I had what I could honestly say was the best sex I'd ever had.

Of course, I couldn't admit this at the time, worried that I would come across either as inexperienced or overly keen.

'Did you enjoy that?' Rich asked afterwards, snuggling into me.

'Sure,' I said, keeping my voice neutral. 'Did you?'

'That was fucking amazing,' he said, and I was thrilled by the sincerity with which he said it.

'Better than go-karting?' I asked.

'Definitely. Probably more tiring, though. You'll have to be very gentle with me for the rest of the day.'

I looked at the clock when he said this. It was still only four. There would be time, I thought, to have a 'rest of the day', to talk and snooze and have sex again before he left for the airport. He didn't seem in a rush to get rid of me and I had no inclination to leave. I had been with a couple of guys up to that point, but never had I experienced this: a hung-over afternoon with nothing planned and nothing needed, nothing except each other's company and each other's body. And it was with that thought that I fell asleep next to Rich for the first time.

I heard a key in the front door and looked up from my phone. It had got dark while I'd been scrolling. Polly, my other housemate, eased open the door and stepped inside, silent and careful as a cat burglar. She didn't spot me in the gloomy front room. Not wanting to startle her, I watched her close the door, remove her shoes and spring up the stairs to her room with a controlled lightness that made me wonder if she was a trained dancer. I'd never ask her, though. I probably wouldn't see Polly for another month. That was just how it was in this house. We paid the bills, took the bins out when they were full, and remained strangers. If Tony and I found ourselves in the kitchen together, we'd exchange updates as each of us prepared his own meal, but nothing too deep. And that was fine, I reassured myself, because I didn't need my house to be a home, not when I had a boyfriend, and everything that came with him: friends, a social life, not to mention an alternative place to sleep when I needed a break.

As I washed my plate, it occurred to me that I was now the age Rich was when we met, and the idea of a twenty-one-year-old student – the same age as hopeless Billy – trying to seduce someone my age felt laughable. It was a miracle that not only had I not scared him off, but I was still with him all these years later. I had to do whatever it took to keep hold of Rich, and if that meant completely ignoring everything Jax had suggested (honesty, limitations, self-respect), well, that was a price I was willing to pay. Miracles don't come along that often.

I messaged Rich again: *How about I come round tomorrow? Can make you dinner and we can chat x*

Sure, he replied, *I'll leave a key out xxx*

Chapter Five

'I thought Rebecca was due back this morning,' said Billy. His face was flushed, and he had rolled up the sleeves of his thick jumper so high that they were almost wedged into his armpits. His blond hair, usually floppy, was plastered to his forehead.

'So did I,' I said, and glanced at the door, willing Rebecca to run in and explain that she had overslept after a late flight. 'Why don't you take off the jumper, Billy? You look a bit warm.'

'That would be great,' he said, 'although I'm not wearing a T-shirt underneath. Do you think that would be a problem?'

On mornings like this, when the sun came blazing in, the café's large windows made the place into a greenhouse, and the heat rising from the coffee machine felt like it was coming from an open fire. All the same, I didn't think a topless barista would be looked on kindly.

'Probably better to leave it on in that case,' I said. 'Let's try to get through some of these orders.' A line of six or seven tickets stretched across the counter beside the coffee machine. Customers stood with arms crossed, some of them checking their phones, one or two staring pointedly at the large clock that hung on the wall. When Rebecca was there, charming the queue and helping with espresso shots when necessary, I got a real buzz off this kind of pressure, looking down the list of tickets and figuring out the quickest way of making them disappear. In her absence, though, it felt like a hellish game of Tetris, one that I was playing after having my thumbs chopped off. I tapped a shot of used coffee out of a portafilter and handed it to Billy. 'Could you do me three shots, please, two doubles and one single?'

'Sure thing.'

The bell rang from Hugo's kitchenette. As if enchanted, Billy walked towards it, the portafilter still in his hand.

'No, Billy,' I said, as I poured enough milk into a jug to make two semi-skimmed lattes and, with luck, a flat white. 'Pavlov doesn't need you right now. I do.'

'Right,' he said, and started measuring out a shot of coffee while I twisted open the steam wand. The bell rang again, and Billy shook his head with quiet defiance. 'Pavlov,' he said, laughing softly.

Hugo refused to leave his inner sanctum during service, believing that mixing front- and back-of-house duties was the kind of thing that would lead to societal breakdown. This was particularly galling when the only order he had in front of him was for two slices of toast. In recent days, I had begun to ignore the sounds of his bell as a matter of principle.

'When Rebecca does get back,' I said, 'we really need to talk to her about Hugo running his own orders.'

'Too right,' Billy replied. He was still measuring out the same shot of coffee. He raised it to eye level and peered closely at the grounds.

'That looks fine, Billy,' I said. 'I'll need two more shots in a minute.'

'It's sort of like looking at a desert when you hold it up close,' said Billy. 'A tiny circular desert of very dark sand.'

One of the customers who had been staring at the clock sighed and made a great show of looking at his watch. The material of his pink shirt was not made for days like this: the two large sweat patches under his arms seemed to be expanding by the second.

'Actually,' I said to Billy, 'why don't you make that pot of tea?' I closed off the steam wand and slid a ticket towards him. 'I'll do these shots.' The milk I had just steamed would start to cool and separate while I ran the shots, but at least the customers wouldn't be aggravated by the sight of Billy contemplating the coffee like a myopic philosopher.

As Billy filled the teapot, the bell rang again, this time with an insistency that suggested Hugo was reaching boiling point. Billy looked to me with a touch of fear in his eyes.

'Fine,' I said. 'Go on.' As Billy disappeared, I turned to the clock-watching customer and placed a coffee in front of him. 'Semi-skimmed flat white?' I asked, with a triumphant smile.

He looked back at me with blank fury. 'It was a skinny flat white,' he said. 'Not semi.'

I felt like a magician who had failed to guess the correct card.

'Did anyone order a semi-skimmed flat white?' I called, trying not to sound too desperate.

'I'll take it,' said a woman from the back of the queue. 'Mine was full-fat, but I really don't mind.'

'Great,' I said, as she ran gleefully to the counter. 'And two semi-skimmed lattes?'

The man who had ordered the skinny flat white turned pale and started to tremble as another customer picked up the two lattes.

'You're going to serve *all of them* first?' he said, with a psychotic intensity that would have made De Niro proud.

'I'm going to give them their drinks, then make yours straight away,' I said slowly, in the tone I imagined I would use to talk someone in off a ledge.

As I turned back to the coffee doser, the bell rang again. Somehow I could tell that it was Billy this time, perhaps crying out for help. I looked back in the direction of the door, praying that Rebecca would return and put some rules back in place.

'What the *hell* is that ringing?' my friend at the front of the queue asked.

'Search me,' I said, and then, as it continued, 'Any plans for the weekend?'

'Well, at some point, I was planning on leaving this café,' said the man, bobbing on his toes as he spoke. 'And you?'

I'm going to follow you home and drown you in a bucket of zero-fat milk, I thought.

'No plans,' I said, smiling. The man's sweat patches had almost reached his nipples by now. Over his shoulder, I saw Uncle Al walking past the door. For someone meant to be keeping an eye on the café, he seemed to be studiously avoiding the crowd inside.

Billy was back at my side.

'Hugo wants to see you,' he said, as I poured the flat white. I hated skinny milk. Because of the low fat content, I found it impossible to stretch properly, so the drink would always turn out lumpy. I wanted to give the man at the front of the queue a love heart on his flat white, just to spite him, but the best I could manage was a blob with a tail.

'Where's the toast?' I asked Billy, then turned back to the man, who by now was hovering a few inches off the ground. 'Skinny flat white, enjoy.' He snatched it from my hand and grabbed a fistful of sugar sachets.

'That's the thing,' Billy said, as the man stalked out, 'Hugo wants to talk to you about all that.'

Over at one of the tables, a woman was waving at us, clearly wondering when she would be served. She had, I noticed, stacked the plates and cups of the last customer to one side. Her companion was sweeping crumbs into his hand. All of a sudden, the music we were playing seemed terribly loud.

'I'll talk to Hugo later,' I said. 'Go get the toast, and bring that tea wherever it needs to go. I'm just going to …'

I stepped out from behind the counter, much to the dismay of the waiting customers. I skipped past the tutting queue and over to the window. As Al passed, I knocked on the glass. He jumped, then glared when he saw it was me.

'Re-be-cca?' I said, mouthing the name with my eyebrows raised.

Al merely shrugged, and walked on.

'Fuck's sake,' I muttered, and turned to dash back behind the counter. In doing so, I collided with someone who, I instantly realised, was a lot heavier and more grounded than I was. I bounced straight off him and fell back against the window, which fortunately was double-glazed, or I would have ended up sprawled on the footpath outside.

'Jesus,' I said, blinking up at the wide, firmly planted man I had run into. 'Sorry.'

'That's okay,' said the man, looking at me with a wary expression I instantly recognised.

'Gym pass,' I said, still slumped against the window.

'Sorry?'

'You left your …'

I picked myself up and jogged back behind the counter to grab the card. His fade was fresher in the photo, but it was definitely him. 'James?'

'Yes?'

'You left this,' I said, and passed him the card. 'Someone handed it in.'

I waited a moment for a thank-you, but he was staring at the card as if I'd passed him a tablet of hieroglyphics, so I returned to the coffee machine and the never-ending row of tickets. Billy was taking someone's order, so I was flying solo again. I flicked on the grinder and looked back at the queue. The guy with the gym pass – James – was still there. He was about my height, but his bulk obscured my view of the other customers.

'I was wondering,' he said, leaning on the counter, 'if I could speak to the manager.'

Oh, God, I thought. Another angry customer.

'I'm really sorry,' I said, over the whine of the grinder's burrs, 'we're a bit understaffed this morning, did you order a …' I looked down at the tickets, hoping they would give me a clue, but I couldn't tell which ones I had already made and which I still had to do.

'No, no,' he said. 'I was actually wondering if you're hiring.'

'I wish,' I said, 'but you'll probably need to drop in another time with a CV or whatever.'

'Any time in particular?'

The bell started to ring again. I sighed. 'Any time that isn't rush-hour,' I said.

James's eyes widened, but then he nodded. 'Sure,' he said. 'I'll call back when you're calmer.'

I scoffed and turned away from him, nodding along to the music in an effort to show just how calm I could be. As I prepared the next round of espresso shots, I noticed him pouring a glass of water from the jug we kept near the window, stuffed with mint leaves and lemons.

'Here,' he said. He leaned across the counter and left the glass next to a stray portafilter. 'You look like you need it.'

His round face briefly lifted into a smile. Then he turned and left. I tried to think of something to yell after him, but the milk jug was starting to burn my hand.

'Oat milk cappuccino to go?' I called instead. As the grateful customer scurried off with their drink, I knocked back the water. The guy might have been making a dig, but he wasn't wrong.

Once I had got through all the orders and filled the dishwasher, I went to see Hugo. He was staring at a saucepan of baked beans, and didn't look up when I came in.

'Busy,' he said, when I coughed quietly.

I turned to go, and he said, 'Waste, man, terrible waste. Toast went cold, had to throw it away.' He stepped on the pedal of the bin to his left, and indicated it with a nod of his head. 'Take a look,' he said.

I stayed where I was.

'Hugo, we've been working really well together while Rebecca's been away,' I said. We hadn't, but in the quiet late-August period, this hadn't been a problem, and I thought it would be better to pretend. 'We've been a team,' I went on, 'but Billy and I were really rushed off our feet just now.'

'I heard you talking,' he said, 'telling Billy to stay out there. Don't do that again.'

I felt caught out. I hadn't known Hugo could hear anything happening outside his den – I always assumed the music covered our conversations. With his back to me, he poured the beans onto a slice of toast. He turned, looked me in the eye, and rang the bell. We stared at each other while Norah Jones crooned away in the background. I could feel a faint thumping in my head.

'What table?' I asked eventually.

'Table three,' Hugo said, and turned away, triumphant.

I picked up the plate and some cutlery, consoling myself with the fact that Rebecca would be back soon, and I could leave her to deal with this. After I had served the beans on toast, I checked my phone to see if she had sent an explanation for her absence, but there was none. I messaged Jax.

How was Michelle's party? Any more smiling with the object of your affections?

Michelle was really touched I could make it, though I'm not sure we actually met. And we've gone waaaaay past smiling, we actually spoke. His name's Aaron.

But you knew that already.

I had a conversation with him, Eoin, can you please just be happy for me and my future husband?

I could hear banging coming from somewhere. I wondered if the people in the flat above the café were having work done. I cleared a few tables as the banging, though still muffled, became more insistent. Then, once again, Hugo's bell started ringing.

'Yes, Hugo?' I said, stepping back into the kitchen.

'That's Billy,' he said. 'He's locked in the toilet.'

'What?'

'The lock's broken. Don't use it.'

I jogged down the stairs, where I could hear Billy calling for help from behind the toilet door.

'Sorry, Eoin,' he said piteously, as I looked around for an instrument to open the lock from the outside. Eventually I found a stray butter knife and used that. Billy stumbled out, bare-chested, holding his jumper and apron in a bundle.

'I was just trying to cool down,' he said, by way of explanation.

I brought him an iced latte and suggested he take an early lunch break. He nodded. He had spread his sweat-soaked jumper out to dry, and was fanning himself with a Lever Arch file from Rebecca's desk. He was surprisingly toned. I was going to ask him if he worked out, but worried it might come across as flirty.

Back upstairs, a fresh queue had formed. I flicked on the grinder and turned to the till. Jax was right, I thought. I had to start standing up for myself. I couldn't just go to Rich in meek acquiescence, no matter how much I loved him.

As I steamed a hot chocolate and began to draw some red lines in my head, Hugo passed, carrying a panini with a generous side salad.

'Just bringing Billy some lunch,' he said, and disappeared downstairs.

'But you won't run a slice of toast?' I yelled after him.

Chapter Six

I fished Rich's spare key out of a hollow brick in the garden wall and let myself into his building. His flatmate, Colin, was away walking the Camino, having given up cocaine and taken up Jesus earlier in the year. His absence left Rich's flat feeling peaceful and ordered in a way that my house – where someone had always left a mess in the kitchen or, at particularly bleak moments, in the bathroom – was not.

Having offered to cook, I had soon begun worrying that this would appear too desperate, that Rich would feel I was silently screaming, 'Love me!' as I fed him spoon after spoon of goulash. But now that I had suggested doing it, I didn't want him to find me sitting at an empty kitchen table, arms crossed, saying, 'Sit down, sweetheart. We need to talk.' I decided to split the difference and make chilli, which he knew I could do in my sleep, but which would keep me occupied so that I could introduce the topic casually, perhaps with words like, 'Oh, by the way, about that seven-year itch of yours …'

I always added red wine to the base of a chilli, and since I had to open a bottle anyway, I decided that a glass would help steady my nerves. I had left Billy to close the café under Al's supervision, and got a text from him as I chopped onions, saying he couldn't get the till to balance.

Looks like we're 40 short, he wrote.

I groaned. I had shown him how to cash-up on three separate occasions. One afternoon, I'd even drawn him a guide on a strip of till roll.

Double count the notes, I replied, *and if it's still out just leave it. I'll have a look tomorrow morning.*

I heard Rich's key in the door as I was adding kidney beans to the pot. This sound would usually mark the beginning of my perfect evening: the two of us with the house to ourselves and nothing much planned beyond dinner, during which I would make Rich laugh by joyfully bitching about whatever horrific customer had ruined my day. Now, though, the sound of the door opening gave rise to the old, almost-forgotten feeling that I was about to sit a particularly tricky exam.

'Heya!' I called out, trying to sound cheerful and relaxed. Rich didn't answer. His keys clanked into the bowl by the door, and I heard him walk into the living room. I turned the heat down and followed him.

'Oh, my God, it's hot,' he announced, peeling off his jacket and dropping it behind him.

'Tube pretty rough?'

'Fucking awful. It's like a science experiment: how many people can we cram into a forty-degree oven before a riot breaks out?'

'Sounds hellish.' I picked up the jacket and turned the sleeves the right way round, thinking that my decision to make chilli might have been the wrong one.

'And then a guy got his head caught in the doors, so we were even more delayed.'

'In the *doors*?'

'He stepped on at Oxford Circus just as they were closing. Tall guy, and you know the way the carriage curves in at the top, so you can't quite tell how low you need to duck?'

'Yeah,' I said, though given that I was a good three inches shorter than Rich, I rarely had to consider this.

'Well, he misjudged it and he was caught right in the middle of them.' Rich bounced the sides of his hands off each other. 'Bang.' He sat and started taking off his shoes.

'What happened?'

Rich started to laugh. 'He went cross-eyed and fell backwards.'

'What – back onto the platform?'

'Well, no, into the crowd behind him – it was busy, remember?' He was really laughing now. 'A bit like he was crowd surfing at a concert. They eventually passed him back out of the way.'

'Was he unconscious?'

'I'll say.' Rich had clearly been trying to impress the interview panel with his best Queen's English, because he was telling me the story in the clipped, matter-of-fact tone of an RAF pilot telling the chaps back at base that his best friend had snuffed it.

'Jaysus,' I said, leaning into my own accent as if in defiance of all this English disinterest. 'Was he okay?'

'Oh, I'm sure he was fine.'

'You don't seem very concerned.'

'Well, he was one of those twits who holds up a train with five hundred people on it, just because he's too important to wait two minutes for the next one,' Rich said, now taking off his socks.

'You don't know that. Maybe he was just unfortunately tall.'

Rich laughed again.

I bristled. 'Grand so. I won't expect any sympathy from you if I ever get maimed on public transport.'

I left his jacket on the back of a chair and went to the kitchen. Some of the chilli had got stuck to the bottom of the pot. I gave it a forceful stir to dislodge it. I hated hearing Rich like this, callous and uncaring, like the jogger who'd skipped over me after my fall. It was so unlike him – but then, I thought, how well did I know him, given how blindsided I'd been by him the night before last?

I sensed him standing behind me.

'Sorry,' he said. 'It wasn't very kind of me, laughing about it.'

'That's okay, I just needed to stir this.'

'And thank you for picking up my jacket. I was going to do that.'

'You're welcome,' I said, and then, sensing that I was being irritable, I added, 'I'm sorry, I didn't ask how the interview went.'

'Okay, yeah, they seemed positive.'

We stayed silent for a moment, and I could tell Rich was waiting for me to move the conversation on.

'Did all your extracurriculars come up?' I asked.

In the past couple of years, Rich had taken on as many additional duties as he could – safeguarding, outreach, fund-raising – so that he could argue his case for being ready for anything a new, larger school might throw at him. I couldn't believe he could take on so much extra and still keep up with all the friends he did. I only had the café to worry about, and I still never felt like there was time to do much else.

'We didn't discuss them much,' he said. 'It was largely asking what I would do in such-and-such a scenario.'

'Great.' I gave the pot a stir, trying to think of another question I could ask about the interview. Just as I had done at Jax's house the previous evening, I was avoiding the subject that was keeping me awake and occasionally making it difficult to breathe.

'Did you get your bike back?' Rich asked, after another minute.

I shook my head. 'I called in, but the guy said it would be another week. Apparently that make of wheel is out of stock.

That's why dinner's a bit behind,' I added. 'I was sort of rushing to get here on foot.'

'You didn't need to rush,' he said. He came closer and rested his chin on my shoulder, reaching his arms around me from behind. I winced as his chin dug into the bruise I'd got from falling off the bike, but I didn't move, not wanting him to let go of me.

'Thanks for making dinner,' he said.

'That's okay.'

'How long will it be?'

'About fifteen minutes. Or whenever.'

His hand slid down towards my waistline.

'When is Colin back from his travels?' I asked, laying down the wooden spoon.

'Next Tuesday. It's just us.'

I turned and kissed him briefly, before undoing his belt.

It was fun and familiar and playful. It was safe and it was exciting. It was in the *kitchen*, for God's sake, on tiles and against the sink and by the fridge. We knocked over Colin's copy of *How to Cook* and I banged my head on the recycling bin. It was great.

And through it all, I couldn't help thinking that this was not the sex of a couple on its last legs. This was not boring or going through the motions. Sure, this wasn't the uncharted territory of an anonymous hotel in Dublin, but that wasn't a bad thing.

And I was thinking, *Isn't this enough?*

I kept telling myself to bring it up, but it was Rich, after showering and eating, as we were cleaning up, who said, 'So did you think any more about what I asked the other evening?'

I took a deep breath. 'Yes.'

'And …'

'I'm open to the idea.'

A smile flickered across his face. 'It sounds like there's a "but" coming,' he said.

'Well, there is. I think we should trial it for a fixed amount of time.'

The smile returned, wider now.

'What?' I asked.

'You sound like you're in a board room, planning some kind of PR strategy.' He looked happy, and I could tell how much he'd been hoping it would go this way. I briefly considered putting up more of a fight, but it was too late for that, or so it felt.

'As I was saying,' I said, 'I think we should talk about it again after a while and see if it's making us happy.'

'Sure. How long is "a while"?'

'Three months,' I said, trying to sound firm but reasonable.

'Fine.' He opened his mouth to say something else, then closed it again.

'What?'

'Just wondering if I should get my diary, or whether we can book the meeting room closer to the time.'

'You should do stand-up, you really should.'

'Thank you. I'm going to Edinburgh next year.'

'Also, I think we should use protection,' I said.

'Oh.' That wiped the smile off his face. 'I mean, yes, obviously,' he said, recovering.

'Gonorrhoea is on the rise in London,' I said authoritatively, feeling delighted with myself. Take that! I can mention all the STIs I like because I'm being mature! And rational! You stupid prick!

'I don't plan on getting gonorrhoea,' he said.

'No one *plans* on getting gonorrhoea,' I snapped. I had finished another glass of wine with dinner. 'Who thinks, I'd really love to ruin my underwear with some green stains, I'd better go sleep around until I get a dose of *that*?'

'What do you mean "sleep around"?' he said.

Oops. I'd overplayed my hand. I reckoned I should probably drink some water.

'Are you sure you're okay with this?' Rich asked.

'Sorry,' I said. 'I am, really.'

He came close and hugged me. I closed my eyes, and wished I could keep him like that, wrapped in my arms.

'I think this will be really good for us,' Rich whispered in my ear.

I felt his arms tighten around me, and knew he was waiting for me to agree.

'Me too,' I mumbled.

Chapter Seven

By the time we reached Caledonian Road, I was almost certain our legs weren't touching by accident. I looked at the man sitting beside me, who seemed to be reading the ads on the opposite side of the carriage. As I watched, he bit his bottom lip and sighed. Either he was mightily aroused by the prospect of a multivitamin for those who were tired of being tired, or he was giving me some kind of now-that-I-have-your-attention show.

I had brushed against him as I sat down at Covent Garden, unbalanced by the train taking off. I mumbled an apology and he smiled, his eyes glittering behind dark liner. Opposite us was a guy clearly just out of a late-evening gym class, who was taking large gulps of a protein shake. As I opened my bag and took out my book, I noticed the gym bunny adjusting his shorts. His eyes were closed and he was nodding along to music I could just about hear escaping from his earphones. Eyeliner sighed. I took all this in but didn't draw a link between any of it, and instead opened my copy of *Mrs Dalloway*.

Virginia Woolf held my attention until just after Holborn, when Gym Bunny readjusted what seemed to be seriously uncomfortable shorts and Eyeliner gave a soft laugh. I looked at Gym Bunny properly. He was wearing one of those vests so loose, with such a plunging neckline and such massive gaps at the sides, that it left very little to the imagination.

His pecs were massive, his arms were swollen like Popeye's, and in general he looked stuffed full of balloons ready to pop. And, also, his eyes weren't fully closed. As I watched, his eyelids lifted ever so slightly. He knew he had an audience, and now he had an audience of two. He rubbed his stomach through the thin material of his vest, and Eyeliner spread his legs so that our knees were touching. I looked down at my knee, then left it there, feeling the pressure of him against me.

I read for another minute or so. Then, when the two repeated their signals, I closed my book and coughed gently, my first move in this three-way chess match that I was almost sure I wasn't imagining. I glanced down the carriage, ready for the look of disgust on another passenger's face, or for someone to spring to their feet, point and scream, 'Perverts!' at the sight of such a shameless carry-on in a public place. But the carriage was quiet. Everyone else was looking at their phones, unaware of the erotic triangle forming nearby. It reminded me of those foreign films that TG4 used to show in the early noughties after their Irish-language programmes ended for the night. I would watch them alone with bated breath, knowing there was always the chance of seeing an arse or, in the *really* foreign ones, a nipple.

I opened my book again, but I was no more reading about what Clarissa and her friends were up to than Gym Bunny was catching forty winks. When he adjusted his shorts again, I put my book away and pressed my leg against Eyeliner's, wondering if I was welcome at this peep show. He responded by leaning an elbow on the arm rest between us. Welcome aboard.

Gym Bunny got off at King's Cross without so much as a backward glance, and I wondered if it had all been my imagination. Maybe the guy was like Rafael Nadal, doomed to be forever fiddling with underpants that just wouldn't fit right. But if I had been imagining things, my neighbour was a fellow fantasist: as the doors closed, he gave a faint tut and crossed his legs. I glanced at him and rearranged mine so they were closer to his. After a minute or so, Eyeliner uncrossed himself, and we resumed our definitely-not-accidental contact.

In the week since Rich and I had opened up, I hadn't spent much time thinking about whether or when I would hook up with someone. Instead, I was seizing every opportunity to text Rich and ask what he was doing, then scrutinising his responses to see whether they could have been written mid-coitus. This evening, he was visiting his mum in Kent, where she had moved three years previously. But, I thought, there were no doubt plenty of men in Kent ready and willing to help him celebrate his newly won liberation from monogamy.

And now, as I nudged a stranger on the Tube, it occurred to me that this was fine. I was allowed to do this. Maybe the guy beside me was interested. Sometimes guys were interested in me. And I could – I glanced at Eyeliner – be interested in him too, if I wanted to be.

And I was. Kind of. I would definitely pick Rich over him, but he was a good-looking guy, probably a few years younger than me. I noticed that, as well as eyeliner, he was wearing a little bit of rouge, which gave him a somewhat doll-like appearance. That wasn't something I would usually go for, but he was undeniably attractive, with defined cheek-bones and classically Latin features. The phrase 'sallow skin' entered my head, a term my family used to describe anyone with a healthy tan, but which in the UK, I had learned the hard way, meant something akin to jaundiced.

I was getting off at Wood Green, and as we approached Finsbury Park, I wondered whether Eyeliner would be going that far. It crossed my mind that he might be a pickpocket, and I surreptitiously checked to see if my wallet and phone were still there. They were, so I decided to give him the benefit of the doubt, crossed my arms and let my fingers graze against him. He shifted slightly in his seat, bringing us into closer contact. My heart started to beat faster. I was picking up someone from the side.

At Wood Green I stood, gave him a glance and stepped off the carriage. He followed me onto the platform, and my heart rate climbed higher. This had all been good, innocent, slightly weird fun, but now I was unnerved, and even felt a bit vulnerable. Was this a risky thing to do? Was I going to end up a newspaper headline? 'Man Strangled After Torrid Night of Leg-grazing'?

But, as he fell into step beside me, I said, 'Do you live near here?'

'The next station,' he said, in a Spanish accent, 'but I got off early to say hello.'

We reached the escalators. I stood on the right and turned to look back down at him. He really was pretty. That was the word for it. Rich was handsome, and this guy was pretty.

'Good night?' I asked.

'What?'

'Did you have a good night?'

He shrugged. 'Okay, yes, had some drinks with my friend …' He shrugged again.

Compared to the erotic charge I'd felt on the Tube, this was all a bit flat, as if we'd turned up the lights in the club too bright.

'Well,' I said, as we stepped off the escalator and moved towards the gates, 'do you have a long walk home from here?'

I was ashamed to realise that I had adopted that classic tactic of talking to a non-native English speaker slowly, loudly and with a lilt of an accent, as if I too was speaking in a foreign language.

'Yes, it's a long walk,' Eyeliner said. We passed through the turnstiles and lingered outside the station. Wood Green was, as ever, a neon smear of traffic and shops.

'Maybe your place is close,' he said. He had a half-smile and a hopeful look in his eyes. It was a genuine proposal, and the more he spoke, the less threatened or worried I felt. Instead, I was feeling excited. Fuck it.

'Yeah, it's close,' I said. 'There's an off-licence on the way. Do you like wine?'

I woke up with a gasp. I always do when I've been drinking the night before. I glanced to my right, confirming that I hadn't imagined bringing home a stranger and staying up until 3 a.m. I decided to go in search of coffee, thankful that I wasn't due in the café until the afternoon. Rebecca still wasn't back, but I had finally given myself a morning off, suggesting to Uncle Al that he could always call in and see if Billy and Hugo needed a hand.

On the floor by the front door was a postcard, with a selection of pictures from the Isle of Man on one side. I flipped over the card and saw that the signature at the bottom was Rebecca's.

'Hey, man,' said Eyeliner, who had materialised from nowhere.

'Fuck!'

'Sorry.'

'No, no, I—Where did you come from?'

'Up the … upstairs?'

'Oh. Yes.'

We stood gawping at each other. I became aware that I probably wasn't looking my best, standing there in baggy boxers, bathed in the half-light of the grey morning. Eyeliner had put on last night's shirt again. Like me, the shirt looked a bit worse for wear, but it was still flattering on him, and his sticking-up hair was quite sexy, whereas mine looked more like a hedge.

'Sorry I scared you,' he said.

'No, no, you … I was just …' I waved the postcard. Jesus, I thought, I must really be hung-over. I was struggling to form sentences. He smiled pityingly.

'Do you want a coffee?' I managed.

'No. I'm going to meet a friend, have coffee with her.'

'Cool, sure. Water or anything?' I really wanted to get rid of this guy before my housemates woke up, so why was I trying to bribe him into staying with a selection of hot and cold beverages?

'I should go,' he said firmly, and I realised I was standing with my back to the front door, blocking his escape route.

'Sure, sure,' I said, shoving the postcard down the back of my boxers and unlocking the door. 'Thanks for … um …'

'Thank you for letting me stay.'

'Course.'

'Maybe we do it again some day.'

I smiled and gave him a little bow as I opened the door, like the hotel concierge seeing off a high-profile guest.

'But …' He hesitated, and I closed the door a little in order to hide my torso from the outside world.

'Yeah?'

'It's a little embarrassing,' he said, and my stomach dropped. Oh, God. He was a hustler. He rode the Piccadilly Line every Friday night until someone invited him home. He had expected to find the money on the nightstand.

'Your sheets,' he said, and I wondered if he was demanding payment in linen.

'Yes?'

'I, uh, I have …' He mimed a firm tug with both hands.

'You stripped the bed?'

'Yes, it was … wet.'

My stomach hadn't returned to its usual position, but I was relieved to learn that the situation wasn't illegal or dangerous, merely gross and embarrassing.

'Sure,' I said, wondering if I'd missed something either spectacular or disastrous during last night's activities.

'Because I pissed myself,' he announced, as if saying it as loud as he could was the only way to break it to me.

'You ... pissed yourself?'

He nodded. 'In the night.'

'Oh.' I didn't have much else to say.

'The ...' He gave a gentle push down on some imaginary springs.

'Mattress?' I offered.

'The mattress, yes, it seems to be dry. Pretty dry.'

'Oh. Good.' No wonder he'd turned down the coffee – he was probably worried he'd be at it again on the Tube.

'It does not happen often,' he said, and I decided it was time to open the door again.

'Well, I'm glad to hear it,' I said, ushering him out. 'Don't worry, I needed to put on a wash anyway.'

He turned to me on the front step and smiled, a little dimple forming on his right cheek. Weak bladder or no, he was a beautiful man.

'You're very sexy,' he said.

'Cool,' I said, unused to receiving this kind of compliment. 'Yeah.'

He gave me a kiss on the cheek, zipped up his jacket and ambled off.

I stumbled back up the stairs and into my room. The sheets were in a ball at the end of the bed, and a large stain had spread across the mattress. That would have to wait until later, but for now, I grabbed the bundle and ran downstairs to the washing machine. I was rooting around under the sink for detergent when Tony walked into the kitchen.

'There's a postcard falling out of your arse,' he said.

I'd forgotten about Rebecca's card, which had become dislodged from my boxers in my bleary-eyed confusion.

'Oh, cheers,' I said, and left it to one side while I poured the detergent and started the machine.

'Has Rich left?' Tony asked.

I hesitated. I hadn't gone into the whole open-relationship situation with my housemates. It wasn't really their business and, although we'd lived together for years, we weren't that close. I barely saw Polly, and a week could go by without Tony and I exchanging more than a few words. On the other hand, I was now bringing strangers home and letting them piss the bed, so maybe it was out of order not to let Tony know.

'Rich is off with his mum this morning,' I said, which was true, just not the answer to Tony's question.

He nodded, poured himself a glass of water and looked out at the square of overgrown weeds we called the back garden. It was odd to see Tony still: he usually clattered about the place, chomping on protein bars and singing Lana Del Rey. He clearly had something to say, so I hovered by the washing machine and waited. I was getting cold in just my boxers.

'You were … you guys were a bit loud last night,' he said eventually.

'Oh, sorry.'

'No worries, it's just that you woke me up—'

'Wow. I mean, sorry.'

'No, mate, fair play, just …'

God, I thought, I could remember it being lengthy, but how loud had it been?

'I'll keep it down,' I said.

'Cool,' said Tony. We chatted about weekend plans for a minute, then he went back to bed. I poured myself a glass of water (I was beginning to distinguish a headache emerging from the general wash of tiredness) and took it, along with the postcard, back into the living room.

Rebecca's postcard wasn't the chatty missive I had been expecting:

Owen [she never spelled my name right],

Will be abroad longer than expected. Do <u>not</u> let Al close the cafe. Pay y/self from the till and keep records. Will sort payslips on return.

Rebecca

How bizarre. I went to refill my glass of water, wondering what could have happened to her, and why she thought Al would shut down the café. At least it wasn't my problem that morning.

As I was making my way upstairs, thinking I might even get back to sleep for an hour, I heard my phone ringing. When I checked, I saw I had seven missed calls from Billy. He must have been ringing while I dealt with the sheets and apologised for all the groaning and moaning.

'Eoin?' I could hear the desperation in his voice when I rang him back, but I refused to be moved to sympathy just yet.

'Billy, what's up?'

'Well, I couldn't get the grinder to the right setting.'

'Sure thing,' I said, before he could get any further. 'I can talk you through that. Pull the handle towards you to start.'

'No, but the thing is, I couldn't get into the safe either. I couldn't see where the keypad is.'

'There's no keypad on the safe,' I said, avoiding the temptation to tell him we'd gone over all this five fucking times since his cash-up mistake the previous week, which I had never managed to correct and which had left my own cash-ups inaccurate ever since. 'It's opened by a key, which is in its own security box behind Rebecca's computer. You should have a text with the code to that on your phone.'

'Listen, Eoin, it's super busy –' his voice became faint for a moment as he told someone he was so sorry and would hopefully see them again '– so it would be great if you could come now. Otherwise …'

'Where's Al?'

'Dunno.'

'Where's Hugo?'

As if in response, I heard a faint ding in the background.

'Billy, how are you taking payments if you don't have any change?'

'Contactless.'

'What do you mean, contactless? The card machine's broken.'

'Oh, yeah.'

I glanced at the postcard, which I'd dropped onto my bedside locker. Rebecca had a lot to answer for.

'Sorry, Eoin,' said Billy.

'Listen, don't let people leave without paying. If they don't have exact change, round it down, but take *something*. I'll be there in half an hour.'

'Cool. Half an hour.'

'Sure.'

'Cheers. Only … if you could maybe … step on it … that'd be, like, even better.'

I let him hear my jaw clench in response.

'Sorry,' he said. 'See you when I see you.'

I hung up and turned to face my mattress, bald and grey and still showing signs of dampness. Giving it a proper clean would have to wait. I went to find some painkillers.

Chapter Eight

My hair was still wet as I set off for the Quarter Turn. The blast of hot water in the shower had made my skin tight and dry, and the quick, violent scrub I'd given my mouth had left my tongue raw and the nerves in my teeth throbbing.

The sensation of being squeaky clean on the outside but jumbled and sore on the inside reminded me of other mornings like this: mornings after blurry, fumbled nights which left me feeling like a different person somehow. My first kiss, the first time I'd had sex, the first time I'd had sex with a man: all of them had been followed by a morning like this, when the sun felt brighter than usual and I found myself wondering if some sign of the night's events was stamped on my face.

I'd once asked Rich if he'd ever felt this way, and he said he'd never heard a better expression of Catholic guilt. He'd only just moved back to London, and we were drinking by the Thames on an August bank-holiday weekend, people-watching and having the kind of rambling, far-reaching conversation you only get to after a solid six hours in someone else's company.

'It's not guilt,' I said, 'Catholic or otherwise. I just mean that you wake up, and you're a different person.'

'No, you're not,' Rich said. 'Look, for example, this chap in my school and I—' He stopped and laughed, seemingly surprised by his own memory. 'Jesus, I haven't thought about this in years.'

'Who was this? Your first kiss?'

'Not quite. The two of us, we never actually kissed, we just …'

'Did stuff.'

He laughed again. 'Exactly.'

I watched a strange, startled smile spread across his face, one I'd never seen before, and I thought it was amazing how many times you could find something new to love in someone. I resisted saying as much, worried that Rich would think it was just the three cans talking.

'You never kissed him?' I asked instead.

'I tried once,' he said. 'He brought a stop to it pretty quickly. And we never did it again.'

'Wow. Did he ever come out?'

'No. And that's what I mean,' he said, as the strange smile vanished, and he assumed his usual expression of thoughtful confidence. 'I don't think you do something and then have to carry that for ever as an identity or a … label or whatever.' He sipped his beer. 'The guy's married now, I think. And I'm …'

'You're stuck with me.'

He leaned over to kiss me. 'I am.'

Well, whatever Rich might have thought, I couldn't deny feeling like a different person right now. Specifically, I was now the type of person who got turned on by a guy in a muscly top and brought home a bedwetter, all after having a meltdown only a week ago at the prospect of my boyfriend doing the same thing.

And yet I couldn't stop grinning. The further I got from the awkward goodbye and the stained mattress, the giddier I felt at the thought that I'd actually picked up a gorgeous man, on public transport at that. And from what I could remember (the bottle of wine had blurred some of the memories), it had actually been a lot of fun. I had forgotten what it was like to have sex with anyone who wasn't Rich, whose favourite positions I could glide through, like a well-practised set of scales. Eyeliner I had needed to figure out, to try stuff on, until he made the noises that had woken Tony. By the time the Quarter Turn came into view, I found that my walk had become a strut. Then, when I saw that today's milk delivery was still sitting on the doorstep, it turned into a run.

Customers were stepping over the milk bottles as they warmed gently in the late-morning sun. I picked up the crate, noticing that some enterprising soul had made off with a bottle, and stepped into the café.

It was about as disastrous a scene as I'd anticipated. It looked a lot like someone had exploded a bag of coffee behind the counter, covering every surface in a three-metre radius with beans. There were no pastries on display and no music to cover the sound of a highly irate queue. The cafe's three two-seater tables and its large central dining table were totally covered with dirty plates, teapots and takeaway cups. There was a smashed milk jug in the middle of the room, its fragments ground into the floor. A pigeon flew in through the open door behind me, and a woman screamed.

'Right,' I said, walking behind the counter. 'We need a reset.'

'Where did you get those?' Billy asked, as I set down the delivery. 'I've been looking for milk all morning.'

'Ladies and gentlemen, I'm so sorry,' I called, 'we've had a technical hitch, and we're going to have to close for half an hour or so. See you all at –' I glanced at the clock '– midday.'

There were groans and sighs, as if the assembled crowd had been dying to sit in a filthy café while a pigeon sipped milk from a puddle on the floor. I turned back to Billy. 'You clean, I'll set up the till. Start with that,' I said, pointing to the broken jug.

'How?'

Billy looked ready to cry, so I tried not to snarl at him, but I didn't quite manage it.

'Pick up the big pieces with your *fingers*. Then mop up the milk. With a mop.'

In the kitchen, Hugo was sitting on a small stool, filling in a crossword. A mug of tea steamed on the prep counter beside him.

'I heard you,' he said. 'Closed till midday. Good idea.'

'Why didn't you help?'

'You said Al would come,' he said.

'And when he didn't?'

He shrugged. 'Billy's a good worker.'

'So why does the café look like it's been hit by a tornado?'

Hugo took a sip of his tea with the self-possession of a man completely secure in a job he didn't care about. 'Tornado,' he repeated. 'That's a good one.'

I didn't trust myself to reply, so instead I returned to the front of the café, where Billy was now trying to shoo the pigeon out the door. A handful of customers were still peering in, shaking their heads. One woman had her phone out and seemed to be filming Billy's efforts. Leaning against the counter was the guy with the gym pass, the one who had come in last week.

'Rush hour?' he asked.

'Not quite,' I said, 'but unfortunately we're closed for the next half-hour.'

'So, no chance of an interview? I brought a CV this time,' he said, waving it in the air. He seemed highly amused by the situation.

A sarcastic cheer came from outside. Billy had successfully got rid of the pigeon.

'And stay out!' he yelled at it, before marching back into the café, beaming. I gave him a thumbs-up.

'Now the milk, please,' I said to him, and turned back to the job applicant, whose name I had now forgotten. 'I'm sorry, um …'

'James. I actually wanted to ask you if you need a hand right now.'

Billy slipped in the puddle of milk. Nearby cutlery rattled as he hit the floor. The crowd outside gave another cheer.

'Look,' I said to James, trying to wade through this waking nightmare as best I could, 'I'm afraid we're not taking on any staff at the moment.'

James glanced over his shoulder to where Billy sat, rubbing his wrist and whimpering softly. He turned back to me. 'Can I say it looks like you should?'

'The owner is actually away—' I began.

'What the fuck is going on?' said Al, barrelling through the front door. 'Why are there people queuing outside? Why aren't we open? What the fuck you doing down there, Bill?'

Billy's face was flushed, and he whispered, 'I think I've sprained my wrist.'

'On second thoughts,' I said to James, deciding that if he was so determined to annoy me, he might as well be doing something useful at the same time, 'help me clear a few tables, and then we can do a proper interview this afternoon.'

'Okay,' he said, 'but shouldn't we mop up that milk before someone else slips in it?'

'Sure,' I said. 'There's a mop and bucket down those stairs, just beside the toilet. It's—'

'I'm sure I'll find it,' he said.

'Thank you, James.'

'You're welcome.'

'I'm Eoin, by the way,' I called after him, as he clattered down the stairs, pulling off his jumper as he went.

*

'Not a great day for you boys,' said Trevor, as I served him his cappuccino. We had managed to re-open and get through lunchtime. The security box with the key to the safe had fallen down behind Rebecca's desk, and Billy and I had agreed to hide it in a gap under the bottom step of the stairs to prevent this from happening again. James had mopped up, stacked plates and wiped down surfaces in silence, the look of mild amusement never leaving his face.

'Not our finest hour,' I said to Trevor, 'but we got it under control.'

'Under control? Ha! I don't call losing five–nil under control.'

I decided he was talking about either a high-scoring football match or a low-scoring game of rugby. 'Sometimes you're just beaten,' I said.

'Wise words,' said Trevor, pulling a sports section from his stack of weekend papers. At the counter, Billy was prodding his wrist tentatively.

'You'd know if it was broken, Billy,' I said, as I added Trevor's cup to the crowded dishwasher and flicked it on.

'I dunno, man,' he said, and waved his phone at me. 'I've been reading about this guy in the States. He had a broken foot for three years and he never knew.'

'Fascinating.' I glanced at my own phone. Rich had messaged to say he would be back from his mum's this evening if I wanted to hang out. I put it away without replying.

'Hey, Eoin.' Billy leaned in to me. 'Do you think I could sue the café?'

'Why?'

'Well, it was a workplace accident.'

'You slipped in milk you were trying to clean up.'

'Yeah. Isn't that negligence?'

'Whose negligence?'

'What?' Billy seemed confused.

I sighed. 'Go ahead and sue, Billy,' I said. 'I'm sure Uncle Al will be delighted to hear about it.'

Billy's face fell. We'd only just got rid of Al, who had been stomping about while we cleaned up, telling us exactly why this was unacceptable, how disappointed Rebecca would be in us. I finally sent him to get some change from a neighbouring shop, emphasising how much better he'd be at that kind of thing than me.

'Do you reckon he'd know?' Billy asked.

'Will Al know if you sue the café? Probably, Billy.'

I made myself an espresso and picked up James's CV.

'I'm going to take a break,' I said. I left Billy cautiously stretching his wrist and went outside, where James was sitting with an oat flat white.

'So,' I said, as I sat down opposite him, pretending I had conducted many such interviews in the past, 'tell me a bit about the last place you worked.'

'Well, I'm an actor.' James looked at me carefully. 'Is that a problem?'

In a word, yes. I had worked with an actor at the pub in Kentish Town. Tilly had had a habit of dropping out of shifts with no notice in order to attend auditions, and insisted we come to see her perform at a scratch night, which took place above a pub in Islington. This was in the early days of seeing Rich, and I asked him along, thrilled with the chance to appear artsy. I began to regret my decision when I realised that a scratch night consisted of half-finished plays performed on a bare stage. In addition to Tilly's self-penned monologue, we had to endure three other half-hour plays, one of which concerned a missing bag of cocaine that was eventually discovered under Rich's chair, much to the merriment of the cast, if not the audience. The improvisation that followed was so unforgettably painful that, to this day, Rich would sometimes break a moment of silence between us by grabbing my shoulders and saying, 'Got my coke, mate?' with the same look of deranged glee the actor had worn as he scrabbled about between Rich's legs.

'Not a problem,' I said to James. 'Just don't drag me to any scratch nights.'

James gazed back at me blankly, and I wondered why the things I said to him kept sounding so harsh. I let a laugh out through my nose to show him what a light-hearted messer I was, then tried to look interested as I asked about his last acting job.

'I did a couple of episodes of *Doctors*.'

'Cool!'

'Not really,' James said, 'but thank you.'

'Do you mainly do TV acting?'

He winced a little and said, 'Not as much as I'd like.'

'Sorry, I'll mind my own business.'

'That's all right,' he said, though I noticed that he didn't discourage me from doing just that.

'And have you worked in a café before?'

He tilted his head from side to side, like this was a phil-osophical conundrum. 'I worked in my auntie's café when I was younger, in my teens.'

I nodded, my heart sinking.

'And to be honest,' he said, swirling his flat white, 'that was attached to her church, like it was sort of a community centre as well.'

He'd poured hot water out of an urn, was what he was saying. One of those steel cylinders with a tea towel drying on top of it. 'Sounds fascinating,' I said.

'Thanks,' he said sharply.

'I'm sorry, that sounded sarcastic.'

'A little.'

'I promise you, I do think that's interesting. I'd imagine it's been quite a source of material for you as an actor.'

'Yeah,' he said. 'Some of the characters come in use in improv classes and so on. You ever worked somewhere like that?'

'I haven't unfortunately,' I said, adopting what I hoped was a look of sincere regret. Was *I* being interviewed? It felt that way. 'Any more recent service-industry work?' I asked.

'I did some time with a catering company.'

'Oh, I did a bit of that. It's demanding stuff.'

'And it was a sort of theatre thing as well, like we had to dress up according to the cuisine.'

'That sounds horrendous,' I said, and panicked that he would take offence again. In fact, he smiled for the first time.

'Horrendous, yeah,' he said. 'It was themed by the country, so one week I'd be serving pasta and pretending to be a mobster. Then they did a Caribbean night and that's when I left the company.'

I laughed again. He didn't. I looked down at his CV for inspiration.

'Fair enough. And do you have any acting work coming up?'

'Nope. I was a bit spoiled in my first few years out of drama school because I booked this tour and then … ' He stopped, and wiped the back of his hand across the table, as if cleaning a blackboard in order to start a fresh maths problem. 'Anyway. Yes, I'm very available, for as much work as you have.'

Glancing inside, I spotted Billy in screensaver mode, staring into the middle distance. 'Well, you really saved our necks today anyway,' I said to James. 'How about three shifts a week to start?'

'Sounds fine.'

I paused, then decided to be honest. 'I should mention that we're not quite sure when the owner is getting back from holiday. I'm sort of filling in as manager.'

'Right.'

'So until she's back, I'm afraid it'll be cash-in-hand.'

'Is that legal?' he asked.

I sighed, wondering if he behaved this way in auditions. If he did, it was no wonder he was an out-of-work actor. 'I'm not a lawyer,' I said, 'but I reckon we'll get away with it for a week. We'll keep everything written down and sort out payslips later.'

'Sure,' he said, and raised an eyebrow. Either mild suspicion was his default expression, or he was finding this all a bit odd. 'What's the owner's name?'

'Rebecca,' I said, 'and I promise you she exists. I'm not luring you into a front for a money-laundering business.'

'I believe you,' said James. 'I mean, if you're the public face of a sinister gang, they've chosen well.' He took a sip of his flat white. 'You look pretty innocent to me.'

I couldn't tell if this was a dig or not.

'Right,' I said, choosing not to dwell on it. 'Well, thanks again. See you on … Monday, at nine? Schools are starting back this week, so we'll probably have a bit of a mid-morning rush.'

'Cool,' he said, and finished the last of his coffee. 'See you then.'

As he stood, his thighs knocked against the table, so I had to grab my espresso to keep it from spilling.

After he left, I stayed where I was, not quite ready to go back inside. I closed my eyes for a minute, the late night and the frantic start to the day finally catching up with me. I remembered that I still had to reply to Rich's message. I wasn't sure what to say, or whether it would be strange to see him mere hours after saying goodbye to my first new bedfellow in years.

I heard Al's snuffling, and opened my eyes as he sat down where James had just been. He threw two bags of pound coins onto the table between us.

'You got everything under control now?' he asked.

'Ah, yeah, just about.'

'Doesn't look great, things getting out of hand like that.'

I folded James's CV in half and tried not to let the annoyance show on my face. I should have been at home all morning, maybe even lying in a park, not cleaning up someone else's mess.

'Well,' I said, 'we got it sorted.'

'Seems like you're the only one who knows what to do around here.'

'I wouldn't go that far,' I said.

'I would. Billy's gonna brew tea in a watering can one of these days, you mark my words. I dunno, son,' he sighed, 'you told me he was getting better, and he ain't.'

I stayed silent. Yes, I had lied about Billy doing well, but what did Al expect me to do?

'Seems to me,' Al said, leaning in close so that I had to turn my head away from the smell of TCP, 'that we should think about shutting up shop for a few days, till Rebecca gets back.'

Rebecca's postcard flashed through my mind. How had she known?

'Isn't she due back any day now?' I asked. Al shrugged. 'And, anyway,' I continued, 'yer man is coming in for a few shifts this week.'

He gave me a quizzical look.

'My man?'

'James,' I said. 'The guy who was helping out for the past few hours.'

Al didn't seem happy. He glanced over his shoulder, perhaps expecting James to be lingering there, waiting for his approval. 'Who gave you permission to be hiring and firing?' he asked.

'Well, Rebecca actually arranged for him to come in – for James to come in, I mean – for his trial shift last week,' I said, aware that babbling wasn't making this sound any more convincing. 'And I postponed it because she wasn't back yet, but I can't keep asking him to wait, can I?'

I knew that this patchy web of lies could be torn apart by a single message from Al to Rebecca, but the tone of that morning's postcard suggested the two weren't in contact right now. If Rebecca was telling me to pay myself from the till, I reasoned, she obviously trusted me enough to keep things rolling until she got back. Besides, Rebecca deserved my loyalty. She could be a demanding boss, but she never blamed me when I made mistakes, she was always quick to jump in when a customer was being a pain in the arse, and on more than one occasion she had given me an advance on my wages, assuring me that she'd always do what she could for me. If she and Al were in some sort of battle of wills, I knew whose side I was on.

'So,' I continued, 'we'll stay open, see how this guy gets on, and then we can decide what to do when Rebecca comes home.' I wondered if Al would fly off the handle at being disagreed with. To my relief, he just sniffed and looked off across the road, as if he was staring at distant snow-capped mountains rather than a shuttered charity shop and a murky launderette. I took this as silent acquiescence, and went back inside.

Trevor was asleep in his usual spot, his new cappuccino barely touched. Two women, each sporting an impressive bump, discussed whether their pregnancy-yoga teacher was still up to scratch since moving studios. Billy was doing a crossword with Hugo at one of the tables. I started to sweep the floor. My lower back was aching, and the image of Rich's bed began to form in my head, like a mirage in the desert, painfully enticing and unreachable. It was only when Billy lifted his legs to allow me to sweep under his chair that I realised the absurdity of the situation.

'Get up,' I snapped, 'both of you.'

Billy looked up, like a puppy getting a finger wagged at him, while Hugo remained intent on the crossword. I decided I'd had enough for one day.

'Rebecca has put me in charge of wages while she's gone,' I said, 'and this counts as an unpaid break, so finish the crossword, if you like, but don't expect any money for it.'

'Sorry, Eoin,' said Billy, jumping up and grabbing the broom. 'I'll finish sweeping.'

I knew he would make a terrible job of this, but I was content with the gesture for now. Hugo remained seated.

'Are you done for the day, Hugo?' I asked.

'Fucking busy lunchtime,' he said, hauling himself up. 'Me and Billy have a stressful start to the day, then the big man arrives and says no breaks, no fun, no talking …'

He wandered off into the kitchen, muttering under his breath as he went. My phone buzzed in my pocket. It was Rich again, saying he could meet me at the café when I was done. I replied saying I'd absolutely love that. Whatever awkwardness I might feel seeing him so soon after sex with a stranger I'd just have to live through. Although, I thought, I'd have to insist we go to his, what with the soiled mattress and—

'Feck it,' I said, and Billy looked up from his ineffectual sweeping.

'What?'

'I left my sheets in the wash.'

I sat at the dining table that dominated the café floor and looked back towards the counter while I waited for Rich. Thanks to all the cleaning and restocking we'd done during the break in service, shutting down hadn't taken long, and I'd been able to send Billy home about twenty minutes after we turned the sign to Closed. I was passing the time until Rich got there by filling in our health and safety log, which no one had touched since Rebecca left. I was alternating between three different-coloured pens to give the impression of temperatures being checked several times daily, rather than invented in one fraudulent burst of enthusiasm.

I rarely sat down in the Quarter Turn, and it was odd seeing the place from a customer's perspective. With the café empty and the surfaces clean, I could appreciate how airy and soothing the stripped-back Scandi aesthetic was.

I looked around and amused myself with an old project of mine, trying to think if there was any way I could convince Rebecca to add a bookshelf without disrupting the style of the place. I had raised the idea before, wondering aloud if the café could seem a bit sterile and impersonal. Rebecca said she'd consider it, but never mentioned it again. Perhaps, I thought, as I eyed some empty space and thought about the shelf that could go there, I could promise to keep any books I sourced to a uniform size, and wrap the covers in a light blue paper to match the colour of the coffee cups. It was the kind of craft project I could rope Jax into, and I could maybe even circulate the titles according to the season.

As I mulled this over, my eyes came to rest on the tip jar by the coffee machine, which, in the name of minimalism, Rebecca refused to label as such, and as a consequence often ended up being used by customers as a bin for tea bags and sugar packets. I closed the logbook and went to count the coins. I was surprised to find it was empty. I wouldn't have expected many tips from this morning's chaos, but I thought we would have been left the odd bit of change in the past few days, particularly since the card machine was kaput and everyone was paying in cash.

I heard a knock behind me, and turned to see Rich waving through the glass door. Rather than the awkwardness I had anticipated, I felt a rush of excitement, and practically ran to let him in.

'Risteárd, *mo stór*,' I said, as I pulled the door open and held out my arms. I knew the Gaelicised name and over-the-top endearment would be lost on him, but trusted that he'd pick up on the spirit of it.

'All right, my Irishman,' he said, stepping into my arms. 'What's got you so poetic?'

'Just good to see you,' I mumbled into his shoulder.

'You too,' he said. 'I've brought you something.'

He steered me out the door, and I saw my bike propped up against a lamp-post, the new front wheel gleaming.

'Ah, Rich,' I said, stepping out to look at it, 'you're very good. How did you know it was still in the shop?'

'I didn't. I was just passing. I dropped in and gave your name.'

I lifted the bike by the stem and gave the front wheel a spin. The sight of the shiny new rim whispering past the brake pads made me shiver with delight, and I realised how much I'd missed it.

'Thank you,' I said to Rich, passing him the bike and digging out my keys to lock the café behind me. 'I meant to call about it this morning, but I had to come in early.'

'Shouldn't you turn off the lights?' Rich asked, as I turned the key in the lock.

'Sorry, yes,' I said, unlocking the door again. 'Just in a rush.'

He shook his head while I opened the door and flicked off the lights. I told him about my unexpected early start as I pulled down the shutters, conscious that I was dancing around the part of the story where I'd woken up beside another man.

'Right,' I said, once I'd snapped the last padlock closed. 'Shall we?'

'Sure,' he said, 'your place or mine?'

'Let's go to yours,' I said immediately. 'I can give you a backie?'

'Are you joking?'

'Why not? The tyres are probably as strong as they'll ever be. You just have to trust me.'

Rich eyed the bike suspiciously. He wasn't much of a cyclist and he had probably pushed it all the way here. It occurred to me that loud and unfamiliar sex was great, but real love was picking up a bike from the shop.

'You sure you can manage it?' he asked.

'We'll be grand,' I said. 'I'll stick to the quiet roads. And you can wear the helmet.'

I unclipped it from where it had been dangling from the handlebars and put it on Rich's head. I saw him wince as it disturbed his hair.

'I probably look like an idiot,' he said, as he climbed onto the saddle from behind.

'You look gorgeous.' I swung my leg over the crossbar and placed one foot on a pedal.

'What should I hold?' Rich asked.

'You can hold onto the saddle, or you can hold onto me.'

'Oh,' he said. 'Simple choice.'

He placed his hands on my hips and gave me a squeeze, then leaned forward to give me a kiss on the nape of my neck, the peak of the helmet bumping gently off the back of my head. For the first time, I could picture how our relationship might work with this new arrangement: the thrill of the unfamiliar, and the comfort of the man I loved.

'Keep your legs spread,' I said, 'or the oil will get on your trousers.'

I pushed down hard on the pedal and we wobbled off. Rich gave an uncharacteristic yelp, and for a moment, I thought I'd lose control. But then I dropped a gear, and soon we were picking up speed.

Chapter Nine

'Just feel that, Eoin.'

'What am I feeling for?'

'Isn't it so much softer?'

'It just feels like wool.'

Jax snatched the ball back from me. 'What do you mean, "feels like wool"? Does burned Nescafé just "taste like coffee"?'

'I don't think you *can* burn Nescafé. It tastes like soil no matter what you do.'

'You see, that's my point. This,' she shook the ball of wool in my face, 'is like a fine, perfectly brewed espresso shot, and you're just pretending to be ignorant of the fact.'

'I like the colour.'

'Me too.' She turned it over in her hands. 'Perfect for a scarf, to go with my long coat.' She put the wool back on the shelf and turned to leave.

'Aren't you going to buy it?'

'From John Lewis? Are you insane? I'll find it online somewhere. I just wanted to see how it felt to the touch.'

She led the way out of the store and onto Oxford Street, where we were hit by a dry, angry wave of heat. It was late Friday afternoon, and the whole of central London felt on edge, as if everyone was furious that they weren't standing in a cold shower. As we waited for the lights to change, a cyclist bellowed at a pair of tourists who tried to cross the road, before disappearing into an impossibly narrow gap between two buses.

'Let's get a drink,' said Jax.

We crossed into Soho and wandered along a few streets, looking for somewhere that wasn't too crowded.

'How's everything with Rich?' Jax asked, standing on her toes and looking through the window of a place on the corner of Dean Street.

'That's a cocktail bar,' I said, 'I'm vetoing that.' We turned away. 'Rich and I are fine. It's sort of business as usual.'

In fact, the evening at Rich's house after my night with Eyeliner had been wonderful. Somehow the everyday actions of ordering a takeaway and listening to Colin describing his pilgrimage had been the perfect way to rebalance after my silly night and frantic day. And having sex with Rich had felt like returning home after a fun but rainy camping holiday – familiar, comfortable and dry.

'Has he … um, opened the relationship yet?' Jax asked.

'I don't know,' I said. 'We sort of agreed to talk about it in a few months.'

'But you're feeling better about everything?'

'Oh, look, there's a bench freeing up.' I pointed to a space outside a pub, where a couple of suits were reaching for their things. A near-identical pair of office workers were circling, but Jax lunged for the bench before they could claim it.

'Yeah, I'm feeling better,' I said, ignoring the dark looks we were getting. 'I think setting out that trial period helped.'

'I knew it would,' said Jax. 'Mind the spot. I'll get you a drink.'

I resisted the temptation to check my phone while Jax was gone. I had read an article in the paper on my lunch break saying that screen usage was linked to depression and that we should only be looking at our phones for an hour a day. I wasn't feeling depressed, but I had promised myself that I would try to cut back. It would make the early starts for the café tough – the white light from the phone acted like an ignition key in the early morning – but I was sure that I'd feel more virtuous and productive without it. I looked at the drinkers around me, at the film posters outside the post-production office opposite, at the shadow of a building dividing the road sharply in two. This is great, I told myself. I'm in the real world.

'How about you?' Jax asked, as she handed me my pint. 'Have you been opening up?'

'I haven't really been looking,' I said. This wasn't a lie – I hadn't gone hunting for Eyeliner, I just stepped into a lucky Tube carriage – but I knew I wasn't telling Jax the whole truth either. Maybe I didn't want to admit that, after all the agonising I'd subjected her to, it had only taken me a matter of days to jump into bed with someone new.

'You should get on Grindr,' said Jax.

'Maybe,' I said, feeling self-conscious about discussing it in public, and simultaneously prudish for feeling self-conscious. I'd tried a few apps before Rich and I were together, but had always been intimidated by the idea of signing up to a service dedicated to hook-ups.

'Go on,' Jax said, nudging me, 'download it now. We're in Soho, your phone will probably explode.'

'I don't want to create a dating profile in public.'

'Dating profile? It's not Lonely Hearts, hon. Just take a selfie and put in your measurements.'

'I'm not doing that in front of you. Besides,' I added, 'I'm actually trying to cut back on my phone usage.'

'The report that came out today was bullshit,' said Jax. 'I read an article that completely discredited it.'

'Well, I still want to take a break from it.'

'Yeah, well take a break from breathing while you're at it.'

A tall man with a ginger beard was hovering just behind Jax. We made eye contact and I nodded politely at him.

Jax glanced over her shoulder and gasped. Even before she said his name, I knew this was the smiling object of her affections.

'Aaron! Are you—' In her excitement, something caught in Jax's throat, so she was forced to continue in a strangled whisper: 'How are you?'

'Fine, fine,' Aaron said. 'Gorgeous evening, isn't it?'

Jax swallowed heavily and introduced us while Aaron lit his cigarette. I wasn't crazy about his big beard and fade combination, but I could see why Jax liked him. In the few minutes we were talking, he seemed comfortable in saying only a few words without coming across as disengaged or bored. He even asked a follow-up question when I told him I was a barista – most people either glazed over or asked what I really wanted to do. Aaron shook his head in wonder as I outlined the properties and origins of the Quarter Turn's Kenyan blend. Jax beamed.

'Where are you off to this evening?' she asked, as Aaron finished his cigarette.

'I'm going for dinner shortly,' he said. 'In fact, I'd better head upstairs and finish my drink. Gotta ship out soon.'

He went back into the pub. Jax turned to me, her eyes alight. 'Isn't he great?'

'He's very polite. And tall.'

Jax sipped her pint and looked at the film posters across the road. 'Who do you reckon he's off to dinner with?' she asked, after a moment.

'I really don't think I could say.'

'Do you think it's a girlfriend? It's Friday night.'

'It is,' I said, 'and couples often eat dinner together on a Friday night.'

'They do,' said Jax, 'so the question is this: why didn't he *say* he was going to dinner with his girlfriend?'

'What?'

'If I asked you your plans, and you were doing something with Rich, you'd mention him, wouldn't you?'

'Unless …'

'Unless you were either single *or* you were some sort of dirty dog, and you thought it would be better to keep that little detail to yourself.'

'Or maybe he *wanted* us to have this conversation, so he deliberately left it ambiguous,' I said. 'We're just playing checkers while he's playing chess.'

'Are you taking the piss?'

'Sorry, I just think you're reading a lot into it,' I said. 'Have you checked his Instagram?'

'He's not on any of them,' she said. 'Mysterious.'

'Maybe you could ask round the office?'

Jax looked at me with a curious expression, as if I were a rare variety of orchid she'd never seen before. 'I should ask people in the office if he's single?' she said, in a tone of gentle incredulity.

'Yeah. Or ask him.'

'You're unwell, is what you are. You're not well, Eoin. As if I'd walk up to a guy in the office and basically say, "D'you wanna fuck?" Honestly.'

I conceded that I wasn't in my right mind and asked instead about how the supplement was coming together. Jax was doing outrageous hours, but these were made bearable, she said, by the possibility of a permanent position in the future.

'Well, if it doesn't work out,' I said, 'I'm sure they'd have you back at the pub.'

'That's sort of what I picture when I'm flagging at the moment. A lifetime of service-industry bullshit.'

I was about to argue that there were worse fates, but Jax went on, 'Speaking of which, how's the new guy in work?'

'James? He's … all right.'

'Oh, no, have you got another Billy on your hands?'

'Not at all,' I said. 'He works pretty well, I haven't had to explain anything twice, I just …'

Jax narrowed her eyes, in the way that always made me feel she could see straight through me.

'I've spent a lot of his first week worrying that he hates me,' I continued. 'He's lovely to Billy – they'll be laughing away together but when I ask what's up, he just shuts down. And everything I say, he takes it as a criticism. Like, I was showing him how to do the cash-up yesterday, and he seemed to think I was accusing him of not being able to do addition.'

Jax nodded and made some sympathetic noises, but I knew I hadn't convinced her of how annoying it was, working with someone I had alienated within minutes of meeting him.

'And,' I went on, 'he insulted my bike.'

This was stretching the truth a little. Seeing me dismount from my newly repaired bike one morning, James had explained that he didn't trust bicycles, because apparently no one knew, scientifically, why they stay upright when in motion. I argued that this was all the more reason to cycle, because it basically meant climbing onto a miracle machine every day, but James had just scoffed at this.

'Not your *bike*,' Jax exclaimed, unable to stop herself grinning. 'Has he insulted any other inanimate objects?'

'Stop that,' I said. 'Whose side are you on anyway?'

Aaron had emerged from the pub, his jacket slung over his shoulder. He looked our way and waved. I waved back and Jax turned. '*Bon appétit!*' she called.

He smiled and walked off. Jax turned back, grimacing, and let out a low moan. '*Bon appétit?* What the fuck was that?'

'Maybe he likes French. Maybe he finds it a turn-on.'

'I may die,' she said, and shook her head violently, as if she was trying to fling the incident out of one of her ears. It was a gesture I recognised from my own life, but I didn't think I had seen her use it before.

'Have you finished your drink?' she asked.

'I have. Do you want another?'

She hesitated, then stood up. 'I want to follow him,' she said.

'Oh, mate, I don't think that's a good idea.'

'It'll be fun,' she said. 'Honestly, if we were still drinking I'd say let's leave it, but since we've both finished –' she knocked back the last third of her wine '– we may as well have a wee mosey after him.'

She left her glass on the bench and strode off up the road. Someone had already swooped in for our seats by the time I caught up with her.

'What if he sees?' I asked. 'That'll be much more cringe-worthy than yelling a French pleasantry at him.'

'He won't see us,' Jax said, ignoring the blast of a car horn as she led me across Old Compton Street. 'Look, there he is. If we keep this distance it'll be fine. We can always say we were just having a wander.'

'But why?' I asked. We were trotting now, breaking from a walk into a half-run as Aaron bobbed in and out of sight.

'I just need to get this out of my system,' said Jax. 'If he meets a woman, then that's that, and at least I won't be wondering any more.'

'And if he's meeting his parents?'

'In that case, I'll take your absurd advice and ask someone in the office.'

'Maybe he's gay,' I said.

'He's not.'

'Or bi. He seemed very interested in me and my coffee beans.'

Jax slowed down for a moment. 'He did, you know.' She shook it off and picked up the pace again. 'Fuck it, if he's meeting a boyfriend that will *definitely* be that.'

We followed Aaron round the corner onto Greek Street, where he stopped outside a Vietnamese restaurant. We skulked in a doorway, breathing heavily.

'How long are we going to wait?' I asked.

Jax checked her watch.

'It's just after seven. I'm guessing they were going to meet on the hour, so unless she's running late ...'

As she spoke, a blonde woman with a fringe that covered her eyebrows walked past us. She wore a green and white floral-print dress, and had a shiny yellow messenger bag slung over one shoulder. Jax leaned against the wall and covered her eyes with one hand.

'That's her,' she said.

'How do you know?' I asked, even though, for some reason, I knew she was right. The woman crossed the road and waved to Aaron.

'Well?' said Jax, keeping her eyes covered.

I watched as Aaron and the blonde woman kissed each other on the lips, holding it long enough to distinguish it from even the most familiar of platonic greetings.

'Sorry, Jax,' I said.

'Fuck's sake.'

She walked off without a backward glance. I hurried after her.

'Let me get you a drink,' I said, as I caught up with her.

'I'm going to go home if that's okay,' she said. All the energy and excitement she'd had in her voice while we followed Aaron had vanished. 'I'm actually quite tired.'

It wasn't like Jax to let an unrequited office crush ruin her evening, but I could see from her face that she wasn't in the mood to be talked out of it.

'Sure,' I said instead. 'Me too.'

I saw Jax to Tottenham Court Road and walked back down Oxford Street to where I'd locked my bike. Rich was over at a friend's playing poker, and now that Jax had called a sudden halt to our evening, I had nothing much to do besides going home and maybe reading. I took out my phone, leaned against the bike rack and stared at the Download button beside the creepy yellow-and-black mask. My resolution to give up on screens flickered through my mind, but was soon followed by the image of Eyeliner. That had been surprisingly fun, after all, and now that I was back on the bike, I couldn't just rely on sitting next to horny men on the train. I'd give it a few minutes when I got home, I thought, just to have a look. Then I'd delete it.

Chapter Ten

At first glance, the grid of faces, torsos and Himalayan sunsets was pretty underwhelming. I thought for a while about what to use for my own profile picture, eventually taking a half-face selfie, which I felt would lend some measure of mystery without having to resort to an unflattering body shot. Given that my exercise regime consisted entirely of short bike rides and running up and down the stairs in the café, I was under no illusions about using my torso as a selling-point. In fact, I worried that I'd look like a grotesque compared to the models used in the app's promotional photos, but when I completed my profile (Relationship Status: Open) and looked at the parade of men within a few miles of me, I saw that any and all body types were on here.

And when I started getting messages, I realised people had the oddest ideas of how to entice someone into their bed. Sure, bodies come in an infinite variety of shapes and sizes, and penises are, if anything, even more wondrously strange and divergent. But every arsehole is pretty much the same, isn't it? From what I could see (and I was admittedly drawing my conclusions from a small sample group) the variation was usually to do with how hairy someone was, but really, when you've seen one, you've seen them all. And yet presumably rational, reasonable men were contorting themselves, spreading their legs and positioning their mirrors in order to get a perfect shot of their rosebud, which they would then use as a form of greeting.

That said, once I got my first bit of attention, and a profile named Looking Around asked me for full-body pictures, I found that I wasn't above unhooking my own mirror from the wall and trying to find an angle that made some of my curves look like definition. Looking Around went quiet when I sent him the photos, but the next profile I sent them to replied with a tongue emoji and asked if I had any NSFW ones on file.

Hours after getting home from my drink with Jax, I remembered my resolution earlier in the evening to cut back on my screen time. Now, it was nearly midnight, and I had to be up early to open the café. I looked at the copy of *Mrs Dalloway*, which sat on my bedside table, silently scolding me for wasting my time, sending pictures of myself to any stranger who gave me attention, then getting frustrated when the chat petered out.

I decided that I would put my phone away and go to sleep, once I had checked Grindr a final time. On it, I had one new message, from a profile with no picture.

Hi, the message said.

Hey, I replied, and then, because by now I had learned that you saved time by doing so straight away, I sent a few of the pictures I'd taken in the past couple of hours.

lol, whoever it was wrote.

?

And then I got a selfie of James, looking at the camera with an expression somewhere between smug and unimpressed. I squirmed, put my phone down and went to brush my teeth, as if doing so would also scrub away my embarrassment. It didn't, so I went and picked up my phone. James had messaged again.

Didn't even realise you were gay, he wrote.

Really? I was sure I had mentioned Rich to him, or at least made reference to being in a relationship, but then again, my interactions with James had been so frosty and stilted that I'd hardly have felt like getting into it much with him.

Well, surprise! I replied, trying to act as if I was used to this kind of thing.

And you're not that far away, if you're coming up on here.

No, I'm near Wood Green station.

Jesus Christ, I thought. Nearby Underground stations. Not exactly the reason you download Grindr. James obviously thought so too, because he wrote: *Well, I might block you, just so it doesn't get too awkward.*

Good idea, I wrote. I thought about adding, *No dick pics!* or something like that, but decided against it, thinking it would be a bit much with someone I hardly knew.

Don't need my boss's dick pics taking up space on my phone, James wrote, clearly less concerned.

Not your boss, but anyway, see you at work.

And then the conversation disappeared. James had blocked me. I felt better, but still a bit uneasy. James was now the only person, aside from Jax, who knew that Rich and I were in an open relationship. It wasn't something I wanted people to know, and I briefly considered asking James not to mention it to anyone, before cringing at the idea of such a conversation. Besides, who was he going to tell? It probably wasn't even that interesting to him.

I kept scrolling as I thought about this, then decided it was a waste of time. Having promised myself to read and have an early night, it was now late and I had nothing to show for my evening except some clumsily photographed arseholes and an awkward interaction with a colleague.

I didn't care what Jax said. I was starting my screen detox in the morning.

James slammed the door to the dishwasher and looked round the café. The Quarter Turn was clean and peaceful, quiet but for the sound of a four-year-old describing her first week of school to a pair of enraptured grandparents.

'What do you do when it's this dead?' James asked me.

'Well,' I said, 'we do things like restocking the milk fridge, which—'

'No need,' he interrupted. 'It's full.'

'I know that,' I said, conscious of my voice quivering as I spoke. 'I'm just giving you examples.'

I wasn't sure how much more of this I could take. It was a relief to have an extra pair of hands in the café, but the run-in on Grindr last night hadn't made conversation between me and James any less awkward.

'If the fridge is full,' I went on, 'and we're not running low on takeaway cups—'

'We're not.'

'And Hugo doesn't need a hand in the kitchen— '

'He's already gone.'

'Then we usually do a bit of a deep-clean.'

'Okay. Where?'

Wherever gets you off my back, I thought. I was trying to do a stock-take for the third day in a row, but nothing seemed to be adding up. It didn't help that the downstairs storage area, never exactly pristine, had recently descended into a state of deeper chaos than usual. The stack of cardboard boxes containing our takeaway cups and birch cutlery had toppled over, forming a mound of disposables you could bury someone under. I was tempted to send James down there, but guessed he'd be back within a minute, asking five more questions. I looked around me for inspiration.

'Why don't you hop up there for yourself and give that a wipe?' I said, pointing to a shelf over the sink, which was decorated with abstract enamel sculptures. I grabbed a few milk jugs that were scattered across the counter. 'I'll just empty these and get out of your way.'

James sighed as I tipped some surplus milk down the sink. 'So wasteful,' he said, grabbing a cloth out of a drawer. 'Can I say, the amount of food thrown away in coffee shops is actually criminal.'

'Yeah,' I said. Earlier in the week, I would have defended the way we did things, or tried to make a joke about it, but I couldn't be bothered any more. I stepped back as James climbed onto the draining board. Whatever he did, I had noticed, James needed a lot of space around him.

Trevor approached the till.

'Cappuccino, Trevor?' I asked.

'Yes, please, my good man, and that last Bakewell tart.' As he paid, he held up what looked like a battered old magazine.

'I was clearing out the glory-hole,' he said – over my shoulder, James snorted – 'and I came across this. Thought you'd be particularly interested.'

It was a programme from the eighties, for an Arsenal–Tottenham match. My heart swelled. Clearly 'my' team was one of these two, and I could finally get to the bottom of what the hell Trevor was talking about every day. 'That's so nice of you,' I said. 'What particularly caught your eye?'

'Oh, I'll leave you to figure that out,' Trevor said, and gave me a sly wink. 'Good to go behind enemy lines every so often, isn't it?'

'Yes,' I said, deflated. 'It certainly is.'

'Who's the enemy, Eoin?' James asked me, from his perch on the sink. I gazed up at him in horror, while Trevor gave a little chuckle and turned to me expectantly. The silence hung in the air between us.

'Oh, God, I forgot about that lady's long black,' I said, nodding at a woman who was reading by the window. As I turned away, I saw Trevor's smile fade a little. I flicked on the grinder as shame and sadness coursed through me.

Had that been a mistake, or had James done it on purpose? If he wanted to have a go at me, fine, but I really wished he had found a way of doing so without embarrassing Trevor. I was surprised to find myself so upset, but then again, regulars like Trevor were my favourite part of working here. I kept my eyes fixed on the coffee machine as I heard James climb down and wring out the cloth he'd been using.

'Do you want me to plate up that cake?' he asked.

'Sure,' I said, 'but you might want to wash your hands first. It's pretty filthy up there.'

And you can take that as well or as badly as you like, I added in my head, seeing as we're never going to manage a civil conversation anyway.

James ran the orders to Trevor and the woman with the book while I wiped down the coffee machine. Not to worry, I thought. I had never needed to be friends with my colleagues. I had other friends. I had Jax. And Rich. I always had Rich.

'He thinks you support Tottenham, by the way,' James said, as he poured himself a glass of water.

'What?'

'So that means your enemy is Arsenal.' He took a sip. 'Don't worry, I didn't give the game away.'

'Tottenham,' I said. 'Is that the same as Spurs?'

'Fucking hell, mate,' James said, keeping his voice low, 'why didn't you just tell him?'

I realised I had never shared my deception with anyone. 'It sort of spiralled out of control,' I said. 'I had the opportunity to ask him what he was talking about a year ago, and I missed it.'

James tutted. 'Silly,' he said.

'You may have noticed, I'm not the world's best communicator,' I said.

'I don't know, I've met worse. You communicate well enough to keep this place going. That's pretty impressive.'

I glanced at him sharply, hardly believing that he might have paid me a compliment.

'Anyway,' I said, covering my confusion, 'I'm going to read that programme from cover to cover tonight.'

'Yeah, reading a forty-year-old team sheet is really going to bring you up to speed.'

'Oh, fuck off,' I said.

'You fuck off and *hop up there for yourself*,' he said, in a near-perfect Irish accent.

I smiled. 'I'm going to run out the bin,' I said.

'Sure thing,' James said, then sidled up beside me. 'Now that I've finished the shelf, I'll pop downstairs and get stuck into the glory-hole, shall I?'

I ducked behind the counter to hide my laughter.

Chapter Eleven

'She's a cross,' said my sister Ciara, for what felt like the hundredth time that morning.

'A Labradoodle!' squealed the lady who had stopped to ask if she could say hello to Ciara's puppy.

'She's a real mongrel, though,' said Ciara's husband Mark, again for the hundredth time. 'She's no test-tube doggo. Straight outta Battersea, you know?'

'What's her name?' asked the woman.

'Sláinte,' said Ciara.

'That's Irish for "Cheers",' added Mark. I gave Rich's hand a squeeze. As usual, Rich was acting as a man-sized stress ball for me as I endured my brother-in-law.

'Oh, I know,' said the woman, 'I'm half Irish myself.'

'Ah, you've got the old *cúpla focal* so,' said Mark, clearly proud of his easy charm and linguistic skills.

After a few more cuddles with the dog and Irish-language exchanges, the woman moved on. We were walking around Clapham Common, and Sláinte was having the perfect Sunday morning, yelping at bigger dogs and sniffing dandelions.

'I should have got a dog years ago,' said Mark. 'She's an absolute bird magnet. A bird,' he said to Rich, 'is what we'd call a girl.'

'Yes,' said Rich, 'we have that phrase in the UK as well.'

'Gas,' said Mark. 'You never know what's made it over and what hasn't.'

I squeezed Rich's hand again. As this Sunday-morning brunch and walk were a celebration of Ciara's thirtieth birthday (her 'proper' party would be in Dublin, but I wasn't going back for that) I had promised myself not to get too annoyed at any of Mark's opinions or anecdotes. I had made it through brunch, but the two Bloody Marys he'd consumed were making him borderline unbearable.

'How much longer are you two planning on living in London?' asked Rich, gently shaking his hand free of my grip.

'Well, my secondment ends midway through next year,' said Ciara, 'and there'll be an option to extend, but I think that might be enough for us.'

'The general consensus is that you can basically do London in three years,' said Mark. 'Like, we're working our way through *Time Out*'s top hundred things to do, and we're going pretty well.'

'We were up the Shard a couple of weeks ago,' said Ciara. 'Have you been?'

'No,' said Rich. 'We really should.'

'Oh, man, it's so high,' said Mark, 'like you're expecting high but it's, like …'

'Really very high?' I suggested.

'Just *so* far up,' said Mark.

'Sounds amazing,' said Rich.

'It's by London Bridge,' said Mark. 'That's on the Jubilee Line.'

Sometimes Mark left me almost physically winded by the force of his condescension: there was no one he had the slightest hesitation in patronising, regardless of gender, age or class. I had only ever witnessed him being deferential to our father, but that might have been because Dad's own inflated sense of self-importance made him harder to talk down to. What really baffled me was that Ciara, far from being blind to her husband's behaviour, was always quick to laugh in exasperation, as if to say that, yes, he was a bit of a tool, but she was stuck with him now and might as well get on with it. She did so now and said, 'I'm sure they'll find the Shard, Mark.'

'Would you lads think of getting a dog yourselves?' asked Mark. He tended to change the subject whenever Ciara checked him like this.

'I love dogs,' said Rich. 'I have one at my mum's house in Kent. He's an old boy, but I don't think I could get another while he's still around.'

'You'd feel like you were doing the dirty on the dog?'

'Yeah, something like that.'

'Well, it's a great rehearsal for us,' said Mark, 'getting used to having a helpless little thing waking up in the night and pissing on the carpet.'

I glanced sharply at Ciara. 'You're not—'

'No, no,' she said. 'Not yet, anyway.'

'That's the other thing about London,' said Mark. 'You just don't want a family here, do you? The air pollution and all the crime, it's just crazy. And Dublin's expensive, but prices in London are just ridiculous, you're in Zone, like, Seven before you can even afford a house.'

'You really are turning thirty,' I said to Ciara. 'Puppies and babies and property.'

'Don't start,' she said, 'you're making me feel old.'

'Anyway, you should really have a think about it yourself, mate,' Mark said to me, 'like, what age are you now?'

'Twenty-seven.'

'Three years go pretty Speedy Gonzalez, let me tell you. And you have to start asking yourself, d'you wanna grow old in London?'

'I don't know,' I said. I wanted to shut this down while I still could, and looked to Rich, hoping he'd think of a question to steer the conversation onto easier terrain. But either he was as stumped as I was – we'd already asked Mark about work, Leinster and Ireland's respective rugby squads, and their flat – or he was happy to hear me answer questions about my long-term future, up to and including old age.

'Gotta start planning these things,' Mark continued, 'like, the two of you would wanna think about getting a deposit together on a house, wouldn't you?'

I doubted I'd have the makings of a deposit any time soon, even with all the extra hours I had clocked up at the café in Rebecca's absence. Paying for Ciara's brunch as part of her birthday present had already put a hefty dent in that.

'Cos it's all just planning,' Mark continued. 'There's all this shite about people not being able to buy houses because of avocados, but the truth is, you can buy a house *and* eat avocados, so long as you plan.'

'And so long as you work for a multinational,' I said.

'So long as you work with your other half,' said Mark, showing the faintest sign of annoyance. 'You have a few quid put aside, don't you, Rich?'

'I do,' said Rich, and took a sip of his takeaway tea. I hated him a little for not saying anything else, leaving me stranded as the only idiot with a zero-hours contract and a room in a grotty house share, surrounded by three bona fide adults with dogs and savings.

'See? If you lads put your money together, you'd find it's not actually that hard. Like, even renting together is cheaper, and then you can start saving. Why don't you try that?'

'Well, not everyone has such a tremendous sense of clarity,' I said.

Rich finally intervened and asked Ciara if Sláinte was playing fetch yet.

'Oh, my God, she's so useless at it, she basically follows the ball and just curls up next to it,' Ciara said, laughing more than seemed completely natural.

'That's very sweet,' Rich said.

I still felt abandoned. My only true ally was Sláinte, who at least didn't look as if she had much in the way of savings. Rich reached for my hand again, but I stepped away from him and crouched down to rub my new friend's belly.

'Cryptic crosswords are really quite elitist,' Rich said, as we sat on the Tube an hour later. I had never understood it when north Londoners claimed not to go south of the river if they could help it, but I had to admit I was relieved to be getting back to cluttered, grubby Wood Green after all the Lycra and open space of Clapham.

'How do you mean?' I asked, as we pulled out of Oval.

'Well, the clue is, "This mover is so in right now, *n'est ce pas?*" '

'I don't get it.'

'The answer is "Dancer", but that requires a knowledge of French, so that you translate "in" to "*dans*".'

'So?'

'Never mind.'

'I don't see how that makes it elitist.' I wished Mark could see us now. You think you're mature? We're a couple who bicker over crosswords, for Christ's sake. 'It could be,' I went on, 'I just need you to tell me why.'

'No, no, just go back to sulking.'

'Since when was I sulking?'

'Since you stopped talking while we were in the park.'

'What – you think I should have continued listening to Mark give me fucking … life coaching?'

Rich gave a small huff and kept his eyes on the paper.

'What was that?' I asked.

'Nothing.'

'Well, you should get it checked. It sounds like you're short of breath or something.'

'Thanks, I will.'

'It sounded like you were laughing at me,' I said, after a minute. I was being awful and I didn't care. I was still angry at his silence when Mark put me on the spot.

'Well,' said Rich, 'you know exactly what Mark's like, and you just rise to him every time. If I'm laughing, maybe you should be too, rather than having a go at me.'

He was right, but I had no intention of conceding as much. I sat silently fuming instead, until we reached Leicester Square and changed onto the Piccadilly Line. When we reached the eastbound platform, Rich muttered a barely audible 'We're down this way,' before marching to one end of the platform. I followed him. Rich always knew which carriage to board in order to step directly into the exit at the other end of the journey. Most of the time I found this impressive and convenient, but right now it felt domineering and arrogant. Why should I sit in a carriage of his choosing, just to save a few seconds at the other end?

When the train arrived, we boarded and found two seats together. I took my book out of my bag and checked in with Clarissa and Septimus, who were feeling about as glum as I was. I reached the end of the page, glanced at Rich and decided I'd had enough of this. I wanted the argument to be over. He was right, I was behaving poorly, and now I needed to apologise. Do it, I told myself. Simply, sincerely, say sorry.

'How's the crossword?' I asked instead.

'Getting there.' He didn't look up.

'Any more elitist clues?'

He didn't reply. I shifted in my seat so I could get a better view of the paper. He didn't object. If I managed to get one of the answers, I decided, I could share it with him and that would be an apology, or at least the beginning of an apology, without having to open with the word 'Sorry.' But my plan was foiled by the fact that this crossword was nigh-on impossible, and might as well have been written entirely in French for all the sense I could make of the clues.

'"A disaster in the main",' I read aloud, hoping that solving a clue together would be an even more profound reconciliation than giving him an answer myself. He didn't say anything. 'What do you think that could mean?' I asked, waggling my olive branch in case he'd missed it.

'That's what I've been trying to figure out,' he said through gritted teeth.

I gave up on the crossword and sat there, feeling miserable, until we reached Manor House, which was the stop for Rich's flat. I stood up with him, stuffing *Mrs Dalloway* back into my bag and gearing myself up for a proper apology, unmediated by word games.

Rich turned to me, blinking in faint surprise. 'Are you ... getting off here?' he asked.

'Yeah, we said we'd stay at yours tonight, didn't we?'

'Okay.'

The doors opened and he stepped off the train. We walked through the platform exit (opposite our carriage, of course) and over to the escalator. He stood on the higher step, giving me a view of his rucksack, which had a little tuft of grass stuck to the bottom.

'I don't have to come,' I said.

'Up to you.'

We were silent until the top of the escalator.

'Well,' I said, as we approached the gates, 'should I tap out or not?'

Rich turned. 'Eoin, it's 3 p.m., and I'm honestly wondering how much more of my Sunday I want to spend with you.' He was speaking very quietly, which made him sound all the angrier. 'I've spent the day listening to you say how much you were dreading brunch with your sister and brother-in-law, then having brunch with your sister and brother-in-law, then listening to you bitch about your sister and brother-in-law, and *then* listening to you have a go at me when I finally have the temerity to voice an opinion.'

I should probably have just conceded all this, but I hated being given out to, so instead I reverted to my earlier outrage. 'Your opinion,' I hissed, 'was that I should listen to Mark and basically get my shit together.'

Passers-by were turning their heads. Even with the volume turned down, it was clear we were having a spat.

'Fine,' I went on. 'Mark's great, I'm a fuck-up. Happy?'

'That's …' Rich just shook his head and went through the turnstile. I hesitated, then slammed my card down on the reader and followed him out. It had clouded over while we were underground, and the clammy chill of autumn was in the air. Rich jabbed the button at the traffic lights.

'Rich,' I began, but didn't get any further.

'When have I ever implied you were a fuck-up?' he asked. I didn't reply. 'When have I complained about you having less money?' He paused, waiting for an answer.

'You haven't,' I said truthfully. 'And I'm sorry. I can save more, if you want, if you want to save up for a trip or whatever, or a …' I took a deep breath '… a mortgage. If we wanted to buy somewhere. Eventually.'

And then he did it again. He gave that faint, sharp exhalation through his nose, a laugh that's not really a laugh but the performance of a laugh, the respiratory equivalent of a teenager's sneer, a kind of aerated eye-roll. He laughed, if you could call it that, and I walked away.

Back on the Tube, when my pulse had returned to its normal rate, I was struck by the thought that while Rich was busily siding with my brother-in-law about the importance of long-term planning, he was the one who had completely thrown things up in the air by suggesting that our relationship didn't need or merit exclusive access to each other's bodies, and instead was a porous and shape-shifting entity. Painful though it felt to admit it, Mark was right. Shouldn't Rich and I be doing all that long-term planning and pooling resources? This felt like such a good point that I considered turning back and following Rich to his flat in order to make it.

But I was already at Wood Green, and I wasn't sure my argument would sound all that great after a forty-five-minute hiatus in conversation. I trudged home and climbed the stairs to my room, which, I was relieved to notice, was no longer infused with the faint whiff of stale urine.

I flopped down on my bed and checked my phone. Ciara had messaged to say how much she and Mark appreciated brunch, along with a video of Sláinte playing with a leaf. There was nothing from Rich. I was relieved that there were no messages from the café, where I had left Billy and James to fend for themselves, with strict instructions not to indulge Hugo's tantrums or let him leave early, since he would be locking up. Billy's cash-ups had been much better this week, but I texted to remind him of our new hiding place for the key to the safe, just in case.

And then I went on Grindr, which I had been avoiding, for the most part, since my embarrassing encounter with James. What had seemed baffling and a bit desperate the other night now looked exciting and sexy – the perfect way to forget about mortgages and savings and my stupid argument with my stupid boyfriend.

A message arrived.

Afternoon, sir.

I looked at the messenger's profile picture. He had a lean face with high cheekbones, a Freddie Mercury-style moustache, and his lips were curled into an exaggerated pout.

Hi, I replied.
How are you this Sunday?
Horny, I wrote. *U?*

Chapter Twelve

The guy with the Freddie Mercury moustache lived a ten-minute cycle from my house. As I unlocked my bike, I checked to see if Rich had texted while I was in the shower. He hadn't, but reading the date at the top of my phone's screen, I remembered that it was our sort-of anniversary later in the week.

We never really marked it, partly because the date was disputable. Should we mark the day we'd kissed in the George or our first actual date over a year later?

We met for the second time when I moved to London after graduating with a decent degree and no idea what to do next. All year, Dad had been pushing me towards teaching, assuring me that it was far from a dead-end career. 'I don't just mean me,' he said, without a shred of irony, clearly thinking my head would spin at the prospect of becoming a principal. 'I mean you can go anywhere you want, Dubai or anything. Politics even – sure half the Dáil are former teachers.'

In my mind, though, the only fate that seemed worse than standing in front of a classroom of teenagers and asking them to care about Seamus Heaney was standing in front of a parish hall full of adults and asking them to vote for me.

Mam, meanwhile, arrived home most days in my final year with a printout or a brochure for another graduate programme. 'Apparently you don't even need to have basic maths to join the Central Bank,' she said. 'They teach you

all the accounting. What they're looking for are *thinkers*, and
you're a good thinker, Eoin.'

I had occasionally considered doing a master's in English
and maybe becoming a lecturer or something like that, but I
was also aware of my limitations. In my final year, I really did
put my head down, but after watching a few of my classmates
giving presentations in seminars, I had to come to terms with
the fact that I lacked creativity. I could understand all the different postmodernist, feminist, postcolonial, queer theories
that I encountered, and even apply them in a close analysis
of *Five Go to Smuggler's Top* or whatever, but listening to one
classmate bounce between them all and seemingly come up
with a theory of her own was bamboozling. I was afraid of
spending another year and a half in the Joyce Library, only to
discover at the end of it that, despite what Mam might say, I
was still just a mediocre thinker.

In the midst of all this hesitation, the only thing I really
wanted to do was to see how things might go with that crisp
English guy. In the year since Rich and I had met, we had
exchanged the odd message, and once we had even got into a
reconstruction of our afternoon in the hotel, but I didn't really
know what he was doing, or whether he had a boyfriend by
now. But if he was still single, that was one big reason to give
London a go. Plenty of people were doing it – 'Generation
Emigration.' Mam sighed when I voiced the idea – so why
shouldn't I? Moving there felt like a risk – I had friends in
Dublin, after all, from school and college and, more recently,
the group Terrence had introduced me to – but at least it was
a plan. I sent Rich a message saying I might be coming over,
and when I got a reply encouraging me to get in touch if I
did, I booked my flight.

I arrived in London in late August, started looking for
work and tried to build up the courage to message Rich and
see if he was around. I wanted to appear as a dazzling, sexy

prospect when I got in touch, rather than a scared little boy fresh off the boat (or the Ryanair plane to Stansted), so I decided I would only message him once I'd found work. I scoured job websites, and to save money (which was disappearing at an alarming rate), I walked to interviews and trial shifts, telling myself cheerfully that I was getting exercise and giving myself a feel for the city. One day, I walked for three hours to get to a pub in Holborn, where I was told on arrival that they weren't looking for anyone who didn't have two years' experience behind a bar. I trudged home, stopping along the way to buy a Tesco Meal Deal, which I promised myself would be my dinner as well.

That evening, I stared at the ceiling of my bare-walled bedroom and considered going home. I had been in London just under a month and couldn't imagine staying. Walking everywhere had indeed given me an impression of the city, and it was a pretty poor one, of grotty shops on the bottom floor of the omnipresent Victorian terraces, peopled with grim-faced, downtrodden commuters. Having visited a couple of times in my childhood, I had assumed that London would feel like a slightly inflated Dublin – wider river, bigger domes, places named after common nouns – but the size of the place meant there didn't seem to be any centre or hub to it, just an endless network of roads, half of which seemed to be named after my childhood villains, like Cromwell. Why was I here? Why was I putting myself through this?

So I gave in and got in touch with Rich on Facebook, framing my arrival in London as a spontaneous lark. I told him I hadn't found a job yet as if it was part of a hilarious picaresque, rather than a depressing failure. I wrote six or seven drafts of the message, then finished by asking if he had time for a drink with a poor struggling Paddy in the big city. Having sent it, I closed my laptop and went to drink tea and eat the remains of my Meal Deal in the kitchen. By the time

I came back to my room, Rich had replied. He was out of London for the year, he said, doing a placement at a school near Maidstone, but he would be in Central for a few hours on Saturday if I wanted to go for a coffee. Or, he added, we could always book another hotel room.

Having read this, I immediately looked up what and where Maidstone was, and was relieved to discover it was only an hour or so out of London. I didn't quite know how to reply to his message, wondering if he really was suggesting another sleazy afternoon in a hotel. I wasn't sure I wanted to set that precedent, and I definitely couldn't afford it either. I suggested a coffee and, hoping it was a clear enough joke, added that we could look up a hotel if we needed to.

That Saturday, I felt excited, but also dreaded that I would bore him, or give away how much I had thought about him since we first met. I had a nagging feeling that, to him, I was at best a curiosity, at worst a casual ride, to be forgotten as soon as the sex was finished.

When he rounded the corner, my heart was pounding like Elmer J. Fudd's at the sight of Bugs Bunny in drag. Rich looked, if anything, more handsome than I remembered, with his beard more grown out and a more relaxed, product-free haircut. I regretted not taking his suggestion of a hotel room more seriously.

When he reached me, I held out my hand in a spectacularly awkward, formal gesture. He brushed it aside and gave me a swift kiss on the cheek as we hugged.

'Shall we?' he said, opening the door of the café.

While he ordered, I got ready to share my most hilarious anecdotes from the past year or so, and reminded myself that I should only mention my degree if it came up, but to impress on him how well I had done if it did.

'So,' Rich said, sliding an Americano across the table to me, 'how's London treating you?'

I took a breath, ready to let rip on the anecdotes, and then met his eye. He was really asking. 'Rich, it's awful,' I said.

He gave a sympathetic grimace. 'It really can be,' he said.

And that was when I started to cry. I had never cried in public before, and it was a real thrill, perching on a stool and accepting Rich's offer of a napkin to dry my tears.

After a couple of minutes, I got my breath back and explained my worries – grubby flat, no mates, lack of any direction – a little more calmly, but the breakdown had lasted long enough to make the rest of the date unlike any other I'd been on.

Perhaps because I had unintentionally set a precedent for soul-baring honesty, Rich admitted that teaching was proving to be more of a challenge than he had anticipated. He had worried about lesson plans and how best to explain the principles behind the maths he was teaching but, really, it was all about crowd control.

'I honestly think two-thirds of my time is spent keeping them from punching each other,' he said. 'We're three weeks into the school year and all I'm thinking about is the half-term break.'

'Reckon you'll be back in London, then?' I asked, hoping I could see him again soon.

He smiled, perhaps guessing what I was thinking. 'For someone living off Meal Deals, you're looking good.'

'So are you.'

Under the table, he pressed lightly on my foot with his, then said, 'I wish I didn't have to go.'

My heart sank. 'Where are you off to?'

'Meeting pals, going to the theatre.'

'Very nice,' I said, trying to hide my disappointment.

'Yeah, it will be. I'd rather mooch around with you, though.'

'Well,' I said, deciding I might as well stick my neck out, 'you could always come over to mine after the theatre, unless you have to rush back to Maidstone.'

'You're free?'

'As a bird,' I said. Then, suddenly worried that all this honesty would backfire and scare him off, I added, 'But no pressure, just if you'd like to … whatever.'

He tapped a finger on the table as he considered this. 'Sure,' he said eventually.

'Cool,' I said, 'though I should warn you, my room looks like what you'd expect from a recent immigrant who hasn't yet acquired the finer things in life.'

'Finer things like …'

'Like a laundry basket,' I said, 'or curtains.'

I woke up early the next morning still broke, still unemployed and still very far from feeling like London was anything but a colossal grey warren of disappointment. But on the other hand, I was waking up next to the warm, dozing body of someone who had texted to tell me he had left the theatre at the interval, complaining of a migraine, and could he please come and inspect the hovel I claimed to be living in? And that much made me feel a lot less stupid, and a lot less lost.

It turned out Maidstone wasn't all that hard to get to, and in the following months, as I picked up bar work through Jax and subsequently moved on to my first barista job, I found a way to get down to Kent for a night or two at a time. It was a relief to have something to say when a colleague asked what my plans for the weekend were, even if that meant turning down their invitations to nights out or house parties.

While it was all casual enough, and primarily physical for the first few months, I found that once you cry in front of someone in a café, you've formed a deeper bond, and when his year in Maidstone was over and he found work in London, it only seemed a formality to declare that Rich and I weren't just dating, but were in fact a couple. An exclusive couple.

★

Well, I thought, as I pulled up outside Freddie Mercury's house, happy anniversary Rich.

I checked my phone. Still nothing from Rich, but on Grindr, Freddie had written: *Message when you get here. I'll come out.*

I briefly considered whether this was risky or not. I should have done some due diligence on this guy, or at least told someone where I was going.

I opened my emails, entered the address into a new message and saved it in my Drafts folder. Then I messaged Freddie.

Here.

At least if I'm killed, I thought as I waited, they'll know where to find the body.

Chapter Thirteen

'Sorry,' he said. He let go of me and hung his head, admitting defeat. He looked a lot less like Freddie Mercury in the flesh.

'That's okay,' I said lightly.

'No offence. You're a really good-looking guy.'

'Oh, well, I didn't think it was to do with me.'

'It's not. You're really good-looking,' he repeated. Then, gesturing in my direction, he said, 'Do you want me to …?'

The offer hung in the air, sad and sheepish. Whatever fire I had left in me guttered and died. 'That's nice of you to offer,' I said, 'but I'll just … go, I think.'

'Are you sure?' he asked. 'I feel bad, letting you leave without getting anything out of it.'

He made it sound so transactional. It reminded me of when we messed up a food order at the café and offered a coffee on the house while the customer waited.

'Don't feel bad,' I said, keeping my voice light. 'You don't owe me anything.'

There were no pictures on the whitewashed walls of his room, just the odd pockmark where a wad of Blu Tack had taken a chunk of paint away with it.

'You can just … take care of yourself, if you want,' he said. 'I'll watch.'

'That's okay,' I said, 'really.'

I went to put on my clothes, but he was up on his feet now. I threw a quick glance at the door, and noticed there was a key in the lock, which I hadn't seen on my way in. This guy was quite tall, and even though he was skinny, it would take a lot to get past him. I thought again of the address saved in my Drafts folder. I should have sent it to Jax.

He must have guessed what I was thinking because he said, 'Look, I'm not forcing you, or anything, but do you wanna just …' he shrugged '… you wanna just, y'know, lie down together for a few minutes?'

No, I thought, *that's a terrible idea. That sounds awful.*

'Sure,' I said. It felt like the quickest, least confrontational way out of there.

We lay down. I stared at the ceiling, and the bare bulb that hung from it. I wondered how long I'd have to lie there.

'Can I ask you something?' he said, after a few minutes.

'Sure.'

'Are you from London? I mean originally.'

'No,' I said.

'Me neither.'

'Liverpool?' I guessed. Northern English accents tended to blend together for me.

He laughed gently and said, 'Close enough. How about you?'

'Dublin.'

'That's in Southern Ireland, right?'

'Yeah,' I said. 'Why do you ask?'

'Well, I was wondering, right … How'd you make friends?'

'I beg your pardon?'

'In London, when you're not from here, how do you meet people?'

There were net curtains stretched across the bottom half of his window. A heavier set, dusty pink, hung limply from a string pinned to the wall above. There was a faint smell of damp in the room. I had been looking for a vengeful shag to get over my anger with Rich. This wasn't what I'd had in mind.

'Well,' I said, 'I guess you meet … flatmates?'

He laid his head on my chest with a sigh. I tried not to flinch. The gesture seemed far more intimate than anything we'd done so far.

'I don't know anyone in this building,' he said. 'We each kind of keep to our own room.'

It sounded a bit like my house, with Polly sprinting for the door in the morning while Tony and I nodded to each other in the kitchen.

'How many rooms are there?' I asked.

'Six, I think.'

'Don't you meet them as you're going in and out?'

'Never even seen anyone in the corridor.'

'You could knock on someone's door,' I said, as if I had ever tried this at home.

'Did that. No one's ever in. I heard some shouting one time, big argument in some language I didn't understand.'

Ironed shirts hung on a clothes rail, which stood where a wardrobe should have been. Underneath was a row of shoes: brogues, colourful high tops and runners. It was all very neat. You'd have to be neat, in a room this size.

'How about work?' I asked, gesturing towards the shirts.

'I'm in recruitment. It's all a bit cliquey in the office, and you're kind of left on your own a lot of the time.'

'Maybe,' I said, trying my best not to sound like a grandmother, 'maybe you could join a club.'

'What kind of club?'

'A … sports club?'

He looked up at me hopefully. 'Are you in any clubs?'

'No … no, I'm not.'

What *did* I do? I asked myself. He raised his head off my chest and I took the opportunity to wriggle away from him.

'Do you have friends?' he asked.

'Of course I do,' I said, feeling defensive.

'So how did you meet them?'

'I moved over to be with my boyfriend,' I said. 'I suppose I made friends through him. But I've been in London for years now – you just get to know people, I guess.' Well, you might do, I thought. For all the people I'd met through work in bars and cafés, I didn't really have much of a social circle to show for it. I'd found that, once our shift was over, colleagues I'd spent the past eight hours laughing and gossiping with became strangers, dashing off to their real lives while I went to meet Rich and his friends, who remained just that: *his* friends.

The front door opened, and we listened as someone with heavy footsteps climbed the stairs and unlocked the door on the other side of the landing. Six rooms, I thought. Six people, at least, and none of them speaking to each other. How many other rooms like this were there in London, with bare bulbs and skirting boards coated in a layer of sticky dust, where single people lay on battered divan beds, swiping and messaging until it was time to sleep?

'Bit lonely,' said the not-quite-Liverpudlian. This was not the way to recover a lost erection, and I wondered if his heart was really in it. Mine certainly wasn't.

'Sorry,' he said again.

'No worries. I might have to go soon, though.'

'Gotta get back to the sports club?' There was an edge of bitterness to the question.

'Yeah,' I said, and I swung my legs off the bed.

'I was well up for it, when we were messaging,' he said. 'I didn't want to be a time-waster or anything.'

'It's just how it goes.' I stood and started buttoning up my jeans. I hadn't even taken my socks off.

'Let's do it another time instead, yeah?' said Freddie.

I will never see you again, I thought.

But aloud, I said, 'Sure.'

Outside, I pulled out my phone.

I'm so sorry, Rich, I wrote. *I'm a complete idiot. Let me know if you're around to talk later. x*

He still hadn't replied by the time I got home. Maybe he'd had better luck than me.

Chapter Fourteen

Outside the Quarter Turn, Uncle Al was holding court. He and a few other men sat around a table with their jackets zipped up, tapping cigarette ash into coffee cups. I was at the next table, eating lunch and trying to conceal the fact that I was listening to them.

'Down by the bins, I saw him,' said one man. He was remarkably thin, with a receding hairline and a tawny moustache. He reminded me of a Quentin Blake illustration. 'Shuffling around, like he was just passing the time of day.'

'Yeah,' said Al, staring down into his empty espresso cup.

'But, Al, it's midnight, yeah? Twelve o'clock in the night, and he's hanging around the bins, casual as you like, just like we are now.'

Al coughed up some phlegm and looked around him.

'You want a tissue, Al?'

Al shook his head, hoisted himself up and wandered over to the side of the road, where he spat into a drain.

'Feeling a bit chesty, eh?'

Al nodded, a pained look across his face.

'Anyway,' said his friend, returning to the subject of the mysterious figure by the bins, 'I went down and told him to fuck off and all.'

I took a bite of my sandwich and wondered how much longer I could eavesdrop before someone told me to get lost. I wished I had brought out my book, which always helped me to appear invisible while listening to Al and his pals trading stories.

'But, Al, when I asked him, he said he hadn't seen her—'

'Cold weather, isn't it, Eoin?' Al said. The rest of his table turned their heads as one.

'Chilly enough,' I said. 'Sure, listen, the clocks will be going back before we know it.'

'They will,' said Al, and then, after looking at his watch, as if expecting the hour hand to spin backwards on cue, he added, 'Why don't you finish your lunch inside, mate? Save you getting cold.'

I stood and went back in. I could feel the group watching me as I went.

I sat at a spare table and checked my phone. It was Tuesday, and still no word from Rich. Couples fight, I reminded myself. It happens, and it's not the end of the world if it takes him a few days to reply. It was the start of term, so he'd have a lot on his plate. Plaguing him with messages might just annoy him more.

I checked that no one could see my screen, and opened Grindr. I didn't know why I was back on it. The app had been nothing but frustrating, and hadn't I resolved to cut back on my screen time? But even as I thought this, the grid of faces shuffled, and I felt a spark of excitement at the sight of a new selection of men in the vicinity. My eye was caught by a profile picture featuring a pair of smiling faces.

Hey, I wrote to what I presumed was a couple. *How are u?*

'Careful,' said James. I hadn't noticed him clearing the table behind me. 'That's definitely not safe for work.'

I covered my embarrassment by laughing. 'I swear I'm not on this as much as you think.'

'No judgement here,' James said, stacking a couple of plates. 'Happy hunting.'

I watched him return to the till. My phone buzzed as a reply came through.

Looking for a 3rd, wrote one of the two smiling men. *U around in a bit? Pics?*

I thought about my answer while I joined James behind the counter, where he was making a coffee. As he poured the milk, his lower jaw jutted out, a picture of childlike concentration. With a flick of his wrist, he lifted the jug, leaving the tip of a love heart on top of the coffee.

'Nice,' I said. 'That's a lovely-looking flat white.'

'Thanks,' said James, squinting at the order ticket. 'Shame they ordered an Americano.' He moaned in frustration and slumped dramatically over the coffee machine, then leaped backwards with a yelp. 'Shit!'

A grandmother, who was feeding a baby in a pram the size of a small tractor, tutted softly.

'The coffee machine tends to be quite hot,' I said, as James examined his forearm.

'I noticed,' he said. 'May I offer you a flat white?'

'I'd love one.'

'You sip that, my darling,' he said, handing me the cup, 'and I'll take a bash at making the drink this nice lady ordered.' He winked at a woman who was talking on the phone near the counter, and hummed as he tapped out the grounds and cleaned the portafilter basket.

'Mind if I watch?' I said, standing behind him.

'Please do. I'm definitely going to fuck up something. Now,' he said, turning to the grinder, 'I noticed that shot was running a bit fast. So if I want to make it run longer …' He turned round to me, eyebrows raised.

'Then you make the grounds finer,' I said. I leaned past him and tapped the adjustment ring on top of the grinder. 'Pull that towards you.'

'Show me.'

'Flick on the grinder first.'

The high-pitched buzz made the waiting lady turn away and put a finger in an ear. I reached past James and pulled the ring forward by a couple of notches. I noticed that he smelt of sweet detergent. He placed his hand on my arm and began humming 'Unchained Melody'.

'Shut up,' I said, stepping away.

'Am I making you uncomfortable by re-enacting *Ghost*?'

'You are. I don't like being reminded of nineties romantic dramas.'

'I'd call it a comedic romance,' said James, as he measured out a shot of coffee and tapped it gently on the counter.

One of the pregnancy-yoga ladies arrived, scrolling through her phone. She looked a little lost without her companion. Even her voice was softer than usual as she ordered her decaf cappuccino. She stepped to one side as James strode past her with the Americano, and I was struck again by the phenomenon I'd started to notice around him. James moved with a physicality somewhere between that of a bear and a penguin, all swaying bulk and powerful limbs. And yet people, animals and even inanimate objects tended to part before him, like the Red Sea. It was amazing to watch.

'Excuse me?' The pregnant woman was looking at me expectantly.

'Sorry?' I said.

'I gave you five pounds,' she said.

'Oh, sorry,' I said, and rooted in the till for change. 'Your buddy isn't here today,' I added, as if she hadn't already noticed. 'Was she sick of the yoga?'

'No,' she said, and her mouth tightened as she clenched her jaw. 'She's in the hospital. I think she's going to be induced this afternoon.'

The wobble in her voice told me that this was not a welcome development. This, I thought, was why I must never, ever engage in anything beyond the blandest, beigest exchanges with customers. 'Oh,' I said. 'Well, I hope it all goes okay for her.'

She nodded and turned away.

'I'm such a fucking idiot,' I said to James, when he rejoined me at the coffee machine.

'Why?'

'Don't look now, but I've basically made a customer cry,' I said, as I measured out the decaf espresso shot.

'Oh, mate,' he said, 'you must stop insulting pregnant women.'

'Shut up,' I said, twisting on the steam wand. 'I feel awful.'

'Well, you just make her the creamiest, velvetiest cappuccino she's ever had,' he said, and gave my shoulders a squeeze. 'Redeem yourself through frothy coffee.'

'It'll take more than coffee to redeem me,' I said, as I poured the milk. After skinny milk, my greatest nemesis was decaf: I could never get the shot to run long enough, so the crema was always thin and disappeared as soon as the milk hit it, rather than gathering around the edge of the cappuccino foam the way I liked it to. Nevertheless, James gave an appreciative whistle as I lifted the jug.

'Just look at that dome,' he said. 'It's a thing of beauty.'

'You run it over,' I said. 'I can't bear to look at her again.'

James spun away with the cappuccino. I started wiping the surface around the coffee machine, keeping my eyes down. I wanted to watch James, I realised. I wanted to see how he'd bustle across the room without spilling a drop, and the ease with which he'd speak to the woman I had made cry, the smile he'd give her.

The incident with Trevor had pierced the tension between me and James, and since then, I could appreciate how good he was with people. He learned customers' names and spoke to them in a disarming, personal way that was completely different from Billy's dazed casualness or my own efficient courtesy. I no longer felt I had made a massive mistake in hiring him and instead began to feel relieved when his shifts came around, even looking forward to them.

I decided to give the floor behind the counter a sweep. James was standing with the pregnant lady by the door. The sounds of the café were just loud enough to drown out his voice, until he laughed, a high-pitched squawk that would probably carry no matter where he was. I focused on the floor.

'She loved it,' he said, as he joined me behind the counter.

'Good,' I said. 'Thank you for serving her.'

'Where did you learn to make coffee that well?'

'Ah, stop.'

'Take the compliment, Eoin, and answer my question. Did you just pick it up?'

'The last café I worked in, the supplier insisted we had to get proper training before we could serve their coffee. I have a certificate and everything.'

'Is it framed?'

'No, but I have it stuck on my fridge, right next to my fingerprint painting. Anyway,' I said, 'I was being serious when I said your flat white was excellent. You've basically mastered it in a week.'

'Well, I've been watching a lot of coffee videos.'

'Really?'

'Oh, mate, I'm all about the World Barista Championships. Have you watched them?'

I leaned on my brush.

'I used to watch them while I was going to sleep. I actually applied for a job at the café where England's last champion works.'

'How was that?'

'A total disaster.'

I set the brush to one side and started looking for the dust-pan, which Billy seemed to hide in a new and inexplicable place each day.

'A disaster how?' James leaned against the counter, his arms crossed and his back to the café, the kind of pose that would drive Rebecca mad if she saw it.

'I had to audition,' I said, 'and I mean audition like you would. There were three of them on the interview panel, standing on one side of the counter with clipboards. They each placed a different order and watched while I made them.'

'That doesn't seem so hard.'

'Would you help me find the dustpan, please?' I said, rooting around in the lower shelves. 'I don't know how we keep losing it in a space the size of a piano lid.'

'So come on, what happened?' James asked, stepping over me and opening the cupboard where we kept the bags of coffee beans.

'Well, they also asked me to play some music, to give them a flavour of my personality.'

'Oh, my God, this sounds like the audition from hell.'

'And then when I started—'

'Hang on,' James said, shutting the door to the cupboard with a bang so hard that all the cups on top of the coffee machine rattled, 'what music did you play?'

'I'm not going to tell you.'

'You *have* to tell me.'

I paused in my hunt for the dustpan to look up at him. He gazed down at me, his hands on his hips.

'You should know,' I said, after a moment. 'The café was in Shoreditch so I thought they'd like some hipster irony.'

'What did you play?'

I sighed. '"Spice Up Your Life".'

By the time his shrieks of laughter had subsided, I had found the dustpan, swept up, emptied it into the bin and washed my hands.

'Oh, my days,' he said, 'that's such an insight into who you are.'

'I don't even like the Spice Girls,' I said, which set him off again. 'And don't tell me that's an insight. I hate when people make judgements like that.'

'Fair enough,' he said. 'I'm sure you have many hidden depths.'

'Anyway,' I said, 'the audition went downhill from there.'

'Speaking of which,' said James, 'I've had an audition of my own come in for this Friday. It's for a BBC thing, filming next year.'

'That's class,' I said.

'So is it okay if I don't do my shift on Friday?'

That would mean another double shift for me, as I had been hoping James and Billy could manage the first half of the day between them. There was still no sign of Rebecca, and I was now ordering food and disposables in her name from the computer in the cellar. I'd given James a spare key so I could have the odd extra hour in bed in the mornings, but Sunday in Clapham had been my first full day off since Rebecca's holiday started four weeks ago, and I was beginning to feel it. Still, given that James was under absolutely no obligation to me or the café, and was the only thing keeping it together, I wasn't really in a position to say no.

'Yeah, fine,' I said. 'Do you need the whole day off?'

'I do, yeah.' He looked apologetic, but there was a finality to his words.

'Well, sure,' I said. 'Break a leg.'

'Thanks,' James said, and then, as Billy entered the café, 'Oh, thank the Lord, that means it's quittin' time.' He gave

Billy a friendly dig and disappeared downstairs. I took out my phone and sent the couple a few of my photos.

Nice, came the reply. *Wanna join us?*

I gave James a wave on his way out and allowed myself to watch him leave.

Sure, I wrote back. *I finish work in a couple of hours.*

I stared up at a painting of Mother Teresa, who was praying with an expression of barely suppressed glee. She held a set of rosary beads coiled around one hand like a pious knuckle-duster. On the opposite wall, a triptych of Padre Pio charted his progress from young heart-throb to rosy-cheeked old uncle, stigmata tastefully concealed beneath a pair of fingerless gloves.

'You like them?' asked the man stretched out beside me. The profile had been named 'T & D' and I hadn't asked who was who when they buzzed me in.

'Who's the painter?' I asked eventually.

'I am.'

'Wow, you've done quite a lot,' I said, turning to look at another canvas hanging over the headboard, in which an extremely muscular Jesus gazed down at us.

'These are only the beginning. There are more in the living room, and I give them away as presents as well. Every year I do one for my mother, for Christmas.'

From the ensuite bathroom came the sound of D (or T) turning on the shower.

'She actually held an auction to mark the thirtieth year of me painting them. She sold quite a few, but she said she found it too hard to say goodbye to them all.'

I looked back to Mother Teresa. I recognised the pose, and guessed that the painting was copied from the poster that had adorned the wall of my primary-school classroom.

'They're quite religious,' I ventured.

'Yes, the one I'm working on is a portrait of the Pope.'

'Can I see it?'

'I don't know … It's a little private, and I hardly know you.'

And, in fairness, he didn't, even though I'd made him come only minutes ago.

'Please?'

I wasn't sure why I needed to see an incomplete portrait of an elderly Jesuit, but it didn't stop me asking.

'Okay, but only because you're cute.'

He lifted himself off the bed and ambled out of the room, adjusting his pink jockstrap as he went.

'Why religious?' I called after him.

All the portraits had an uncanny paint-by-numbers feel to them. Skin was rendered in a maximum of three shades, and the figures were dressed in garish clothes that clashed with brightly coloured backgrounds.

'It's my way of praising Jesus,' he said, returning with another canvas. 'I paint him and his followers.'

I wondered if I had missed a note of irony. 'Well, that's great,' I said, and then, when he turned the canvas round, 'Oh, yes, it *does* look like him. You've really got the eyes down.'

'I'm not happy with it,' he said, placing it on a dresser and stepping back to assess it, 'but I'll work on it some more. Do you want a shower?'

'No, thanks. I'll have one when I get home.'

'Are you sure? He'll be finished in a minute.' He knocked on the door of the bathroom. 'Wrap it up in there. Our guest wants to shower.'

'Honestly, that's okay,' I said, and started to pull on my boxers, but the shower had stopped. 'Coming,' we heard through the door.

'Do you guys … entertain often?' I asked.

'We entertain when we see someone we like. I'd say that's
… once a month? Do you think?' he asked the other, who
came out of the bathroom towelling his hair.

'What?'

'We have visitors around once a month.'

'Something like that. Oh, God,' he groaned, catching sight
of the unfinished portrait, 'he's been boring you with his
painting.'

'He *asked* to see it,' said the artist, 'and actually, he thinks
I've really captured Francis's eyes. So there.' He grabbed the
canvas and turned to leave the room.

'I'm teasing,' said his partner, dropping the towel and
intercepting him at the door. 'I'm teasing,' he repeated, and
kissed him gently, as if to say it a third time.

I looked away, feeling like an intruder, which was odd,
given the half-hour we'd just had. I'd been quite awkward at
first, not really knowing what I should be doing or where I
should be looking, but the two of them seemed used to it, and
were no more put off by my presence than they were by the
crucified Jesus hanging above us.

When they separated, the artist gave the other a playful
pat on the arse.

'Go on, then, get a towel for him,' he said, nodding in my
direction.

'Honestly,' I said, as the dripping man turned back to me,
'you're grand.'

He smiled, and picked up his own towel. 'Suit yourself.'

'Have you guys anything else planned for the evening?' I
asked, as I turned my T-shirt the right way round.

'Well, we placed a Deliveroo order just before you got
here, so it should be arriving before long.'

That might explain the rather sudden end to all the activity, I thought. Even a threesome isn't worth letting the curry
go cold. I watched as he continued to dry himself.

'Are you T or D?' I asked. 'I think I missed it in all the excitement.'

'I'm T,' he said, and shook out his towel. 'I think that's your sock.' He pointed to a corner of the room.

'Oh, great,' I said, crawling towards it. 'And what does the T stand for?'

He laughed gently, as if I'd made a whimsical joke. 'Tom,' he said.

'Do you guys always do this together?' I asked.

'Why? Would you prefer one of us on our own?'

It so happened I'd probably have chosen him over D, but I thought that would be a bit rude to admit. 'Oh, no preference,' I said instead. 'Top marks all round. You make a really good team. I was just curious.'

'Why, thank you,' Tom said. 'Is this your first time with a couple?'

'Could you tell?'

Tom laughed again. 'You're very cute,' was all he said.

'Now this,' D said, coming back with a new canvas, 'I honestly think this is in my top five, one of the best I've ever done.'

I squinted at the portrait of a heavily pregnant Mary while I put on my socks, trying to see what distinguished it from the others. 'The light ...' I managed, after a moment.

'Exactly!' said D. 'I just never know when I'm going to get it right.'

There was a buzz.

'Food's here,' said Tom, and threw his towel in the direction of a laundry basket. He went to answer the intercom, leaving D and me gazing at the canvas.

'I'm Eoin, by the way,' I said, cramming on my runners.

'Dean,' he said softly, eyes fixed on the painting.

We continued our silent contemplation of the Blessed Virgin until Tom returned and gave a little wave from the corner.

'Sorry to interrupt,' he said, 'but do you fancy staying for dinner? We always order too much.'

'No, no,' I said. 'I should be going. Thanks for the …'

I gestured vaguely towards the bed.

'Any time,' said Tom, and went to get my jacket

Dean giggled a little, his eyes still on Mary. 'He likes you,' he said to me, sounding like a twelve-year-old gossip in the playground.

I scanned the room for any possessions I'd left behind, and tried to figure out the best way to respond to this. 'Well,' I said eventually, 'I like … the both of you.'

Dean continued to giggle as Tom returned with my jacket and showed me out.

It was only when I was in the corridor that I began to regret turning down the invitation to stay for dinner. For one thing I was starving, but more than that, I wanted to be around Tom and Dean, to see how at ease they were together, and maybe to ask them how they made it work so well. Did they also see other people separately, or did they only have threesomes when both of them were present, and did they take breaks from it when one wasn't in the mood? The contentedness they'd shown during and after sex made me feel jealous, and I had to remind myself that I did have a boyfriend of my own, albeit one who (I checked my phone) still wasn't texting me.

I reached the lift just as the Deliveroo driver walked out of it with a bag. It smelt warm and inviting, and I considered going back to Tom and Dean with it.

'That way,' I said instead, pointing my thumb back in the direction of their flat, before stepping into the lift.

Chapter Fifteen

Jax looked surprised when she opened the door.

'Sorry,' I said. 'Am I early?' I held up a plastic bag. 'I bought wool, knitting needles and a bottle of wine.'

'I wasn't expecting you,' she said. 'But, great, come in. I'm having a baking nightmare, and I think quite a few people are coming this week.'

The icing was refusing to spread. It sat in a large teardrop shape on top of a sponge cake, stiff enough to support the wooden spoon sticking out of it. Jax's flatmate Claudia was taking a photo of it as I entered the kitchen.

'I don't understand,' Jax said, 'I definitely followed the recipe.'

'No, she didn't,' Claudia said to me. 'There's chickpea juice in there. It smelt like arse.'

'It's the same as egg whites, just vegan,' said Jax. 'And I didn't hear you complaining about the hummus I made.'

'The hummus is excellent,' said Claudia. 'I just don't think that fart-water makes for good icing. Hi, Eoin,' she said, looking up from her phone with a smile.

'Well, aquafaba aside, why won't it spread?' asked Jax.

'Has the cake cooled?' I asked.

Jax gave the sponge a cautious prod. 'Partly, why?'

'I don't know. It just seems like the kind of thing that goes wrong in baking. Not letting stuff cool.'

'You're right, let's leave it for a while,' said Jax, backing away from the cake. 'I don't think the others will be here for half an hour or so – maybe it'll sort itself out in the meantime. I'm so glad you could come to Stitch and Bitch,' she added. 'I didn't think it was your thing.'

It wasn't, but on my way home from Tom and Dean's flat the previous evening, I had decided I should find a way of occupying myself that didn't involve sleeping with men I had met on Grindr.

'Nights are drawing in,' I said, 'and I'll need something to pass the time. But you'll have to teach me how to start.'

'Great. Step one is opening the wine you brought. Is Rich coming?'

I didn't answer, concentrating instead on the bottle's plastic cap, which gave a satisfying crack as I twisted it off.

'Oh, God,' Jax said. 'What now?' She glanced at Claudia, who was writing a caption for her photo of the icing blob and giggling, then looked back at me, wincing in anticipation.

'Ah, no,' I said. 'We just had a bit of an argument. We're not really speaking.'

'Are you okay?'

Jax seemed wary. I guessed she didn't want me sobbing through the evening's knitting circle. 'I am, actually,' I said. It was weird not being in touch with Rich from one end of the day to the other, but compared to the terror I'd felt when he first suggested seeing other people, I was feeling oddly calm, bordering on numb. I wondered if the wild time I'd had with Tom and Dean had anything to do with this new-found stoicism.

'You sure?' Jax asked, as I divided the bottle between three glasses. I was hoping the wine would help me stay relaxed as the rest of the knitting group arrived.

'I guess. I'd prefer not to be arguing, but …' I shrugged my shoulders. 'Cheers.'

'Oh, you guys'll be over it in no time,' Jax said, as we clinked glasses. 'Rich can come to the next one.'

'Fucking hell, Eoin,' Claudia said, looking up from her phone at the glass I'd poured for her. 'I'm going to be pissed.'

'I'll finish it if you need,' I said. 'Who else are you expecting?'

'Well, Claudia's sister's coming,' said Jax, 'and she's bringing baby Ella.'

'Oh, that reminds me,' said Claudia. 'Venetia's doing that insufferable thing of claiming that her baby is smarter than average for her age, so be sure to point out all the ways the child is really dumb.'

'That seems a bit harsh.'

Claudia took a gulp of the wine and nodded. 'It is, and I do worry that it'll give Ella a complex, but it's also highly entertaining.'

'Anyone else coming, aside from Venetia and her stupid baby?'

'That guy from the paper's coming, isn't he?' Claudia asked Jax.

My mouth dropped open, and Jax gave me the tiniest shake of her head.

'I just mentioned it to him the other day,' she said. 'He might call in.'

'He's interested in knitting?' I asked.

'Probably as interested as you are, Eoin.'

Claudia's resolution to take her niece down a peg or two seemed to weaken when Venetia and baby Ella arrived just before eight.

'Oh, my God, she's *grown*,' she exclaimed, seizing Ella while Venetia flapped out of her cardigan and dragged in a bag of baby essentials the size of a fridge.

'I'm absolutely quivering for a wee,' said Venetia. 'Nice to meet you,' she added, as she bounced past me in the direction of the downstairs toilet.

'Would you like to?' Claudia said, offering me the baby as if it was a drag on a joint.

'Oh, I don't know,' I said, feeling like the square who didn't really do drugs.

'She won't mind,' called Venetia from the toilet. 'She's very independent, really.'

'Yeah, very independent,' Claudia said, bundling Ella into my arms. 'Sometimes she can be left alone for a whole ten seconds.'

Ella's head rolled around on the top of her neck, and I raised one hand to steady it while keeping her pinned to my chest, utterly terrified that I would drop her. She raised her eyes to me in what appeared to be a mixture of alarm and curiosity. Tiny bubbles of spit dribbled from one corner of her mouth. I tried to think of a cooing noise, but none came to mind, so I just smiled and hoped she'd recognise the expression of dumb goodwill. She wriggled, raised one arm and thumped my collarbone with all the force of a heavy blink.

'She's strong,' I said.

'Oh, I don't know,' Claudia said. 'She's got absolutely no core strength.'

'Actually, the doctor said her muscles are highly developed for her age,' said Venetia, flicking soapy water from her hands as she emerged from the toilet.

'My turn,' Jax said. 'Pass her over, Eoin.'

Jax was still holding Ella while telling me how to form a purl stitch when the bell rang. If Jax was disappointed that it wasn't Aaron, she covered it well, and welcomed a miniature hurricane in the form of her friend Crystal and three of Crystal's employees, all of whom had been working as children's entertainers at an upmarket wedding that day.

'Sorry we're late,' said Crystal. 'I had to swing by my nana's house for more needles – I didn't expect this lot would all come.'

'Sorry to crash, but we have brought vegan cheese,' said one of her team.

'And actual cheese,' said one of the others. 'I'm Jonno, by the way.'

At least, that's what he might have said. He might also have said his name was Tommo, but by the end of a round robin of introductions, handshakes and air kisses, I had completely forgotten who everyone was, and even began to wonder if I had Venetia's name right. In addition to a selection from the cheese board, the team of entertainers had been given some leftover Champagne at the wedding. Fuelled by bubbles and vegan Wensleydale, they began recounting the outrageous behaviour of the bride's uncle, who had been escorted from the venue before the end of the cocktail hour.

'I was playing Simon Says with the kids,' said one of them (Gordie? Badge? The fact that they all had nicknames wasn't making things any easier), 'and I kept having to tell them to close their eyes.'

'Simon says, "Avert your eyes from the drugged-up rello,"' said Jonno/Tommo.

'Simon says, "Let's move into the next room."'

'Simon says, "Avoid the crying bride."'

The wine had backfired: I couldn't keep up with the knitting or the conversation as names and references and in-jokes swam around me. I became aware of how little I was saying, and then concerned that I was coming across as the weirdo in the corner, muttering to his needles. Jax and Claudia kept throwing me lifelines in the form of explanations or questions, but all I could do was smile, in much the way I had when confronted with Ella, who was now being passed around the circle, like a parcel in one of the games Crystal and Co. had played earlier. I bent my head and tried to concentrate on the knitting (Jax and I had decided a simple scarf was probably my best bet) but I felt like I was dropping stitches, the sight of the wool was making me itch, and when I looked up to ask Jax for her advice, I was confronted with what looked like six or seven masterpieces, as the group compared chunky jumpers and bobbled hats.

I was reminded how much I struggled in groups. A line of customers I could deal with: no matter how angry or irritating they were, the relationship between us was clear. But among people I didn't know, I could feel myself shrinking into the background. With Rich it was different. With him there, I could always just talk to him, at least for a minute, to remind myself that I wasn't completely incapable of forming sentences. Now, without him, I somehow felt like a lost little boy.

When Ella ended up in my hands again, I decided to take her for a walk. She seemed perfectly content in the babble of conversation, but Venetia made encouraging noises as I stood up, as if it was the baby and not me who needed a few minutes away from the group.

'Here,' she said, throwing me a small towel, 'just in case she spews over your shoulder.'

I paced the quiet of the kitchen, feeling grounded by the weight of Ella in my arms, and distracted by the task of finding something she'd be interested in (the magnets on Jax's fridge turned out to be a hit). I wondered if all kids offered this kind of comfort to adults, or whether Venetia was correct in thinking that Ella really was exceptional.

My phone buzzed in my pocket, and I shifted the baby from one arm to the other so that I could reach for it. I was hoping it was Rich, but as soon as I unlocked it, I saw it was a Grindr notification. I clicked on it and was met with a photo, taken in a changing-room mirror, of someone's jogging shorts tugged down to just beneath his arse.

The doorbell rang, and I heard Jax going to answer it. I closed out of the photo and put the phone back in my pocket, feeling a bit weird about looking at it while holding a baby.

'Sorry, pal,' I said to Ella, and took her for a second look at the fridge magnets, which fortunately had lost none of their appeal.

'Aaron is here,' Jax said, as she came into the kitchen. 'He's just meeting the others. Shall we have another go at this cake?'

Rather than sorting itself out, the icing had assumed the appearance and consistency of mashed potato. Jax smushed it over the top of the sponge, which started to disintegrate under the pressure, while Ella stared at her efforts.

'When did knitting come up in conversation with Aaron?' I asked.

'We had a coffee the other day,' said Jax. 'It wasn't planned – we were both just taking a break at the same time. I think we could be friends.'

'Has he mentioned his girlfriend yet?'

'No.' Jax shook a few berries onto the icing. 'Is that a problem?'

'Absolutely not,' I said. 'You guys are just friends.'

I knew that if our roles had been reversed, Jax would have told me what she really thought, but I didn't feel like fighting with more than one person I loved at a time, so I kept my mouth shut.

'Right,' she said. 'It looks a complete mess, but it's not going to get any better. Coming?'

'Sure,' I said. 'I've probably hogged Ella for long enough.'

As if in agreement, Ella opened her mouth just wide enough for a little waterfall of regurgitated milk to cascade down her chin.

'She just can't hold her booze,' said Claudia, as I passed Ella back to Venetia in the living room.

The team from the wedding mustn't have had much to eat, because Jax's cake was demolished in minutes. Even Claudia agreed that she couldn't taste the chickpeas.

'The smell doesn't really linger,' said Aaron.

'Are you vegan?' asked one of the women whose name I had forgotten.

'My girlfriend is,' Aaron said, carefully squishing the last few crumbs onto the back of his fork, 'I've been giving it a try for the past few months.'

I kept my eyes on my scarf (I was now on row number three) and resisted the temptation to catch Jax's eye. However, I couldn't help sneaking a look at her when Ella ended up with Aaron in the evening's final round of Pass the Parcel. When Ella reached up to tug Aaron's beard, the look on Jax's face was one of startled awe, as if she had opened a bread bin and seen the face of God.

As I left, I thought about texting Rich. I wanted to be reminded that I wasn't just the quiet one at the party, or the spare wheel at the end of a threesome. But I knew that was wrong. I should be getting back to Rich because I wanted him, not because I needed him. That was how adults behaved, I told myself. Still, after I'd unlocked my bike, I checked my phone, just in case he'd got in touch. He hadn't. But Rebecca had.

Chapter Sixteen

James answered on the fifth ring, just as I was beginning to despair. I could hear a lot of noise in the background.

'I'm sorry to call on a Friday night,' I said. 'Are you in the middle of something?'

'Can you speak up, Eoin? I think the signal's not great.'

'Actually, I'm whispering.'

'What? Hang on.' I heard him move, telling whoever he was getting past that he'd be right back, and then the noise became quieter.

'Why are you whispering?' he asked.

I took a deep breath, not totally ready to admit why I was calling. 'I'm trapped,' I said.

'Trapped? Where?'

'In the café. In the downstairs toilet. You know, the one by the office?'

'I know where the toilet is, yeah. How come you're trapped in there?'

I wondered how much I could explain over the phone.

Rebecca's email had clearly been sent in a rush, with groups of words running together and several passages written in block capitals. In it, she explained that there weren't enough funds in the cafe's current account to pay some of our suppliers, and now they were threatening not to deliver. She promised she would be back next week, but in the meantime, she needed me to lodge some money in the overnight safe of a nearby bank. *And Eowan,* she wrote, *it's VVV IMPORTANT THAT YOU DO THIS DISCREETLY!!! I wont bore you w/ details, but there's a LOT of family stuff going on, so I neED AL NOT TO KNOW.*

Rebecca hadn't specified that I should come back after hours, but having slept on it, I had decided that it made sense to count the money when the café was closed and there was less chance of being intercepted by Al. And when I let myself in, pulling down the shutter and locking the door behind me, it made sense to leave the lights off. And when I heard the rattle of the shutter being lifted upstairs, it made sense in the moment to slam the door to the safe shut and run for the nearest hiding place, which happened to be the staff toilet. It was only as I was turning the lock that I remembered Billy's confinement a few weeks previously.

'The lock is banjaxed,' I said to James, hoping that a full explanation could wait. 'I was wondering if you could … help me?'

'Um, I'm not that close by actually. Could you ask Uncle Al? He might be free.'

'Actually,' I breathed, 'Uncle Al is upstairs, in the café.'

'Right …' I could picture his furrowed brow as he tried to piece all this together. 'Does he … often come to the café after hours?'

'I don't know, but the point is it's quite late, and he doesn't know I'm here. And also,' I said, accepting that I'd just have to trust him, 'I have a bag of money in here with me.'

There was a pause. I worried that I'd lost the signal.

'That's a sticky one, yeah,' he said at last, in an admirably mild tone. 'How long you been in there?'

I looked around my cell. I hadn't noticed the crack in the wall before, which ran from floor to ceiling in a gentle arc. 'A while,' I said. The first few minutes of my imprisonment had been spent trying in vain to get the lock working without making any noise. The next half-hour had rushed by in a black vortex of despair, at the end of which I had decided that I either needed to call someone or get ready to sleep in the toilet.

'So,' said James, 'how can I help?'

'Well, I think I gave you that spare set of keys.'

'You did.'

'So if you could let yourself in and then … let me out?'

'How long will Uncle Al be there?'

If I hadn't been depending on James for my freedom, I would probably have said something sarcastic in response. How the hell was I supposed to know?

Instead I said, 'Hopefully he won't be long.'

'Okay, I'm on the way.'

'Honestly, though, if I'm interrupting anything, don't worry about it.'

'Babe, you're stuck in a toilet, yeah?'

'Yes, I am.'

'So I'll come and let you out of the toilet.'

He hung up. I sat on the toilet seat and prayed that Al wouldn't come downstairs and notice my bag, which was sitting on the desk next to Rebecca's ancient computer.

I hadn't asked James where he was, so I had no idea how long it would take him to get there. I just hoped that Al would finish up whatever he was doing before then. There were two other men with him, and whatever they had been talking about for the past forty-five minutes was certainly prompting a lot of laughter, accompanied now and then by a hacking cough.

I was just wondering whether I should give the toilet a scrub to pass the time when I heard footsteps on the stairs. I lifted my feet off the floor so that I was squatting on the toilet seat and covered the screen of my phone to prevent any light giving me away. Whoever it was took another few steps, and I thought I could detect a faint whiff of TCP through the door. After a moment, the footsteps retreated, and I let myself exhale.

Most of the time, I felt pretty mellow about where I'd ended up in life. And yet, sitting in a cold subterranean toilet with a bag of money that didn't belong to me on my lap, hoping that no one would open the door, I did wonder if all of my life choices had been good ones. Certainly, now that I had time to think, I could admit to making quite a few bad choices this evening. My phone, which mercifully hadn't run out of battery, buzzed.

Be there in 40 mins. x

I placed a gin and slimline tonic in front of James. He was texting someone, but glanced up as I threw two bags of crisps onto the table between us.

'Thanks,' he said.

'Thank *you*,' I replied. 'I owe you a very big favour.'

When he finally let me out it was nearly ten thirty so, rather than going back into town, James agreed to let me buy him a drink in the pub around the corner from the Quarter Turn. I was starving, so I tore open the bags of crisps while James returned to his phone. They tasted incredible. They tasted like freedom.

James finished sending the message and placed his phone face-down on the table. 'So,' he said, 'would you like some feedback on your performance this evening?'

I had explained the bones of my plan, and my subsequent panic, on our way to the pub.

'I don't really,' I said to him, 'but I can sense some coming my way.'

'Mate, if you'd just left the light on—'

'If I'd left the light on, if I'd called out and said hello, if I'd bumped into Al before I let myself in and locked the door behind me ... all of these things were better options than trapping myself in a toilet with a dodgy lock. I can see that now.'

'Can I say something?' James asked, and as always, pressed ahead before I could answer. 'This is looking very suspicious.'

'What – me?'

I wondered whether James would feel compelled to tell Al.

'No, the whole thing, this Rebecca woman, who's technically my employer even though we haven't met or signed a contract. And just generally. I mean why would Al be meeting people in the café after hours? It's all looking pretty shady.'

'What do you think I should do?'

He shrugged. I noticed he was wearing a nice bright T-shirt under his jacket, and I felt a pang of guilt for dragging him away from his night.

'Actually, never mind,' I said, 'do you want to get back to your friends? It's not all that late, and you're not in till the afternoon tomorrow.'

'Nah,' he said. 'Now that I'm out this far I'm not sure I could be bothered. There was a lot of talk about going to G-A-Y, and I'm not quite ready for that.'

'I haven't been there in years,' I said. In fact, now that I thought of it, I hadn't been there since my very earliest days in London, when Jax and I went with the crowd from the Kentish Town bar.

'Lucky you. Speaking of which,' he said, as he leaned back in his chair, 'how's your man?'

'Who?'

For reasons I couldn't put my finger on, I didn't want this conversation. I'd been avoiding any mention of relationships or sex with James.

'Who?' he echoed. 'The other half of your open relationship.' He was speaking at a normal volume, but to me it seemed as if his voice was booming around the quiet, unfamiliar pub. I shrank a little into my chair.

'What's his name?' asked James.

'Rich.'

'And what does he do?'

'He's a teacher.'

'Very nice.' James looked at me a while longer, then burst out laughing.

'What?'

'Nothing, you just seem to be in agony talking about your boyfriend.'

'No, I'm not. Why? What other questions do you have?'

I was turning red, I could feel it, and dropped my gaze to the sticky rings of beer on the table in front of me.

'Nothing, no more questions,' James said. 'Interrogation over.'

'Are you seeing anyone?' I asked.

'No. Well, I'm seeing plenty, just not dating.'

'How long have you been single?'

I expected him to tell me to mind my own business, given that I had effectively said the same to him. Instead, he peered into the middle distance and started counting on his fingers. 'Eleven months … yeah, nearly a year,' he said, 'since my heart was broken.'

'Really? Heartbroken?'

He took another sip of his drink and tilted his head to the side. 'Yeah,' he said. 'When I fall, I tend to fall hard.'

'Right. How did it end?'

'He was fucking around,' he said, looking me directly in the eye.

'Oh. So you weren't in an open relationship?'

'Nah. I couldn't do it. No offence.'

'None taken.'

'But it would drive me crazy, I'm sorry. Anyway, I should have seen it coming.'

'Why?'

No matter what the scale or subject matter was, James always prepared for an anecdote by stretching and pursing his lips, like a Homeric bard about to begin an epic. He did so now, and cleared a space on the table in front of him.

'We met at a party, and we were talking on these patio chairs in the back garden. Summertime, warm, some dickhead was playing a guitar and everyone was bonding over how much we hated him. And, anyway, me and André, we were getting on well, when he told me he didn't believe in love. I assumed he meant he didn't believe in love *at first sight*, which I definitely agree with, but he actually meant that he had no qualms about fucking other men, even when he'd committed to a relationship.'

'I'm sorry to hear that.'

'Thanks. Fucking poet as well,' he spat, and drained most of his drink.

'A poet?'

'He did spoken-word stuff, got a book deal after winning a few big slams.'

'Wow, an actual published poet.'

'I know. I think that's what attracted me to him, in a way. I mean, we all know fucking writers, yeah?'

I didn't, but I nodded.

'Every Tom, Dick and Harriet's got an unpublished masterpiece in their bottom drawer, or a devised fringe show with their mates, but André was actually living off it.'

'You find success attractive.'

'I just love seeing people get their shit together and work.'

'Do you think your break-up inspired any poems?'

James shook his head. 'He's been working on a verse novel about Epping Forest.'

'Set in Epping Forest?'

'No, Epping Forest is the protagonist, and all the trees speak together like a Greek chorus.'

'Well, I think you're well shot of him, because that sounds shite.'

'It does, doesn't it?' James slumped forward onto the table. 'I'll never be a muse,' he cried, into his crossed arms.

'Can I get you another drink as a consolation?'

I had speeded up my own drinking to match his.

'Fine,' he said, without looking up.

As I stood, the gentle buzz of my first drink crept over me. I felt a little giddy from the novelty of talking to James outside work, hearing him open up about himself, as if we were actual friends. It was only as I was ordering the next round that I became aware of the silly smile on my face. When I came back from the bar, James was sitting up again, watching me carefully.

'You look taller outside work,' he said.

'Why do you think that is?'

He shrugged. 'Maybe you're not weighed down with so many responsibilities. Which reminds me, look at our little Bill,' he said, showing me a picture of Billy pulling a face with a blonde-haired girl. 'Isn't he adorable, all grown-up and out on the town?'

'He is,' I said. 'Poor, useless, pretty Billy.'

'Shady bitch!' crowed James. 'I *knew* you had it in for him.'

'I don't have it in for him.'

'Well, I notice you haven't given him a key.'

'No, no, he's just …' I was smiling again, trying to find the word.

'He's just useless,' said James.

'He is.'

'Bit rich coming from the man who trapped himself in the toilet.'

'To idiots,' I said, raising my glass.

'To idiots.'

We were quiet for a moment after that. James's phone buzzed. The friends he'd left were asking him to come back.

'Sorry,' I said, 'I shouldn't have got you that second drink.'

'This I can finish whenever,' he said, rattling the ice cubes in his glass. 'Do you want to come?'

'I have work in the morning.'

'You've never worked hung-over?'

'I have,' I said.

'Well, then.'

'That doesn't mean I want to inflict it on myself again.'

'Fair. But if you want to come, I have a friend who isn't looking for anything serious. I could introduce you.'

'I'm not on the hunt for anything like that.' Besides, I thought, I'd had enough of it this week.

'You could have fooled me, lurking on Grindr like that.'

'You're the lurker,' I said, 'with your faceless profile.'

'Anyway,' said James, 'I wouldn't insist on you fucking my friend. I was just trying to sweeten the deal.'

'You're sweet enough.'

'Oh, I bet you say that to all the girls,' he said, in a mock-ney accent. Then, as if remembering something important he had been meaning to do, he put his drink down, leaned forward and asked, 'What do you want to do, Eoin?'

'What – in life?'

'Yeah. Where do you want to be?'

'I don't really do five-year plans.'

'Neither do I. But I know where I want to be.'

'Where?'

'On the stage, darling,' he said, sweeping one hand through the air. 'Where else?'

'Ah, yes.'

'So? What do you want to do?'

I stared into my drink while I considered my answer. So much of the time, this question came with a weight behind it that I couldn't stand, whether the person asking it was Mam, Mark, or a curious regular at the café. Usually it came with the assumption that the café was where I was biding my time, before my real life began. His attraction to ambition notwithstanding, I felt as if James would accept my answer if all I said was that I wanted to remain a barista, and one day manage to do a swan pattern in a flat white.

'I'd like to run a café,' I said.

'Well, congratulations, babe, you're doing that now.'

I shook my head. 'Not a café like the Quarter Turn.'

'You mean, not a front for Uncle Al's criminal gang?'

'I mean, not just a café. I'd like it to be a bookshop, with a café in it, and a bit with a book exchange, a decent menu, that kind of thing. A community hub, I guess.'

I stopped, thinking of how ludicrous this must sound to James, in much the same way my suggestion of getting a mortgage had sounded laughable to Rich. But James just sat there, nodding, seeming to accept the fantastical idea that I could start a business.

'And will you have jobs for unemployed actors with zero experience?' he asked.

'Only the ones who show up on a Friday night when I've made a complete hames of things.'

'I think that's quite a sweet idea,' he said, 'although I do wonder what kind of community you imagine in your hub.'

'A bunch of book-loving nerds like me, I suppose. Anyway, that's as close to a plan as I have.'

'Well, you're doing a great job at the moment,' he said. 'I'm sure you could run your own place.'

'Cheers.'

'I mean it. Right …' He drained his glass. 'Coming?'

He winked, and I noticed he had a small scar just beneath his left eye. I wanted to know how he'd got it. In fact, I wanted to know pretty much everything about him. I winked back and downed the rest of my pint.

Chapter Seventeen

We emerged on Tottenham Court Road an hour later and split the last of the vodka and Coke we'd mixed on the Tube. James had insisted we catch up with his friends, who, no doubt, were seriously hammered by now.

On the way into Central, he talked me through who we were going to meet, including another ex of his (not the poet). Guy was a French horn player who had been studying at Guildhall while James was training there as an actor.

'Wait,' I said, 'Guy is French, or he plays the French horn?'

'Both,' said James. 'We were kind of poison when mixed together, but in the best possible way.'

'What's the best way of being poisonous?'

'Oh, we were like something out of an Italian film. I literally threw a plate at him once, and later that night we had sex in a stairwell.'

'Jesus.'

'Haven't you ever had a relationship like that?'

'Not really. I've always valued my crockery too much to throw it at someone.'

We'd come out of the wrong exit at Tottenham Court Road station, so James steered me towards the pedestrian crossing, and I draped an arm over his shoulders.

'Do I smell like a toilet?' I asked, remembering where I had spent the first half of my evening.

James pressed his face into my shirt and inhaled. 'You don't,' he said. 'You just smell like the café.'

'Spoiled milk and stale coffee?'

'Don't worry,' he said, 'no one's going to be smelling you.'

In the queue, we shivered and looked at our phones. James said he would message the others and see if they were already inside. I saw that I had a message from Rich, who was breaking his five-day radio silence to ask how my evening was. He didn't even reference the lack of contact. I looked at my previous grovelling message and remembered how much I'd have given for him to reply then, rather than just over an hour ago, when James and I had been starting on our second drink and talking about lurking on Grindr. In my reply, I decided not to go into too much detail about the toilet door and instead said I had been working late, and had gone for a drink afterwards. I didn't mention that I was now queuing outside a club.

Well, if you want me to meet you, I'm free, he wrote.

Tnx, but I have work in the morning, should probably go home soon.

Sure thing. Speak tomorrow? x

I looked up. We were at the front of the queue, and for a moment I wondered if I should go home, or for that matter to Rich's house. Wasn't now the time to make up properly?

'Come on,' said James, and the thought skipped out of my mind.

I felt impossibly plain and dishevelled when we stepped inside. There were just so many beautiful men with sculpted bodies and perfectly executed fades. Everyone was sporting immaculate trainers, along with jeans that showed off all the effort they put into leg day.

James's friends were even more intimidating. The infamous Guy, who yelled, 'Toilet boy!' when James introduced us, was wearing a knee-length cardigan over a string vest,

gigantic yoga pants and boots. He was far from the aloof
muso I had pictured James attacking with a plate, but every
bit as gorgeous as I had expected.

After a few minutes, during which I was grilled on my time
trapped in the café, James and I went to get a drink. It was
hard to hear, so James leaned in close and shouted in my ear,
'Guy's giving you the charm offensive.'

'What does a charm offensive look like?' I shouted back,
looking him in the eye. This was happening a lot this evening,
I realised, the two of us locking eyes without saying anything.
I turned away, trying to manoeuvre into the barman's eyeline.

James squeezed my shoulder. 'I'm going back to the others, I'm just taking up space here.'

'Sure.'

I resumed my battle for space at the bar. A young guy next
to me smiled, and I smiled back.

'Wanna buy me a drink?' he yelled.

I laughed. 'Not really.' He left.

Jesus. I hadn't thought I was so old and desperate-look-
ing that younger men thought I'd buy them a drink for
the pleasure of being flirted with. I shook my head and
focused on getting served, attempting to ignore the feeling
that I was an outsider there, embarrassing myself just by
showing up.

James was dancing with some of the others when I got back.
The forcefield I'd noticed in the café, which kept him from
colliding with anyone, was still in effect, even in a crowded
club. I knocked back most of my drink in the minute or so I
spent watching him.

Guy sidled up to me. 'Smoke?' he said.

'Sure.' I didn't smoke, but welcomed the excursion.

'You don't dance?' Guy yelled, as we inched our way
towards the door.

'Never,' I replied. 'I can't.'

'I'm sure you can,' he said. He held the door open for me, and I took a deep breath of fresh air ...

I was smoking and explaining the Irish education system to Guy.

'The Junior Cert is a bit like GCSEs. Do you call it Le Brevet?'

I was back inside, yelling to another of James's friends about the rude guy at the bar. 'I don't mind getting older, but I didn't think I was totally ancient yet.'

My drink jumped out of my hand, like a puppy that just doesn't want to be held any more.

'I'm so sorry,' I yelled, to no one in particular. 'That's so embarrassing!'

I was back in the smoking area, talking to two Germans about the Irish education system. 'It's not like the UK. We call A levels the Leaving Certificate. How does it work in Germany?'

I was accepting a drink from James. 'I haven't seen you in ages – you drag me all the way here and then disappear!'

I was kissing Guy in the smoking area. His mouth tasted like an ashtray.

I was talking to Guy on the way to the bar.

'Can you knit?' I yelled at him.

He could.

I was wandering around alone, leaning on surfaces, telling myself I was soaking in the atmosphere.

I was in the toilets, leaning against the wall and concentrating hard on not missing the urinal. The smell of stale piss and cleaning products has been the bouquet of my evening, I thought.

I was watching James, from a distance, dancing with someone I didn't recognise. I looked down, and noticed that one of my legs was drenched in beer. How had that happened?

I was back in the smoking area, taking a breather. A breather from what? I couldn't remember. The guy who'd asked me to buy him a drink was pointing at me and giggling with a friend.

James was kissing the man he'd been dancing with, while Guy glowered from a distance. Where had I left my jacket?

I was on a night bus, checking my pockets to make sure I still had my phone, my wallet and my keys. I pulled a half-eaten Yorkie Bar out of my jacket pocket. How had I got hold of that? And did I say goodbye to anyone before I left?

It was around 4 a.m. when I got home. I was due in the café in three hours. I filled a pint glass with water and drank the whole lot while standing over the sink. I filled it again and downed that. The second pint didn't sit particularly well. I wondered if I was going to be sick, and decided the best thing to do would be to sit up for a while, maybe eat some toast and then see how I felt.

I sat on the couch in the living room, staring into space for a while. Then I took out my phone. I had a missed call and several messages from James. The last one read: *Guessing you left. Guy's pretty disappointed. Get home safe, give me a text if you get this. x*

I closed my eyes and let the wave of shame wash over me. When it receded, I wrote back.

Classic Irish Goodbye, sorry. Tell Guy I say sorry, was feeling pretty ill so had to leave. Thanks for inviting me along, I had a great night. See you tomorrow x

I opened Facebook, found James and trawled through his photos until I found some of him and Guy, taken when they were together, looking like students. James had bulked up in the years since then. His soft, round features had settled into something more solid and steady. He and Guy looked happy, sitting in what looked like London Fields on a group picnic. I jumped forward to James's more recent photos, some of which, I guessed, featured the poet who didn't believe in love. Then I just looked through James's photos until I was feeling less nauseous. I decided I could almost trust myself not to throw up if I lay down in bed. But, I thought, why not have a look at Grindr first? I'm sure no one's even on it at this hour.

Half an hour later, I was brushing my teeth while standing in the shower, getting ready to go out again. I'd be knackered in the morning anyway, so what was the difference between an hour's sleep and no sleep at all?

I stepped out and started towelling off. I checked my phone as I did so, and copied the postcode of the guy I'd been chatting to into Citymapper. It would be a five-minute cycle, followed by maybe an hour's activity, then (I checked the map again) a fifteen-minute cycle to the café. What a plan.

I closed the front door behind me, turned to where my bike should have been, and realised that it was still outside the café, where I had left it when James and I went to the pub, nearly six hours ago.

Never mind, I thought, a five-minute cycle couldn't mean more than a fifteen-minute walk. I would still have plenty of time.

I checked my phone. My hook-up was requesting more pictures.

On my way, I wrote. *See you soon.*

You said that before, he replied. *Getting bored now.*

Sorry, I'll be there in ten.

I put the phone away and started to run. It was getting bright. After a few minutes I slowed, thinking it wouldn't be a particularly sexy move to arrive covered with sweat. I belched. Best to get that out of the way before I arrived. I broke into a gentle jog again, which I kept up until the map showed my blue dot almost next to my destination.

I opened Grindr to ask the guy for his house number. There was no sign of our conversation. He had blocked me.

I slumped against a wall and let myself slowly sag to the ground. The footpath smelt damp and fresh, with a hint of soil. I closed my eyes. It was chilly, but not so cold that I felt an immediate need to get up. I lay there, feeling the sweat on my back drying. Somewhere at the back of my brain a headache was being born, which I knew I would carry until I could go to bed in nine or ten hours' time. I wished James was there. He'd find it hilarious, I thought, and that would make the whole thing worth it. Odd, how he'd been the last person I'd wanted to meet on Grindr, and now he was the first person I wanted to hear about my misadventures. It felt good, knowing there was someone who wouldn't judge my behaviour or compare it to what I'd done or said in the past.

I picked myself up and plodded back to the Quarter Turn. My bike was still locked outside, my helmet hanging from the handlebars. I let myself in.

It all felt a bit surreal, going through my usual motions when I hadn't been to bed and was (maybe) still drunk. I flicked on the coffee machine, and while it was heating, I stumped downstairs to get the float out of the safe.

I turned on the light and knew, before I even took in the room, that someone had been there. I stepped further into the office and saw some papers strewn across the floor. I was suddenly afraid, and longed for someone there with me or, failing that, something heavy I could use to defend myself if I had to.

I unlocked the safe, almost certain that it would be empty, but inside, there was the float, in its bag, along with all the takings from the previous month, which I had been trying to keep in order. I breathed a sigh of relief before I realised what was missing: the bag of cash Rebecca had asked me to lodge. I hadn't put it back in there. The moments after my escape rushed through my head: I had been so relieved to be free that I'd practically leaped on James when he opened the door, and so afraid of being caught that I had dragged him up the stairs as fast as possible, desperate to be outside and away from blame. I tried to remember my last moment with the bag of cash, but I didn't land on anything. I fumbled about the room in desperation, turning over stacks of papers and even the computer keyboard in search of what I knew I wouldn't find. My mouth started to flood with saliva.

I ran to the toilet, pulled open the door and retched. The door swung shut behind me.

Chapter Eighteen

My shift finished at three, but I stayed late to sort out every-one's wages. As I counted out stacks of notes and sealed them in envelopes for James, Billy and Hugo, the absence of several hundred quid, as well as the dodgy nature of paying everyone cash in hand, made me sweat. I was handwriting calculations of hours and earnings, which I still hoped Rebecca would con-vert into official documents, even if the prospect of everything returning to how it had been was looking less and less likely. One more week, I told myself. I will do this for one more week, and then either Rebecca will be back or I'll … But I didn't know what I would do. Tell Al to take care of it? Let him close the café? None of this sounded appealing, particularly on a hango-ver. But in a week, I told myself, I'd have to change something.

I was double-checking my own wages when James thud-ded down the stairs. I knew it was him without looking up: his tread was so distinct from Billy's light-footed trot or Hugo's sulky plod.

'Rich is here,' he said, leaning over the banister. 'You're in trouble.'

'What?' I snapped, panicked. 'What do you mean?'

James laughed. 'Joke,' he said. 'You must really be hung-over.'

James was looking fine, no doubt because, with his later start, he had managed to get something close to a full night's sleep. When he got in at midday, he shrugged off my apologies about leaving the club unexpectedly and, seeing how wrecked I looked, suggested I have a power nap in the storage room. I had actually managed to drift off briefly, before I was woken by the sound of Billy falling down the stairs.

'There's no rush,' James said, 'he's sitting down with a latte. You didn't mention that he was handsome.'

'Oh. Uh, yeah,' I said, blinking stupidly at this. 'He is.'

James turned to go back upstairs, and I was about to ask him not to mention our night out to Rich, but I hesitated. I didn't want Rich to know I had been out until dawn, but I also didn't want James to think I felt ashamed or regretful of our night together. And in the moment, I decided that I'd sooner risk Rich finding out. After all, I reasoned, what had I done? Aside from the impulsive and unsuccessful attempt at an early-morning hook-up, it was all pretty innocent: I had gone for drinks with a new friend, it had turned into a few more, and I'd had a drunken kiss with a French horn player. Shoot me.

Rich was on his phone when I emerged upstairs a few minutes later with the wages. In the kitchen, Hugo tore open his envelope and counted out the pile of notes while Billy watched, seeming unsure of whether he should do the same.

'All good?' I asked.

Hugo shrugged as he folded the money and shoved it into his back pocket. He looked doubtful. 'Tax,' he said.

'I haven't done any of that, Hugo,' I said. 'That's just your hourly rate. Rebecca will have to sort out taxes and all that when she gets back.'

'*When* she gets back,' Hugo repeated, with a smirk.

'Enjoy your evening,' I said, as I left the kitchen.

I handed James his envelope.

'If it stays this quiet, you can send Billy home,' I said, putting on my jacket. Rich looked up from his phone. I smiled and gave a small wave.

'Have fun,' James said. 'Hope you recover.'

I walked over to Rich. It felt like I hadn't seen him in months. James was right: he really was handsome.

'This is a surprise,' I said. I could feel James watching.

'Your phone was off,' Rich said. 'I thought it might be easier just to call in.'

'Sorry,' I said, 'I ran out of battery.'

I was still standing, hovering over the table where he was sitting. I didn't want to talk in there.

'Shall we go for a stroll?' I asked. 'I'd love some fresh air.' What I'd actually love, I thought, was my bed and some blackout curtains.

'Sure,' Rich said. 'We could climb up towards Ally Pally.'

This sounded like an impossible ordeal.

'Sounds great.'

Outside, we walked in silence for a few minutes. I wondered if Rich was waiting for me to apologise again for the previous Sunday. I was happy to, if it would end this awkwardness, but I decided to let him give me a steer in the right direction. I hadn't the strength for much else.

'I didn't know there was someone new in the café,' said Rich, eventually.

'Yeah,' I said. 'I thought I'd mentioned training him in the past few weeks.'

'What's he like?'

'Grand, yeah,' I said. In the general fog of my hangover, I couldn't quite piece together what was feeling so odd, why the brief interaction between James and Rich had unsettled me so much. It didn't feel like a classic, groundless case of The Fear.

'So,' said Rich, as we approached Wood Green, 'I have good news and bad news.'

My stomach twisted into a knot. 'Oh, yeah?' I said, trying to stay calm.

'The good news is that I got the job.'

'What?'

'Yeah.'

'That's amazing, Rich!' I said, and turned to hug him. I could smell his aftershave, and feel where my arms slotted in around him, how familiar his shape was.

'Yeah,' he said, as we separated. 'I'm pretty happy.' Then he frowned a little. 'Are you crying?'

'Sorry,' I said, blinking away the tears. 'I just know how hard you worked and—'

'Eoin,' he said, laughing a little, 'are you okay?'

'I'm sorry,' I said again. 'I've just missed you this week. I've hated fighting.'

Rich looked confused. 'What do you mean?' he asked.

'Just after last Sunday I messaged to say how I was sorry for acting like a dick, and when I didn't hear back from you, I assumed you were still mad.'

'I was a bit angry,' said Rich, 'but I knew you were sorry. Don't worry about it.'

It was my turn to be confused. How long had we been reconciled? How hadn't I known about it? Usually we'd have seen each other two or three evenings since Sunday.

'I've spent all week thinking you were still furious with me,' I said, choosing to omit that I had spent some of that time having a threesome and bungling a low-stakes heist in my place of work.

'Oh,' said Rich. 'Sorry, I was just preoccupied with the second-round interview and all that, so—'

'Never mind,' I said. 'Tell me about the interview.'

We were out the other side of Wood Green and nearly at Alexandra Palace station when I remembered. 'Hang on,' I said, as Rich explained the timeline for changing school, 'what was the bad news?'

'Oh, yeah,' he said, and I noticed that he looked bashful, which was an expression I rarely saw on him.

'The bad news is that I have crabs,' he said. 'I *had* crabs, I should say.'

'Oh, feck.'

'Sorry.'

'When did you notice?' I asked. I felt as if I'd been awake for a week. My legs were aching and I was starving. And now I had to go to a chemist.

'Tuesday,' said Rich. 'I was a bit itchy.'

His silent forgiveness began to make a bit more sense. It must be hard to stay truly angry with someone when you know that the next conversation you have is going to be about pubic lice. But it's also hard to tell someone you forgive them just because of the fresh perspective you've been afforded by your experience with pubic lice.

'Couldn't you have told me a little sooner?' I asked. Now that he mentioned it, I had been scratching a lot this week, but hadn't really thought of it.

He nodded sheepishly. We were crossing the bridge over the railway. A train passed beneath us, carrying the first wave of commuter residents into London for their Saturday evening out. Through the hangover, I pieced together that, if he had picked up crabs, Rich had definitely been with another man. At least one other man. And, to my surprise, I was still breathing, still placing one foot in front of the other, still holding his hand. Was it only a few weeks since the very idea of this had reduced me to crying into Jax's embroidery?

'Sorry,' Rich said again, 'it was a bit embarrassing. And I really did have a lot on my plate with the interviews.' He seemed chastened, somehow, even though my reaction must have been milder than he'd anticipated.

We made our way up the hill to Alexandra Palace. Clouds hung above London, like sodden, crumpled-up tissues. I sank onto the steps leading down to the park.

'Tired?' Rich asked, sitting down next to me.

'Yeah,' I said, then decided he'd better hear it from me rather than seeing a stray photo on Instagram. 'I stayed out a bit too late last night.'

'Oh, no,' he said. 'You feeling hung-over?'

I nodded.

'Poor baby,' he said, and put an arm around me. I nuzzled into his shoulder and waited for him to ask where I had been, who I had been out with, what time I'd got home. But he stayed quiet. This was how it was now, I supposed. I didn't ask who he'd got crabs from, and he didn't ask about my night out, or the almighty hangover that it had taken me nearly forty minutes to bring up.

'I suppose I'd better stay at mine tonight,' I said. 'I don't want to give the crabs back to you.'

'Yeah.'

'That's a shame,' I said. 'I'd quite like a night with you.'

'Me too.' He rummaged in his pocket. 'I brought you something.'

It was a tube of insecticide cream.

'Wow,' I said, reading the box, '"Five per cent permethrin". Five per cent! You really are spoiling me.'

'Just don't expect any birthday presents this year,' Rich said.

It felt good to kiss him again.

Chapter Nineteen

On my bus back from Ally Pally, I messaged Tom and Dean to let them know about the crabs. I got a curt reply, after which they blocked me. That felt like a bit of an overreaction, given how much fun we'd had while they waited for their meal to arrive. The Freddie Mercury lookalike was a lot more understanding, and even suggested a second meeting, promising he would keep his head in the game this time. I was trying to figure out a nice way to decline his offer when Jax messaged.

You up to much this evening?

This kind of message wasn't quite on a par with 'Could do with a chat,' but it certainly merited an instant reply.

Incredibly hung-over, I wrote. *Equal parts exhaustion and guilt.*

Same. Wanna pop over for tea?

I really didn't. I had stopped at the corner shop for a frozen pizza, which I was planning on inhaling before a ten-hour sleep. But I could recognise a cry for help when I heard one. When hung-over, Jax tended to shut herself away from others. Hangovers made her furious with alcohol, pubs, capitalism, herself and everyone around her. Back when we lived together, I could tell she was feeling rough when she shut herself in the bathroom and cleaned it for up to five hours. The rest of us would tiptoe around, bursting for the toilet, while she furiously scoured the bathtub, listening to a neo-Marxist podcast and occasionally bellowing, 'Fucking stains!' from behind the locked door. One Sunday Tony pissed into a bottle rather than daring to interrupt. So the fact that she was offering tea suggested that this wasn't the kind of hangover that could be defeated with bleach and vigorous scrubbing.

Sure, I wrote. *I'll be there ASAP.*

Before I left, I applied half a tube of the insecticide cream. It stank, and it felt like I'd smeared myself in glue. To cover the smell, I sprayed on some deodorant and hunted out an aftershave I saved for special occasions. A rebuke of my mother's – 'You smell like a whore's handbag' – echoed round my head.

Because I had gone for that walk with Rich, my bike was *still* locked outside the café, so it was a trudge, then a bus to Jax's flat.

When I got there, Claudia opened the door with the soft smile and whispered update of a palliative-care nurse. She pointed me in the direction of the living room and padded off. I was worried to see that Jax wasn't engaged in any kind of craft, and seemed to be staring through the TV, rather than at it. I suggested some knitting (I had left the three completed rows of my scarf behind on Wednesday) but she just winced and shook her head.

'Did you get any cleaning done today?' I asked.

'I don't deserve clean surfaces,' she said.

'Not true,' I said. 'You deserve sparkling …' I couldn't think of a material. It had been a long day.

'Granite?' Jax offered.

'Sparkling, highly polished granite,' I said. 'Also, can I put a pizza in your oven? I think I might die if I don't have some carbs.'

'Sure,' she said, not moving.

'You can have some, if you like.'

'I don't deserve pizza.'

I stuck the pizza into the oven and made two mugs of tea while I was there.

'I'll drink them both if you don't deserve tea,' I said, placing one next to her. 'What's up?'

'I joined a tag rugby team,' Jax said. 'We had a match yesterday.'

'Is ... is Aaron on the tag rugby team?'

When Jax nodded, I closed my eyes briefly and reminded myself to be supportive before asking, 'Did you win?'

'We won,' she said, 'or so I believe. I managed to get concussed in the first few minutes.'

'I thought tag rugby was non-contact,' I said.

'It is. I slipped and fell into someone's knee. Everything went a bit blurry for a few minutes, but I didn't bleed from the nose and I didn't really have a headache, so I don't think it's full-on concussion. But, basically, Aaron stayed with me for the whole game. We just stood on the sideline and talked while the others played.'

'That was nice of him,' I said.

'He's a very nice man,' said Jax. She sighed deeply and put down her tea.

'Did you go out afterwards?'

'Yes.'

'I wouldn't have thought that was advisable with a head injury.'

Jax clenched her jaw, and I worried she would retreat into the bathroom with a pair of Marigold gloves after all.

'Anyway,' I said, 'how was the night?'

'It was great,' said Jax. 'It was genuinely lovely to get to know the rest of the team, and after the pub closed, a few of us found another one.' She continued in a rush, with her eyes screwed shut. 'And then we were getting the night Tube home, and Aaron and I were the only ones on the Piccadilly line, and my one was northbound and coming first so he waited with me on the platform, and we basically snogged and I feel like complete dirt and I don't think I should go back into work on Monday or leave this house ever again.'

'And the blonde with the fringe that we saw, she's definitely his girlfriend?'

Jax nodded. 'Am I a bad person?' she asked.

'Definitely not,' I said. 'Good people make mistakes all the time. You fancy him, he's taken, you had a drunken kiss. You shouldn't beat yourself up about it.'

'Yeah.' She stared mournfully at the TV for another few minutes. 'Where were you last night, anyway?'

I wondered how much detail I wanted to go into about my evening with James and his friends. Not too much, I decided. 'I've got a mystery for you,' I said instead.

Jax's mood picked up considerably as I laid out my misadventure with the toilet door and the subsequent disappearance of the cash. By the time the pizza was ready to come out of the oven, she had cleared the coffee-table and laid out some multi-coloured pieces of card.

'Right,' she said, tying back her hair as I arrived with the pizza split between two plates. 'Suspects. Motivation. Opportunity. Who has a key to the café?'

'Everyone except Billy,' I said.

'So that's you, Uncle Al, Hugo ...' Jax wrote down each of our names on a piece of card and drew a rough sketch underneath.

'And James,' I added, peering at my card. The picture of me looked like the kind of caricature you get done by the beach. All it was missing was a big dipper in the background. 'Do I really have that big a nose?' I asked.

'No,' said Jax, 'just compared to your chin.'

'And am I a suspect?'

'Not really, no, but including you makes it more ...' Jax twiddled the marker between her fingers.

'Fun?'

'So James is the new guy, right?' Jax asked, writing his name on a new piece of card. 'The one who hates you and your bicycle.'

'That may have been an overstatement,' I said. 'He's not as bad as all that.'

'Okay. Please describe him for the sake of my sketch.'

'Well, he's got a *huge* nose, just like me.'

'Oh, for fuck's sake, you're so sensitive.'

'He's solid-looking, quite stocky, short hair.'

'Brilliant. Just show me a photo,' Jax snapped. 'Some witness for the prosecution you'd make.'

As I took out my phone, I noticed that James had messaged me a photo taken of us the previous night. I looked as if I was carrying a head injury of my own, as I beamed at the camera. I decided not to show Jax that one.

'Aw,' said Jax, when I showed her his Instagram. 'How cute.'

'What?'

'He's like a big cuddly teddy bear.'

I'd never have described James as cute, but maybe that was because I'd met him in person first, and knew he was anything but cuddly.

'Anyway,' Jax was saying, 'cutie or no, he's a suspect. He's the one who let you out of the toilet, yes?'

'Yeah.'

'So there was a period of time when he was alone, in the office, with the safe open?'

'Yes,' I said, 'but I had the cash with me.'

'Are you sure?'

This idea was absurd. Jax would understand that if she talked to James for five minutes.

'Listen, we went for a drink afterwards,' I said. 'Can you imagine having the neck to bring money you'd just stolen to the pub?'

'I can imagine it,' said Jax, as she drew a sketch of James. 'I wouldn't do it myself, but I can imagine a thief doing it.'

The noun did it.

'James isn't a thief,' I said, a little louder than I needed to.

Jax nodded, and added some cross-hatching to her sketch. 'How many drinks did you go for?'

'Enough to give me this terrible hangover,' I said. 'You can take James off the list of suspects.'

'Fine,' she said, though I noticed she kept his card in the pile.

We spent another half-hour debating Hugo and Al's motives. On balance, Al seemed the most likely suspect. He had practically unlimited opportunity, and while his motivation wasn't immediately apparent, there was plenty to hint at dodgy dealings, not least the suggestion that he was on the hunt for Rebecca.

'I have to go home,' I said eventually. 'What should I do about it? What if Rebecca comes back and asks where the hell the money is?'

'Eoin, I know I'm a brilliant crime-solver, and my detective agency is going to be bigger than Precious Ramotswe's, but don't you think you should go to the police?'

'But how dodgy is the whole thing? I'm paying everyone under the table, for one. I know that's what Rebecca told me to do, but I've also hired someone without a shred of paperwork, and ended up alone with him after hours with a bag of money that's now gone missing.' As I spoke, the scale of my misdeeds came crashing down on me.

'Look, for now forget about lodging the money,' said Jax. 'Pretend that nothing's happened, and plead ignorance if Rebecca realises it's missing. You won't be lying. You have nothing to do with the money being taken.'

'But I won't be telling her the full truth.'

'Do you think Rebecca's telling *you* the truth?'

I had no idea. When I saw her email, my in-built defer-
ence to Rebecca had kicked in so that I simply did what she
asked as best I could, without questioning her motivations
too deeply. Now all I wanted was to go to bed.

'I should head,' I said. 'Thanks for the tea.'

'No worries, thanks for the pizza,' she said, 'and for the
distraction. I honestly forgot for an hour that I'm an Other
Woman.'

'Just let me know the next time you're feeling blue, I'll get
myself embroiled in some other criminal activity.'

'By the way,' Jax said, as she led me to the front door, 'I'm
covering a launch for work on Tuesday, I've got a couple of
spare passes if you and Rich want to come?'

'I'll ask him,' I said. 'Sleep well.'

Outside, it occurred to me that I should really go and pick
up my bike from outside the café before it was stolen. After
the last twenty-four hours, a part of me never wanted to see
the Quarter Turn again. But, I thought, that could also mean
never seeing James again. And that felt reason enough to keep
going, regardless of the consequences. I turned for the café.

Chapter Twenty

We had just flipped the sign to Closed when the two pregnancy-yoga ladies walked past the Quarter Turn, one of them pushing a pram. James gasped, and left me counting the takings while he ran to greet them at the door. I watched as he stepped around to look into the pram, gently placing one hand on the new mother's shoulder and another on his chest. After a few seconds, I saw the mother gesture, and James bent down to wave. The mother's friend looked my way and beckoned me outside.

'Congratulations,' I said, as I stepped out. 'Great to see you back.'

'Oh, bless you,' the mother said. 'I heard you were asking after us.'

'Yeah,' I said, not sure my awkward small-talk quite merited this description. 'I'm delighted to see you're both well.'

James gave the baby a final wave, and after a few jokes about free Babycinos for life, the women went on their way.

'That reminds me,' James said, throwing an arm over my shoulders as we stepped back inside. 'I'm still getting job alerts for café work, and I saw one you should go for.'

'Oh, yeah?'

'There's a café in Crouch End looking for a manager,' he said. 'And it sounds like they have that community-hub vibe you were after.'

'Oh, right,' I said, returning to the cash-up. 'I don't know if I'm qualified for that.'

'Yes, you are,' James replied, hunkering down to clean the inside of the dishwasher. 'And you'd learn stuff for when you have your own place.'

I was surprised that James even remembered me talking about running a café. With everything else that had happened on Friday, I'd certainly forgotten mentioning it. 'I'll think about it,' I said.

'Great,' said James, 'you think about it, and once we're done closing, you can apply.'

'I don't have a CV.'

'I've got a template. We'll use that.'

I laughed, and spread the twenty-pence pieces flat on the counter. 'I don't have the experience. Or the references,' I added, thinking that Rebecca was more likely to report me to the police than she was to vouch for my character.

'Put my number down. I'll do you one,' James said. 'I'll tell them I'm an employer of yours from Ireland.'

I sealed the last of the coin bags and wrote down the day's total. For once, the figure matched the one on the receipt, though that was little comfort when we were missing a bag of cash, which I had by now spent hours hunting for down in the storeroom, just in case.

'Long is the day, and many the hour,' James said, in a voice that sounded like Fiona Shaw wearing a gum shield, 'that I would be needing to list the qualities of young Eoin.'

'Eoin Óg,' I said. I usually hated people doing Oirish accents at me, but I made an exception for James.

'Eoin Óg, indeed,' he said, following me as I took the cash and the tablet downstairs. 'Wise, he is, and patient as well. Fair as the—' He stopped, laughing.

'Fair as the …' I prompted him, happy for a distraction from the gap inside the safe where the money should have been.

'Fair as the cream atop a freshly made cappuccino,' James finished, his accent wandering from Skibbereen to somewhere on the Amalfi coast.

'Okay, Seamus Trapattoni,' I said, 'I'll put you down as a reference.'

'You can use some of the jobs I put on my CV as well.'

'Hang on,' I said, closing the safe, 'you lied on the CV you gave me?'

James sighed, crouched beside me and placed a hand on my knee. 'Babe, I'm going to be straight with you. My auntie never ran a café.'

'What?'

'She volunteered in the church's soup kitchen a couple of times a month.'

'And you helped her there?'

He was laughing again. 'I didn't work for her, Eoin. I'm really sorry. I lied.'

'Why would you invent such an unimpressive lie?' I asked, pushing his hand off my knee so that he lost balance and rolled backwards. 'Why not say you'd worked in an actual café, one that served coffee?'

'Because then you'd have been able to check, ask for a reference. You were hardly going to call up Auntie Trish, were you?'

'I suppose not.'

'Also, not being funny, but I guessed you were pretty desperate, considering I arrived when Billy was lying in a pool of milk.'

'I'm such a gullible fool,' I said, standing up and pulling the office chair towards me. 'Forget what I said about running a café, I'd just be swindled by the likes of you.'

'Seriously, though, let me send you that template,' he said, picking himself up and batting the dust off the back of his jeans. 'And you don't need to make up anything. I'm sure you'd be more than qualified.'

I swivelled the chair back and forth while James took out his phone and looked for the document, shuffling his feet as he did so.

'There,' he said, as my phone buzzed. 'I've sent you the link for the job post, and a copy of the template I used.'

He stretched, and I kept my eyes on his face, determined not to look at the gap where his shirt lifted above his waistline.

'I can help you write a cover letter,' he said, 'if you want. I can even get us some gins in a tin if it helps.'

I reached for my phone, thinking that, if nothing else, putting the CV together would be a good prompt to entertain James with my greatest service-industry disasters. But when I looked at my screen, in addition to the email from James, there was a message from Rich: *You on the way? x*

'Oh, fuck,' I said, jumping out of my chair so that it rolled to the other side of the storage area and knocked over a box of wooden stirrers. 'I'm meant to be meeting Rich and his mates,' I said, and looked up at James, wondering how he would react to this.

'How convenient,' he said, crossing his arms. 'Just when I had you convinced, something comes up that you plain ol' forgot.'

'I did forget,' I said, as I sent Rich a message to tell him I was coming, 'and I would have really liked to … I'd have appreciated the help, I just—'

'It's fine,' said James, 'honestly.'

I wondered if I could make out some of the sharpness in his voice I associated with his first week at the café. 'But listen,' I said, 'my friend Jax has invited me to this fashion event tomorrow. I don't know much about it, but she told me there'd be free cocktails, if you want to come?'

I tried to keep my tone casual, but it felt different, asking him to a specific event rather than just hanging out at work or even going out by chance.

'Cool,' James said, after a moment. 'Sure.'

He turned and led the way up the stairs. I followed him, once again forcing myself to keep my eyes up.

I collapsed in the door of the pub, having cycled over in about fifteen minutes, giving the pothole that had wrecked my front wheel a wide berth on the way.

Danni and Shanice weren't there this time, but the rest of the 'Member-Whens were at their usual table. Kev and Olga were sitting on the bench by the window, while Andrew was slumped in his throne. Rich was up at the bar.

'Sorry I'm late,' I gasped, 'I lost track of time.'

I realised I'd interrupted Andrew in the middle of a story, but he barely seemed to notice, raising a single hand in my direction as he spoke. Kev nodded, while Olga gave a slightly more energetic wave. I crossed to the bar, tapped Rich on the shoulder and kissed his cheek as he turned.

'I thought you'd been swallowed by another pothole,' he said.

'Sorry.' I gave him a squeeze around the waist. 'Could I have one of those?' I asked the barman as he placed a pint in front of Rich.

The barman's gaze flicked down to my grubby jumper and back up to my face before he tutted and turned away from us. I glanced at Rich, wondering if he'd noticed, but he seemed more interested in taking a sip of his pint.

'How was work?' he asked.

'Grand,' I said. 'Did you notice the daggers I just got from the barman?'

Rich shook his head. 'I didn't,' he said. 'But maybe he's a bit stretched. He had just served me, after all.'

As if in agreement, the barman slammed my pint down on the bar so hard that some of the beer slopped over the side.

'Thank you,' I said, thinking that Rich was probably right, and I'd just been rude about an overworked server. The barman gave me a pained grimace of a smile and held out the card machine.

'By the way, Eoin,' Rich said, when we sat down at the table, 'Kev and Olga have big news.'

'We're pregnant,' Kev said, while Olga beamed.

'I knew it!' I said, and nudged Rich triumphantly.

Rich looked at me with such an alarmed expression that I wondered if I'd accidentally shouted an insult without noticing.

'I mean, congratulations, both of you,' I said, turning back to Kev and Olga. 'It's just, I actually guessed the last time I saw you guys.'

Olga raised her eyebrows, seeming alarmed to learn that I'd been speculating about her behind her back.

'I just noticed,' I went on, feeling myself begin to blush, 'that you weren't drinking, and I was saying to Rich afterwards, I wondered if that might be the reason.'

I looked around the table for someone who might chime in, but everyone seemed happy to let me dig my own way out of this hole.

'Remember?' I said to Rich, who was once again midway through a sip of his drink, so could neither confirm nor deny my story.

'Oh, yes, well,' said Olga, 'we weren't telling anyone then. We were waiting for the twelve-week scan.'

'Yes,' I said, 'that was what I guessed, when Kev was …' I gestured back to the bar, but stopped, realising that the more I explained, the more I was sounding like a freak.

'Wow, real Poirot stuff,' Andrew said, after a moment, and I could have kissed him for being kind enough to say something. 'You don't miss a thing.'

Rich smiled.

'Yeah,' he said, and ruffled the hair on the back of my head, 'he may not say much, but he's always watching.'

The table laughed, and while I asked Olga how she had been feeling, the thought passed through my head that this was how they all saw me: Rich's quiet boyfriend, who no one had any particular opinion on, and who didn't really have anything of interest to say. I leaned back in my chair and comforted myself with the idea that Jax would be happy to hear I had been right. The conversation turned to who else from the group's wider circle of friends had had a baby, and I let them at it, wondering why I had panicked and rushed to get here. The barman was looking in our direction, and when I smiled at him, he gave another grimace and turned away.

Rich was on his phone, facing away from me in bed, and I was finally getting to the end of *Mrs Dalloway*. As Clarissa turned to her party guests, I had one of those moments of clarity that only ever comes to me while I'm concentrating on a book, when an answer to a problem, or a memory from childhood or, as in this case, a question floats into my mind unbidden.

'Hey,' I said to Rich, 'did you have sex with the barman?'

He turned round to look at me, his phone loose and forgotten in his hand. 'Say again?' he said, but I could tell he was stalling.

'It's okay,' I said, 'I was just thinking, that might have been why he was a bit weird around me.'

'Weird?' Rich asked.

'Rude. Remember, I asked you at the bar if I had done anything to annoy him.'

'Oh. Sure. Uh …'

Rich looked ready to spring out of bed and run for the door at any moment.

'Well,' he said, 'yeah, we … we did fool around, yeah.'

I nodded, and flicked back through the pages of the book. I had known that Rich must have slept with someone, but it was quite a different thing to put a face to it. The barman was almost exactly the kind of good-looking, self-possessed man I had pictured while I was panicking about who Rich would go off with. I felt like I should be devastated, but my main emotion now was curiosity, that the guy had been so aloof with me, and had even bothered to glower in my direction.

'Are you okay?' Rich asked, watching me closely.

'You could have told me,' I said. I put down my book and switched off the bedside lamp beside me. 'I thought I was imagining things.'

'Well, I thought we weren't discussing all that,' Rich said. 'I thought that was what you wanted.'

'Yeah, but that's …' I trailed off, not sure how to put it. Surely it would be better to tell me the truth, rather than let me worry about it.

After another few minutes, Rich put down his phone and turned off the light on his side of the bed. I moved towards him, but he wriggled a little further away. I lay in the dark, listening to the sound of his breath slowing and deepening as he fell asleep.

Chapter Twenty-one

I closed my eyes and leaned into the wind. It was blowing hard enough to roar in my ears and let me experiment with how far forward I could lean before I fell flat on my face. It was the kind of thing I used to do when I was small, and I wondered if kids still did it now. I'd have to ask Rich: he probably saw them do it in the playground.

I heard a train arriving at the station down the hill. I opened my eyes, regained my balance and saw James getting off. I waved, he waved back, and we endured twenty seconds of being too far away from each other to speak as he approached. I adjusted different items of clothing, looked at my phone and generally pretended that I wasn't feeling extremely self-conscious.

Finally he was close enough to say, 'Hey,' and we hugged, as if we hadn't last seen each other a few hours earlier when he'd finished his shift at the Quarter Turn.

'Sorry to drag you out to the middle of nowhere,' I said. 'I didn't realise it was in Leyton until I read Jax's invitation properly.'

'I actually grew up a bit further east,' he said. 'I know Leyton well.'

'Great.' I smiled, struggling to find anything else to say. Why was I being so fucking awkward? James inhaled as if he was about to say something, then held the breath for a moment. 'What?' I asked.

'You look good,' he said. 'You scrub up well.'

'Oh.' I patted the tuft of hair I knew was sticking out at the back of my head. 'Thanks.'

'Did you cycle?'

'Of course,' I said, gesturing to where my bike was locked. 'You look good too,' I added, thinking that I should maybe have said this sooner.

'Thanks. Shall we find this warehouse?'

'Yeah, I think it's about a ten-minute walk, past the building site. Jax said it would be signposted once we were in the general vicinity.'

'Cool.'

'Off we go, then.'

'Off we go.'

I had a vague impulse to reach for his hand. Today in work, I had been feeling nervous around him again, not in the wary, antagonistic way I had been when he started at the café, but in a way that made me feel energised, buzzing, like I would after a triple-shot flat white. It was almost a relief when his shift finished and I was left alone with Billy.

As we walked, James asked if I'd heard any more from Rebecca since the previous Friday night. I hadn't. Every day I woke with a mixture of dread and excitement at the prospect of arriving at the café to find her wiping down the counter, waiting for me to explain (or try to explain) what had happened to all the money she'd asked me to lodge. I felt the conversation would definitely end in me being sacked, but at least it would be over. I hadn't told James about the money going missing, deciding that it would be unfair to burden him with it. Despite my best efforts, though, it was becoming clear that something was wrong at the Quarter Turn. The bakery we got our pastries from had stopped delivering, and without any stock, the café's minimalism was looking more like austerity. Even Trevor (whom I had recently been assailing with random Spurs facts) had looked a bit miffed when we told him we didn't know when the Bakewell tarts would be in again. I tried to shake off my worries by asking James about the various friends of his I'd met on our night out.

'Well, I'm sorry to break it to you, but you're dead to Guy,' he said, 'after the Cinderella routine you pulled.'

'Jesus,' I said. 'I don't even know what he saw in me to begin with.'

'Oh, shut up,' James said, giving me a playful shove that nearly sent me toppling into the hedge we were walking past. 'There's lots to see in you.'

As I steadied myself, I spotted a warehouse lit up in green and blue on the opposite side of a small roundabout, and led the way over to it. At the entrance, a woman wearing a brown waistcoat and some brass goggles strapped to her head strode towards us.

'Good evening, sirs, welcome to the Homecoming celebrations,' she said, with a booming voice that instantly marked her out as an actor. 'Have you journeyed far?'

I looked to James. I assumed he would be more used to engaging in this kind of rapport.

'Oh, yes,' he said. 'Our travels have been wearying, but we're very excited to be here.'

'Wonderful,' said the woman. 'I believe Mr Fogg is due to land within the hour.'

'Great,' I said, trying to get into the spirit of things. 'That's … splendid.'

'Can I see your ticket?' she asked.

I spotted Jax, who was standing just inside the entrance. Next to her, I noticed, was Aaron. Why on earth would she ask him?

'Sir?'

'Yes,' I said, and found the invitation that Jax had for-warded to me in my emails. The hostess produced a phone of her own, branded with a silhouette of Queen Victoria, and scanned the QR code.

'That's some astonishing technology,' James said. 'Wher-ever did you get it?'

'Oh, these gizmos,' said the woman, 'I can't pretend to understand them. They're a recent invention of …' She trailed off, looking worried.

'Brunel?' I suggested.

'Indeed, you got it in one, sir,' she said, 'now enjoy Phileas Fogg's triumphant Homecoming.'

'Look at you,' James said, as we walked away, 'riffing with the actors.'

'In Steampunk, every sentence ends either with the word "combustion", or Brunel,' I said.

'How do you know?'

'I used to read a lot of Steampunk fiction online,' I said, surprising myself with this fact. I hadn't thought about it in years, and I laughed as the hours I'd spent in front of the family computer came flooding back. 'On dial-up internet, I would read Sherlock Holmes fan fiction.'

'So when everyone else was discovering online porn, you were reading short stories set in Victorian London?'

'The two things aren't mutually exclusive. Some of those stories were pretty racy.'

'Eoin!' Jax called. 'You found it!' She was wearing a purple velvety dress. 'You remember Aaron, don't you?'

James and Aaron were introduced, Jax and I going out of our way to make sure everyone knew that our respective dates were our friends and nothing more.

'I'm too scared to go any further than this,' Jax admitted. 'I'm afraid of getting stuck in a conversation with an actor playing a chim-erny sweep.'

'You look really on-theme,' said James, before turning to me in mock outrage. 'Why didn't you tell me there was a dress code?' he asked, adjusting my collar.

'I'm sorry,' I said, 'but I couldn't bear to come in costume. We're both wearing shirts – that's enough of an effort.'

'You're better off,' said Jax. 'I feel like I'm wearing a carpet. It's not embarrassing, is it?'

'It's perfect,' said James. 'A nod to Jules Verne.'

Aaron was looking around the entrance area with a bemused, slightly bored expression, his hands in his pockets, as if he was waiting for a train. 'Can't say I've ever heard of an immersive fashion show before,' he said.

'I don't think anyone has,' said Jax. 'They've taken a bit of a risk in the hope that it gets traction with the influencers.'

'Oh, they'll be all over this,' said James. 'In fact …' He took out his phone and tried to negotiate the four of us into a selfie against a Victorian postbox. Aaron stepped out of the group and offered to take the photo for the three of us.

'Guys, don't look now,' said Jax, as we smiled for the camera, 'but we're being approached.'

'Oh, no. Run!'

It was too late. A man wearing a tall hat decorated with cogs and wheels blocked our path. 'I say,' he rasped, peering at us through a pair of frameless glasses, the lenses of which were painted with clock hands, 'could one of you fine people tell me the time?'

After a while, it became apparent that beyond the general Steampunk theme, there was some kind of story that we were meant to be following as we walked around the warehouse in search of a drink. Every now and then someone would grab me and whisper something about a hidden crossbow or a scrambled compass, but I was always concentrating too hard on nodding politely to take in anything they were saying. All the interaction reminded me of the scratch night with the play about the missing cocaine, and I thought of texting Rich. But we hadn't really referenced it in a while and, anyway, I reminded myself, he'd be prepping for his first meeting at the new school.

'So hang on, are we here to assassinate Phileas Fogg?' Jax asked, as we avoided making eye contact with a stilt walker, who was clearly longing to talk to an audience member.

'No,' said James. 'We suspect that Phileas Fogg is going to assassinate the Queen.'

'How are you so on top of the plot?'

'Because the policeman told us.'

'Wait, I missed that,' I said. 'Which policeman? Shouldn't he have been in uniform?'

'He was an undercover policeman,' replied James.

'Of course!' Jax yelled. 'Well, how the fuck could we have missed *that*?' She grabbed a glass of champagne off a passing tray. 'Thank God there's booze,' she said, 'because the rest of it is a shambles.'

That was unfair. The warehouse was elaborately done up as Victorian-era Plymouth, complete with dockside amusements and a cheery brothel. And whenever they weren't making me jump by whispering in my ear, I could appreciate that the actors were really committing to the fantasy as well, with plenty of wiggling eyebrows and Cockney rhyming slang.

'The only thing that confuses me,' said Aaron, 'is how this relates to a fashion brand.'

An urchin tugged at his sleeve. We all tried to pretend she wasn't there.

'Will there be a runway at some point?' I asked Jax, as Aaron gave in and followed the urchin to a nearby notice board, which was plastered with black-and-white mugshots.

'Doesn't look like it,' Jax said. 'Maybe I'll go and save him,' she added, nodding towards Aaron. She grabbed another drink from the same tray as she went.

'Shall we go with her?' James asked.

'I'd feel like I was getting in her way.'

We watched Jax offer the glass of bubbles to Aaron, who accepted it before introducing Jax to his new friend. The urchin bowed and promptly led them away.

'Are they really just friends?' James asked.

'He has a girlfriend, but apparently he never mentions her.'

'That's odd.'

'Yeah. Jax reckons he's not totally happy.'

'Sounds like it.'

We drank our cocktails in silence, not looking at each other.

'Are you enjoying it?' I asked. 'Or is it a bit of a busman's holiday, improvising with other actors?'

'A bit,' he said. 'There's nothing like watching other people working to remind you that you're not. But I'm enjoying it. It's mad how much money they've pumped into it. I'll be pissed if we don't figure out this assassination plot, though.'

'Didn't your undercover policeman say something about finding a map of the docks?'

'Yeah. He said it was in the opium den, which is just next to that fire exit. I'm going to pee, shall we go have a look when I'm back?'

'Do you want me to grab a drink while you're gone?'

'Yes, please, babe,' he said, 'thanks.' He gave my shoulder a squeeze as he left.

Friends squeeze each other's shoulders, I told myself. It wasn't a big deal. Nor was calling a friend 'babe'. And just because I was smiling at the sight of him crossing the warehouse towards the toilets, that didn't mean anything, did it?

Half an hour later I was dragging James by the hand as we sprinted after the assassin, who had been lurking in the opium den all this time.

'Stop him!' I yelled, barrelling past a huddle of influencers. 'He's after the Queen!'

I was feeling a sugar rush from all those sweet, fruity cocktails we'd been served. The hooded assassin ducked behind a curtain, and a large bouncer blocked our way.

'Sorry, guys, no entry.'

'But he's getting away!' I said.

'You can't go in there.'

'Why not?'

'It's backstage. You need to be in the cast.'

'Oh,' I said, a little deflated by the abrupt end to the fantasy. 'Well, what should we do now?'

The bouncer shrugged and turned away.

'Come on,' said James. 'We just passed a miniature gin palace. We can go there until Phileas Fogg lands.'

He led the way. The influencers I'd barged past stepped back to let him through, glaring at me as they did so.

'Have you ever noticed that?' I asked him.

'What?'

'When you cross a room, everyone gets out of your way. People, dogs, buses, everything seems to flow around you. It's like you're so in sync with everyone, they just glide around you.'

'Not you, though,' James said.

'No. I walked straight into you.'

We stepped into the gin palace, which looked like a fairground hall of mirrors. Distorted, gloopy versions of ourselves looked back at us through dusty glass. Even the ceiling was mirrored.

'I once went home with a guy who had floor-to-ceiling mirrors,' said James, as he sat down next to me. Our table looked out onto the main performance area. I hadn't seen Jax since she disappeared with Aaron and the urchin.

'How was it?' I asked James, peering at the berries in my drink.

'The sex was good, but he really loved watching himself during it all.'

'That sounds a bit too much like a psychopath for my taste.'

'I did wonder if I'd turn up in series of bin bags.'

'But you didn't stop,' I said.

'Oh, no. I thought I may as well follow through. I'd already missed the last train.'

I looked out of the window of our little lean-to. At one end of the warehouse, the lights were focused on a set of curtains, from which came the sound of pistons and propellers. Over the speakers, a voice said, 'Ladies and gentlemen, please gather for the arrival of the eminent Mr Phileas Fogg!'

'It seems like it's all kicking off out there,' I said to James.

'Do you want to go and have a look?'

'No,' I said, 'not particularly.'

'Me neither,' he said.

There comes a point when it's inevitable that, short of a major natural catastrophe, you're going to kiss someone. I realised that here, in this pretend gin palace with smudged mirrors and cracked surfaces, in a matter of seconds or, at most, minutes, I was going to kiss James. My chest tightened. I didn't want to rush into it because this moment, I knew, was the one I'd remember, watching him out of the corner of my eye, wondering which of us would finally lean in.

'How's your cocktail?' I asked.

'Fine,' he said, and put it down on the table beside him.

His mouth was sweet and soft. I trailed one hand across his shoulders, and pulled him closer to me with the other, while the sound of recorded propellers swelled, and the audience began to cheer.

I finally saw Jax again as the last of the models left the stage and Phileas Fogg descended into the crowd to shake hands with various well-wishers. The corpse of the assassin James and I had chased lay slumped against the basket of Fogg's hot-air balloon. I wondered how long the actor would have to stay in that position. James and I had been told the gin palace was closing, and we had split up to find a bar that was still serving when I spotted Jax leaning against a pillar not far from the exit.

'How have you been getting on?' I asked her.

'Fucking … nightmare,' she said slowly, and took a slug from a bottle of water.

'Where did the urchin take you and Aaron?'

'She took us …' Jax shook her head, sighing deeply, and I could see that the gin and champagne had caught up with her. 'We went into this room where someone told our fortune.'

'That sounds intense,' I said. 'What did the fortune-teller say?'

'Eoin, she thought we were a couple – at least I think she did, because she basically told me how happy I'd be with the man in my life, and how my search was over. Happy, happy, happy,' she said, and rolled her eyes with enough force to knock her off balance.

'What did she tell Aaron?' I asked, as I steadied her.

'Pretty much the same thing – that his love line was unbroken, and was only deepening from here on. But then he made a joke about how his girlfriend wasn't here, and her face just dropped, and it got so embarrassing.'

'Where's he gone?'

'He said he needed to dash for a train – he left about ten minutes ago. Or maybe longer. I've been here for a while.'

She examined the bottle in her hand with faint surprise, as if she'd forgotten she was holding it, then took another gulp. I hated seeing her sad, but I couldn't help saying it: 'What the hell did you ask him for?'

Jax blinked at me in surprise, and stepped away from the pillar that had been supporting her. 'I'm sorry?'

'Look, we all make mistakes, the two of you had a drunken kiss on a Tube platform, but like … why did you ask him? It's like you wanted it to happen again. It's stupid.'

The look of surprise left Jax's face as she pursed her lips. 'Aaron and I are friends, Eoin.' She looked me up and down with a disdain I'd never seen on her face before. 'You're familiar with the concept of friends, aren't you? We're actually allowed to have more than one at a time. You should give it a try.'

She turned and walked towards the exit, stumbling as she went. I stayed where I was, winded. I felt a hand on my shoulder, and snapped my head round to tell the actor to piss off. But it was James, looking concerned.

'Everything okay?' he asked, keeping his hand on my shoulder. I leaned gently against it and shook my head.

'I – I have to catch up with Jax,' I said.

'Sure, I'll come.'

'No,' I said, and placed my hand on his arm. 'She's pretty upset. I think we need to talk.'

James tilted his head to one side, the gesture I loved to spot in him.

'I'm really sorry,' I said, 'I've had a great night, I just really need to—'

'Go on,' he said. 'Honestly, it's fine.' He smiled.

I squeezed his arm and drew him into me, kissing him deeply.

'Get a room, boys,' someone said, as they passed us. We broke apart.

'I'll text you,' I said to James, and sprinted for the door.

I ran out of the industrial estate, overtaking other guests on their way back to the station. A car beeped at me as I crossed the roundabout, and I spotted Jax in the distance. She was striding in the direction of the station, her pace slowed by the narrow hem of her dress.

'Jax,' I called, when I was a few metres away. She spun round, and I saw that she had been crying. I slowed down, unsure of what to say.

'Don't you fucking judge me, Eoin. Don't you fucking dare. We're not all getting fucking … chased around a warehouse by a man who's clearly besotted with you, all while you mooch about pretending to be this poor abandoned boy, when Rich is clearly just—' She broke off, and shook her head.

'Clearly just what?' I asked, but Jax looked at her phone.

'My Uber's nearly here,' she said.

'What – Rich is clearly just sick of me?'

She turned away from me, staring at the road. I didn't know what else to say. I checked my phone. One message from Rich: *Hope you had a good night. See you tomorrow. x*

And one from James: *Good of you to see Jax home. Just as well, or I might have asked you to cycle over to my place.*

Jax's car pulled up, and she stepped into it without looking back at me. As it drove off, I replied to James. *Well, she's just got into a cab, so you can ask me now.*

And sure enough: *In that case… wanna come over to my place?*

I looked back in the direction of the industrial estate, and pictured James walking my way. The very idea made me grin. *Yes please*, I wrote.

Chapter Twenty-two

James was sitting on a low wall outside a red-brick church. He spotted me when I was still a long way down the road, and didn't seem to feel the need to adjust himself or pretend he was looking anywhere but at me. All he did was lean forward and jiggle his leg slightly, coiled and ready, like a tennis player at a change of ends. Somehow, even from a distance, I could tell he was grinning.

'Are we going to mass?' I asked, as I reached him and dismounted from my bike.

'Mass,' he echoed, drawing out the flat 'ah' sound I gave the word.

I locked the bike to a lamp-post and stood in front of him, arms crossed, feeling shy again: the kiss at the gin palace seemed a long time ago, and I didn't know how easy it would be to pick up where we'd left off. I was also a bit upset still: Jax's look when she told me I had no friends had been on a loop in my mind all the way from Leyton. How long had she been thinking that? Was I really just a burden to her, and to Rich?

James reached up and gently tapped my forearm. 'Uncross,' he said. 'You're blocking the energy.'

I scoffed, but dropped my arms to my sides. 'What energy?' I asked.

'That's better,' he said, ignoring the question, and reached up to my shirt collar. He tugged on it gently, and I leaned down to kiss him briefly on the lips. Jax's scorn seemed to melt and flow away. 'Do you want to come in?' he asked.

'Into your church?'

'Yeah,' he said, then added, 'I live here,' as if it was the most obvious thing in the world.

'Do you sleep in a confession box?' I asked.

'Not far off. It's a property-guardian thing. There are six of us.'

I stepped back to take in the church, noticing for the first time the building's shabbiness, the boarded-up front door and the branded signage warning prospective scavengers that it was occupied.

'Apparently there's a big dispute about restoring it,' James said, 'and how much of it can be salvaged, whatever. We reckon we've got another year at least.'

'Well,' I said, 'I'd love to see inside.'

'Sure,' James said, but he didn't move, just kept looking up at me from his seat on the wall. I forced myself not to cross my arms again.

'Everything okay?' I asked.

'Absolutely,' James said. 'I'm just a bit nervous.'

'Oh, for God's sake,' I said, refusing to believe that I could make someone like James nervous. 'Come on, stand up.'

'And I'm also just a bit turned on,' he added.

I laughed, and glanced around me for any late-night passers-by. 'I think you'll get away with it,' I said. 'And I promise I won't tell anyone you had a hard-on in public.'

'Fine,' he said. 'Eyes up, please.'

I looked skywards as he stood and adjusted himself, then stepped in to kiss him again. He bit down gently on my bottom lip, and I shivered. 'Come on,' I said again, 'I'm getting cold.'

James led me to a side door and into a kitchen area, which must once have been attached to the church's community centre. A large board still had a copper plate stamped with

'Parish Notices' stuck to the top of the frame. It was filled with photos, mostly done on a home printer, of the people who, I assumed, were the current inhabitants of the church. I recognised a few from my trawl through James's social media, including one of him in black and white, standing on what looked like a half-constructed theatre set.

'So is this like an artists' commune?' I asked.

'It's like a cheapskates' commune,' James said. 'The rent's pretty low, and we've got so much space.'

We left the kitchen and James pulled open a set of double doors with a flourish, showing me into a long corridor, the walls of which looked as if they were built of plywood. Peering up at the vaulted ceiling, I realised we were in the apse of the church, and on either side of us were temporary rooms that had been built where the pews would have been. A holy-water font stood to my right, topped by a goldfish bowl. I followed James to the far end of the makeshift corridor, which opened up into a larger space.

'We use the altar as the living room,' he said.

Light from the road outside entered through tall, ornate windows, illuminating five battered couches arranged around the sides of the altar in a horseshoe shape, roughly following the curve of the walls. An impressive projector sat on a table in the middle, propped up by a stack of magazines and free newspapers.

I guessed that, between the high ceilings and the temporary walls, sound would travel pretty easily, so I kept my voice low as I asked, 'Do you watch a lot of films together?'

James pointed back over my shoulder, where a screen was rolled up and bolted to the plywood wall. 'Every Sunday,' he said. 'We're midway through an Almodóvar retrospective. You should come,' he added.

'I'd love to,' I said, excited not so much by the films as by the idea of sharing a Sunday-night ritual with James.

I turned away and began walking around the edge of the altar, inspecting the barely discernible artwork hanging on the wall. I could sense that James had gone in the opposite direction, and took my time walking around the semicircle, enjoying the feeling of his gaze on the back of my head. We met in the middle of the altar, and stood at either end of the couch that would no doubt offer the best view of the projector screen.

'It's amazing,' I said. 'What's it like living with so many people, though?'

'I love it,' James said. 'Maybe not for ever, but it's nice being in a big dysfunctional family, and we get a new sibling every six months when a room changes hands.'

'Isn't that a bit much?' I asked.

James shrugged. 'I'm an only child,' he said, 'so it's nice for me to have a turn. Whereas you—'

'Whereas I,' I said, 'must have twelve brothers and sisters because I'm Irish.'

'No,' he said. 'I was going to say, whereas you are clearly the eldest child.'

'Wrong again,' I said. 'I'm the baby.'

'Really? You have that responsible-eldest-sibling vibe to you.'

'Shows what you know,' I said, and flopped onto the couch as if in celebration of correcting him. Unfortunately I underestimated how wrecked the springs were, so my attempt at showing off ended with a squawk as I was swallowed by the soft, yielding foam.

'Jesus,' I said, struggling to extricate myself. 'The thing would nearly eat you.' I clawed for the edge of the cushion, and managed to pull myself into a near-sitting position while James looked down at me.

'Yeah, that's the entry into Wonderland,' he said. 'I should have warned you, really.'

He offered me his hand, but instead of pulling me up, he let himself flop forward, knocking the air out of my lungs as he landed on top of me. I let out another squawk, worrying that we'd disturb his flatmates (housemates? churchmates?) with all the noise.

'Well,' James said, as I squirmed beneath him, 'we're stuck here now. Hey, look.' He pulled a grubby pound coin out from behind my head. 'There must be hundreds buried in here.'

I nodded, still too breathless to say anything.

'Here,' he said, somehow managing to wedge his arm beneath me and slide the coin into my back pocket. 'Consider it a gift.'

'I'll treasure it always,' I said to him. 'Now you can take your hand out of my pocket.'

'Fine.' He sighed, and tried to shift his weight to do so, but whether by accident or design, he slipped and landed on me again.

I started to laugh, trying to claw my way out, but between the weight of him and the couch's complete lack of resistance, I could barely breathe, let alone move. I somehow found the strength to roll on top of him, and when he reached for me, I grabbed his arm and pinned it to the cushion. His smile dropped, and I relaxed my grip on his arm, seeing if he would move it. Instead, I felt it press further into my hand, and he let the other drop. We stayed like that for a moment, and then I started to undo the buttons on his shirt, keeping his arm pinned as I did so. My right knee had sunk so low to the floor that I could feel the wooden frame of the couch through a thin layer of material.

'Wait,' said James, as I moved to the third button. 'Can we do this in my room?'

'Of course,' I said, and gracelessly rolled off him, hitting the floor with a thump.

★

We had been in James's room (which, disappointingly, did not have a confession box in it) for a while when I noticed a look of concern pass over his face. He was lying on the far more spacious and supportive surface of his bed, and I was running my hands across the soft curve of his belly when his eyes closed in a wince.

'What is it?' I asked.

He kept his eyes screwed shut and shook his head.

'Come on,' I said, 'what's wrong?'

Ever since I had felt him relax while I pinned his arm down on the couch, I had been trying out variations on this, wanting to see what he liked, and I wondered if I had done something wrong.

'I don't suppose,' he said, opening one eye, 'you have a condom with you?'

I laughed with relief. 'You're joking, right?'

'I meant to buy some. I ran out.'

'When?'

'Last week.'

'Well, sorry, pal,' I said, 'it so happens I didn't bring any with me to see Phileas Fogg.' I rolled over and looked up at the plywood ceiling, where I noticed a wire hanging like a washing line, connecting the overhead light to a power source in a corner of the room. James propped himself up on one elbow and looked at me.

'Are you on PrEP?' he asked.

'I'm not.'

'Me neither,' he said, and rolled onto his back. 'Sorry, has that killed the mood?'

'Not so much that as the face you made,' I said.

'What face?'

'Like you'd been caught with your hand in the cookie jar.'

James flipped over and buried his head in the pillow. He gave a muffled groan of frustration, the kind I'd hear when he made the wrong coffee.

'Oh, come on,' I said. 'We can still have fun, can't we?'

He shook his head, his face still in the pillow.

'So are you going to stay face down for the night?'

He nodded.

'Aren't you afraid of suffocating?'

He shrugged.

'Fine,' I said, and climbed on top of him. 'Well, I can head home if you'd prefer?'

I bent to kiss his neck, just as he shook his head sharply, bumping the back of his skull off my cheekbone.

'Ow!'

'What?' he asked, his voice still muffled by the pillow.

'I bit the inside of my cheek.'

'Sorry,' he said.

'I'm sure you are,' I said. 'Feckin' eejit.'

He started laughing into the pillow then, and kept laughing as I kissed him just beneath his ear lobe, then moved my lips to the nape of his neck and continued down his spine. I could feel his body shaking with laughter as I went, and I wondered if he could feel the smile on my lips.

Chapter Twenty-three

I came out of the wrong exit at Piccadilly Circus, as usual, and was greeted by the sound of a busker murdering Ed Sheeran. I spotted Rich at the corner of Shaftesbury Avenue while I waited for the lights to change. He glanced up from his phone and raised one hand in greeting before returning his gaze to the screen. When I reached him, he gave me an absent-minded squeeze around the shoulders, still typing something with his other hand.

'What's up?' I asked.

'Work,' he said. 'Sorry, there's a safeguarding meeting tomorrow, and the room we booked is …' He trailed off, tapping away while I looked around Piccadilly Circus. I avoided this place when I could, repelled by the hordes of tourists and the dystopian screens glaring down at us all. But after the weird conversation in bed the other night, Rich had suggested we reset things by having a date night, just the two of us, and that merited going somewhere a bit further afield.

'Thank God it's dried up,' I said, while Rich typed. 'It was really lashing earlier.'

'Mmm. Sorry, I'm listening.'

'I mean, I know we're going to the cinema, but still.'

'Done.' He put the phone away and looked up at the darkening sky, blinking. 'Yeah, the kids were going crazy because they didn't get any playtime outdoors.'

'That reminds me,' I said. 'I was wondering, do kids still play with the wind?'

'Play with the wind?'

I tried to demonstrate what I meant, but it was difficult without having a real wind to lean into, and I got shoved by a commuter as I spread out my arms in the way I had the previous evening.

'Most kids tend to play with other kids rather than the wind,' Rich said. 'Shall we go and get the tickets?'

As we stood in the queue at the cinema, I found myself looking closely at Rich, trying to see if some subtle change had come over his appearance that I hadn't noticed. There was something odd about how he looked to me.

'Did you have a haircut?' I asked, cutting off what he was saying about his first visit to the new school.

'No,' he said, running his hand through his hair. 'Well, about a week ago, I suppose. Why?'

'No, nothing, sorry. What were you saying about the principal?'

That was it, I thought, as he explained how cold his new boss had seemed. His hairline had receded and I hadn't noticed. The haircut just highlighted the change. I examined Rich more closely. For years I'd felt like I was attuned to every part of him, that nothing about him escaped my notice. What else had I missed?

'Are you okay?' he asked.

'Sure. Are you?'

'You looked miles away.'

'No, I've been listening. That's bizarre behaviour on her part. Do you think she may have just wanted to check that you knew who was boss?'

'Maybe.' He looked at me for a moment. I smiled and gave him a wink. 'How's the café?' he asked. 'Still no word from Rebecca?'

'Nope. I have a funny feeling I may be looking for a new job soon.'

'Why?'

I considered going into the missing money, and the near-constant sense of dread I was carrying around.

'Ah, it's just a feeling,' I said instead. 'I'm probably worrying about nothing.'

Why wasn't I telling him? Rich and I shared everything. But then again, I thought, that wasn't quite right. I shared everything with Rich, while Rich sometimes went through all kinds of things without telling me. His mum had been in hospital for four weeks the previous year, and I only found out when I texted her to ask if she had any ideas for Rich's birthday present. And now I wasn't telling him everything either. I could feel the ellipses in my stories, the gaps in what I said when he asked what I had been up to since I'd last seen him.

'I forgot to ask,' Rich said, as we turned away from the ticket seller. 'How was Jax's event?'

I thought through the version of the night I could tell him. Thank God for the Phileas Fogg assassination plot, I thought. By the time I'd explained that, the film would be starting.

'I sort of saw the twist coming, didn't you?' Rich said, as the lights came up.

'No,' I said, 'I honestly didn't.' I pulled on my jacket and patted the pockets.

'Lost something?'

'No.'

'It looked like you were missing something.'

'I always check my pockets when I'm leaving somewhere. Haven't you ever noticed?'

'No.' Rich frowned. 'Sorry.'

'That's okay, it's just something I always do.' I told myself to snap out of it and stop being irritable.

'Do you want to go for a drink?' Rich asked, as we left the cinema.

'Would you like to?'

'Yeah, let's go for one,' he said, and led the way across the road and into a pub at the edge of Soho.

After being snippy about the pocket thing, I felt like I should make up for it by complimenting him on spotting the twist. After a few minutes of talking about the clues he'd noticed, as well as how brilliant the cast were and what an icon in the making one woman in particular was, I felt like we were back on track. And then Rich, still smiling at a joke I'd made, looked out of the window, rapped his knuckles on the table between us and said: 'I've been thinking.'

'You have?' I asked, unsure I was ready for whatever new suggestion he might have.

Rich, perhaps inspired by the more suspenseful moments of the espionage thriller we had just watched, took a long, slow sip of his drink before going on.

'I'm not sure about this whole ... open-relationship thing,' he said eventually.

My concern was replaced by bafflement. What had brought about this change of heart? And why would he mention it now rather than on Saturday, when he was passing me the delousing ointment?

'What's changed?' I asked him.

Rather than answering straight away, Rich reached over to a nearby table for a beer mat and, in that sleek, ordered way of his, lifted my glass and slid the cardboard circle beneath it.

'You tell me,' he said, as he replaced my glass.

In the moment of panic that followed, I was somehow convinced that Rich not only knew I had gone home with James the previous night, but was privy to feelings I hadn't even processed yet. The question before the movie had been a test, and now my evasive answering would be exposed.

'Nothing's changed,' I said, and then, thinking of how we had spoken about his fling with the barman, I added, 'I mean, we're still sort of adjusting to it, right?'

Rich pulled his unhappy-clown face while he considered this, and I took a large gulp of my beer, hoping it would at least calm my nerves.

'Don't you feel a bit … distant?' he asked.

'How do you mean?'

'I mean, I don't know if you look forward much to seeing me at the moment,' he said, 'or if you're that bothered when you don't.'

Maybe it was the half-pint of beer I'd just swallowed, but I was beginning to feel a bit steadier. I felt fairly sure Rich didn't know any more than I'd told him about last night.

'Well,' I said to him, 'we're both quite busy just now.'

'We barely spoke last week.'

'That's because I thought you were angry with me!' I said, my voice louder than I'd intended. 'Remember?'

'I remember,' said Rich, dropping his voice so low that I had to lean in to hear him, 'but I've been thinking about that too. If you thought I was angry with you, why didn't you text me?'

'I did,' I said, thinking of the grovelling message I'd sent straight after my attempted hook-up with the northern Freddie Mercury. 'And you said you knew I was sorry. How many messages did you want?'

'There was a time,' Rich said, 'when you'd have been reaching out more.'

This was probably true. In the early days of seeing each other, I'd have to force myself not to message too many times between visits to see Rich in Maidstone. If I succeeded in limiting my texts, I'd allow myself to switch to Facebook Messenger and send an extra update that way, telling myself that spreading it across platforms made it look less weird. If we ever had a tiff or I felt I'd done something wrong, the number of messages would probably increase as well.

'Well, I'm sorry, but that was a while ago at this stage,' I said. 'I'm probably not besotted with you the way I was when I moved here.'

That came out harsher than I'd meant it to, and Rich's face fell. Instinctively, I leaned across the table and took his hand. He was usually the one who did this kind of thing. I'd always been wary of public displays of affection, partly because of my fear of being shouted at and partly because showy couples made me cringe.

'I love you,' I said, 'but I don't love you the way a twenty-two-year-old would.'

He nodded slowly. 'That makes sense,' he said. 'So, what about it? Do you think we should be exclusive again?'

I looked across the pub as I considered this, and spotted the bartender sneak a few wasabi peas out of a jar and into her mouth, eyes watering in delight as she crunched down on them. I turned back to Rich, who was waiting for my reply. 'I'm not sure that's the right question,' I said.

'What do you mean?'

'It's not the most important question about our relationship right now. Like, we've been with each other for all this time, and it doesn't feel as if we're even close to moving in together.'

'Do you want to move in together?'

'Do you?' I asked, starting to feel I was playing emotional table tennis.

'I thought we both liked our own space,' Rich said.

You mean you like your own space, I thought, *and when my first house share ended, I didn't want you to think I was depending on you for a home.* I stayed silent, interested to see if he'd say anything else.

'Also,' he said eventually, 'I might be looking to buy in a few years, so …'

He licked his lips, seeming unsure what the end of that sentence could be.

'Well, there you go,' I said. 'Don't you think I should know that? If you want to buy somewhere? If you … I don't know, want a dog?'

'You don't like dogs.'

'But *you do*. And that's what I mean. Aren't we supposed to be a team? Shouldn't we be talking about this kind of stuff, rather than silly things like sex with other people?'

Rich frowned, seeming surprised to hear me talk about the open relationship like that. I was surprised myself.

'I can't say I was thrilled when you brought up the whole open thing,' I went on, 'but at least I knew it was something you wanted. A lot of the time I'm in the dark, I don't know what you want, and if we don't know what each other wants, well …'

It was my turn to trail off. One end to that sentence, I thought, was that if Rich and I didn't know what each other wanted, we shouldn't be together. But the idea of a world where Rich and I weren't together was frightening. Not sad, I realised, but truly frightening. I looked at Rich, clinging to the sight of him, the lines in his face and the shape of him, like a lifebuoy. From his expression, he seemed to be feeling the same fear.

'I don't want to lose you,' he said.

That's not the same as wanting to be with me, I wanted to say. It's not the same as wanting to marry me or move in together. But the fact that we'd even voiced the possibility of breaking up had rattled me far more than any argument could, and I didn't want to push it any further, scared of what would happen if I did. My hand was still resting on his, and I gave it a squeeze.

'I'd like to be exclusive again,' Rich said. 'Would that be okay with you?'

I kept my eyes on our hands as I thought about what this meant. Stability, commitment, a return to normality: everything I wanted. The thought of James crossed my mind, but I blinked hard, determined not to let it linger. 'Of course that's okay,' I said, looking up and giving Rich a small smile.

He stretched across the table to kiss me, but it was too wide, so he had to come round to my side, hunkering down and resting one hand on my knee as he leaned in.

Chapter Twenty-four

I looked around the café for something else to do. We had closed over an hour ago, and everyone else was gone. The till was balanced, the floor was clean and I had even done an honest-to-God temperature check, but I still wasn't ready to leave. Outside the empty café was the rest of my life, and even though this place wasn't exactly a haven, the longer I stayed busy in there, the longer I could put off thinking about the corner I had backed myself into.

Waking up beside Rich that morning, I had resolved to tell James as soon as possible that I was in an exclusive relationship again. Maybe if I brought it up casually, he would respond in kind. Maybe the night we had spent together really wasn't a big deal to him, and assigning it a significance he didn't share would just make things unnecessarily awkward. No, better to remark on it like a change in the weather. The sun was out, and now it's raining. I was at liberty to sleep with you, but now I'm not. No harm no foul, and now we could get back to being mates. Maybe I could even join James at one of those movie nights. Maybe in time James and I could be great friends. Yes, I had thought on my way to work, it would be fine. I just needed to get it out of the way.

And yet the moment to break the news just hadn't come. I got to the café a bit before my shift was due to start, in the hope I could mention it then, but the queue was almost out of the door and the dishwasher was misbehaving. By the time we sorted that out and got through the morning's dirty crockery, it was time for Billy to take a break, which would have been the perfect time to talk if Al hadn't arrived for an inspection and a never-ending discussion of dress codes (Al being of the opinion that we were far too casual in our appearance, and should adopt a uniform similar to Costa's), and on it went, until it was mid-afternoon and James was asking if he could leave a little early. I was down in the storeroom at the time, searching for some medium-sized takeaway cups in the funeral pyre of boxes.

'Go for it,' I said, feeling relieved that I'd have to wait until tomorrow to tell him. I turned back to the boxes, but then he was beside me, turning my face to his, kissing me gently.

'Sorry,' he said. 'Been thinking of doing that all day.'

'No problem,' I muttered, feeling my face grow warm. I didn't want to admit I'd been thinking the same thing, which might have been another reason I hadn't brought up the situation with Rich. James winked, and clattered back up the stairs.

Reliving this moment on my own after closing, my earlier hopes of a smooth return to friendship seemed a little naive.

Finally, I accepted that there was nothing else to polish or scrub, and wondered what I could do to distract myself. I didn't want to be alone, but I wasn't sure I could face Rich, and neither Jax nor I had messaged the other since the fashion event. I missed her, and was ready to apologise for what I'd said about her decision to invite Aaron, but I didn't want to ring her just because I needed company and advice. Clearly I'd been asking too much of her for a while now.

I tried to think of someone I could invite for a drink at such short notice, but came up with a blank. On impulse, I called Ciara, who sounded a little alarmed when she answered.

'Everything all right?' she asked, clearly worried that we had lost one or both of our parents in a car accident, though in that scenario she would definitely have been the one calling me.

'All good,' I said, acting as if this was something I did all the time. 'I was just calling to say hi.'

'Oh, right,' she said, sounding relieved not to hear that we were orphans.

'How's Sláinte?' I asked.

'She's … uh, she's grand. She's getting better at chasing balls anyway, and she's not whining so much in the night.'

'Are you walking her this evening?'

'Yeah.' Ciara still sounded vaguely wary. 'Why?'

'I could join you,' I said. 'For the walk. You know, just if you … if you don't mind.' Why, I asked myself, was it such agony to suggest I meet my sister for a stroll?

'Oh, my God, of course,' she said. The tone of startled happiness in her voice made me ashamed that I was calling her as a last resort, but I tried not to dwell on it, and arranged a meeting time outside Clapham Common station.

Mark was working late, so Ciara and I walked towards the common with only Sláinte for company as the darkness crept in.

Maybe it was because we were out of practice, but in the past few years, Ciara and I had taken to speaking in a strangely formal way whenever we were on our own. Passing the skate park, we asked each other about work and our respective partners as if we were in-laws meeting at a funeral. It was only when Sláinte ran off to play with the members of an open-air HIIT class that conversation eased up a bit. In fact, Sláinte played a blinder, doing something cute or exasperating every few minutes until Ciara and I were finally talking like human beings.

'Do you think she'll adjust to Dublin when you move home?' I asked.

'Ah, she'll be grand,' Ciara said. 'Sure one park is as good as another for a dog.'

'I wonder if she'll bark with an English accent,' I said. I was so happy to be thinking of something beside myself that I barely heard Ciara's next question.

'What?'

'I said, I don't suppose you'd think of moving back to Dublin yourself?'

I laughed. 'I'm not sure Rich would be delighted about that.'

'I'm sure he could find a job over there.'

'He's only just got a new one here. Anyway,' I said, 'why do you ask?'

Ciara didn't answer straight away. She bounced the tennis ball she'd been throwing, while Sláinte watched, quivering in anticipation. 'I'd find London lonely enough, if I'm honest,' she said, when she finally threw the ball and sent Sláinte scurrying off into the gloom. 'Like, I just thought it'd be worth mentioning to you. I know you've been here longer and you've probably got your own networks, but if I didn't have the girls from college over here, I'd be a bit lost.'

I wasn't aware that Ciara had a group of friends in London. Even when she was sharing her vulnerability, Ciara still managed to be a high-achiever. I'd been here six years, and the closest I had to a network were the people who'd made space for me in their lives because of my link to Rich or Jax. And even then there was a big gap between feeling tolerated and feeling accepted.

'Well, I'm glad you have people you know nearby,' I said. 'And you can always give me a buzz if you're at a loose end.'

I didn't think that was what Ciara was getting at, but I felt like moving the conversation on.

'I just wanted to mention it,' she said again. 'It'd be a different experience, I suppose, if you were back as an adult, and with Rich, and you'd maybe be able to reconnect with your gang from school or whatever.'

I wondered if Ciara had bumped into one of my friends from Dublin, and heard that I'd barely been in touch in the past couple of years. I used to contact them whenever I was back for Christmas, but recently I'd been finding it harder and harder to hear how well they were all getting on, the progress they were making in their lives, while I had nothing to report besides the fact that Rich was well.

'And I know you came over here as soon as you finished college,' Ciara continued, 'but no one would think you were ... whatever ... coming back with your tail between your legs or anything, if you were to come home.'

I considered her use of the word 'home', weighing up if that was still what I felt Dublin was. It must be, because I surely wouldn't use the word to describe London. A pair of joggers overtook us, chatting breathlessly in unmistakably Irish accents.

'Listen to that,' I said lightly. 'Sure we could be in Dublin now.'

Ciara laughed, and went to extricate Sláinte from a tussle with another puppy that was getting a bit snappy.

'Do you want to come back for dinner?' she asked, clipping the lead onto Sláinte's collar. 'Mark should be home by now, and I'm sure he'd love to see you.'

'Yeah,' I said, 'if that's okay?'

On our way back, Sláinte decided she'd had enough of walking, so I carried her, surprised by just how intense her body heat was, even through my jacket.

'How does Mark find London?' I asked. 'Does he know people over here?'

'Well, don't take this the wrong way, but Mark's actually a bit like you,' Ciara said. 'He's pretty happy being a lone wolf.'

I was surprised to hear Ciara describe Mark as a loner, but even more surprised that she thought of me that way. I liked my own company, but I wasn't some kind of hermit, was I?

'But, yeah, I have a feeling he'll be happy once we're home,' Ciara went on. 'I think he mainly agreed to come over because I fancied it.'

Sláinte twitched a little in my arms, her eyes closed, seeming on the edge of sleep. I thought again about Ciara's suggestion of Rich finding work in Dublin.

'When did you decide Mark was the one?' I asked, surprising myself as well as Ciara, who gave a short whoop of laughter that woke Sláinte up.

'I'd say around about the time he proposed,' she said. 'It's the kind of thing that really helps make your mind up.'

'But before that,' I insisted, feeling that since I'd started, I might as well follow through, 'there must have been a point when you knew you were in it for the long haul.'

Ciara and Mark had been together since they were both doing the Leaving Cert, and in my mind, they had been like a rock formation ever since, solid and eternal. This was probably what made me so harsh in my attitude to Mark: I knew I was stuck with him. But surely Ciara and Mark had changed since they were eighteen, and if they hadn't, didn't they want to? When had they decided they weren't going to evolve out of each other?

'Honestly I don't know,' Ciara said, 'though …' She laughed again, softer this time, and shook her head. 'At the end of first year in college, I was completely feckin' stressed out about exams – first-year exams, what was I like? – and Mark was already finished, or maybe he wasn't and he just wasn't thinking of them, but either way, one evening he was meant to be going on a night out with his class, and I called him in a bit of a state, and he just came to the library and sat next to me instead.'

Ciara had slowed down as she spoke, and now came to a complete stop. 'I know he can be a bit of a dose when he wants to be, but he's forever doing that sort of thing for me. He drops what he's doing and comes, even if it's just so he can be there. Anyway, when the library closed and they kicked us out, we went for a drink and I told him I loved him.'

After a second she started walking again.

'What about you? When did you know Rich was the one?'

I didn't have an answer. I used to, I thought. The answer used to be, the first time I met him. That moment he waved at me across a smoking area, like he'd always known me. 'You're right,' I said instead. 'It's hard to put a date on it, isn't it?'

Ciara nodded, and we walked on, getting closer to the flat, where Mark would be waiting to kiss Ciara and shake my hand and play with Sláinte and tell me what he thought of the Leinster squad. I'd nod and laugh and fawn over the dog with the others, and maybe the answer to Ciara's question, to my own, would drop into my head when I wasn't even thinking of it.

Chapter Twenty-five

In the weak light of the morning, I could make out a large figure leaning against the front door of the Quarter Turn. His arms were crossed and his head was lowered, but it was clear that he was awake, and not just some drunk sheltering from the rain. I cycled past him and locked my bike to a lamp-post fifty metres from the café. Whoever this was, I didn't want to deal with him while removing a helmet and digging in my pocket for keys.

The man lifted himself up from his slouch as I approached.

'Morning,' I called, attempting some casual cheerfulness. 'I'm afraid we don't open for another half an hour.'

'Don't care,' he said, 'I came to collect some money.' He towered over me. He had the flattened nose of a boxer, paired with the cauliflower ears of a rugby player who thought scrum caps were for fairies.

'Okay,' I said. 'Who did you want … um, that is, what was it in connection to?' My voice sounded high and fluttery.

'Don't worry about it,' he said. 'You just open up. You got the keys?'

'No,' I said, putting the hand clutching them into my pocket.

'What you got there?'

'My bike keys,' I said. 'I just locked it up. I'm actually just waiting for the owner to arrive.'

This situation was definitely above my pay grade. Covering for my absentee boss by lying to a brick shithouse merited more than the London living wage.

'Mate, open the fucking door.'

'Listen, I actually don't have the keys,' I began, but then, oddly, I found I was lying on my back, and my nose was throbbing as though it had just been punched. In fact—

'Hey!' I heard someone yell from down the road. 'What the fuck are you doing?'

He *had* punched me in the nose! From nearby came the sound of a heavy weight slamming into the steel shutter. I opened my eyes to see Hugo launching himself at the giant, hurling what I assumed was abuse at him in Polish as he did so. A car slowed and honked, and a few people on the other side of the road started shouting. The heavy obviously decided it wasn't worth hanging around any longer and strode off down the residential street, away from the main road.

'Crazy bastard,' said Hugo, and turned back to look down at me. 'What the fuck, man?'

He held out a hand and helped me up. My nose felt about five times its normal size, and was streaming like a tap. I put one hand to it and came away with a streak of snot and blood. My eyes were watering, but I didn't feel dizzy or anything, just stunned.

Hugo was asking me who my attacker was.

'I don't know.'

'What do you mean, you don't know? He punched you in the fucking face,' he said, as if only one's nearest and dearest could do something so intimate.

'I don't know, Hugo,' I said, 'but I think it might be something to do with Rebecca.'

'Well, open the fucking door,' he said, seemingly unfazed by body-checking a heavyweight boxer. 'I'm gonna be way behind on my prep. Fucking arsehole.'

*

When Billy arrived, I told him he'd be doing all the serving today. I didn't want to deal with the customers, the inevitable questions and expressions of concern. I just wanted to get through the day, then figure out whether I had enough money saved up to quit and find another job.

Billy glanced over his shoulder at me occasionally and made sympathetic noises, but I ignored him. If I wasn't making coffee, I was cleaning. Even last week, I would have been wondering how the man who had assaulted me was connected to Rebecca and the café, but now I found I just didn't care. The throbbing in my nose was all I could focus on. There was something almost soothing about the gentle pulse of pain. Once or twice my nose started bleeding, so I tore up a napkin and shoved bits of it up my nostrils.

I looked at my reflection in the stainless-steel surface of the coffee machine. The skin around my eyes had darkened, and my nose was an angry red. I gave it a careful prod, wondering if it was broken. It didn't look bent out of shape, but the swelling would probably hide that.

'Jesus Christ!'

I glanced up to see James standing at the counter. 'You should see the other guy,' I said, with a smile. I'd been waiting all morning, maybe all my life, to say that.

'I would imagine his fist is mighty swollen,' James said, joining me behind the coffee machine. 'What the fuck happened?'

I explained my early-morning altercation.

'Why are you even working?' he asked.

'I didn't want to leave Billy in the lurch.'

Billy, who had been eavesdropping, said, 'Thanks, Eoin.'

'You're welcome Billy. Could you clear that table?'

As Billy grabbed a tray, James said, 'Can I speak to you downstairs?'

We went to the office.

'You okay?' James asked.

I shook my head, and he stepped towards me. His hug was firm, but brief. Considering how affectionate he'd been in bed only a few nights ago, how tender his kiss had been yesterday, it felt strange, this fraternal clap on the back. I couldn't take in the sweet, comforting scent of his detergent, because the napkin up my nose meant I had to breathe through my mouth.

'What's up?' I asked.

James took a deep breath. 'I got a job.'

I blinked, confused.

'Job?'

'A play. It's small, but it's paid, and pretty good.'

'Amazing. I didn't even know you'd auditioned for a play.'

'Yeah,' he said, 'I don't really mention auditions unless I have to – stops people asking how they went. Anyway, I hope it doesn't mess you about too much. Here, I mean.'

I finally caught up with him. He was leaving. 'Oh,' I said. 'Of course. No, no, it'll be fine. I mean, how long will we be open anyway?'

'Well, not being funny, but if you're getting attacked it might be time to move on.'

I nodded. I hated being told what to do.

'Not telling you what to do or anything,' James added. 'And listen, I'll hopefully see you anyway. I mean, I'd like to see you.'

He smiled. Now was the time, I realised.

'One second,' I said, and ran upstairs to check that Billy had everything under control. As I looked around the café, I saw Hugo placing two plates of food on a nearby table, the sight of which made me wonder if I had been punched into an alternate universe.

'I'll be back in a few minutes,' I told him. He shrugged.

'Sorry,' I said, returning to James.

'We can deal with wages and all that another day,' he said.

'Oh, yeah, I suppose we can,' I said. I wondered if he was looking particularly attractive because he was happy about the acting job, or whether it was just in my head.

'I'd like to see you too,' I said. I badly wanted to grab him, kiss him, even though it would probably result in a fresh nosebleed. 'But,' I continued, 'Rich and I have decided to be exclusive again.'

James flinched, the way he did whenever he brushed against the hot surface of the coffee machine. 'When did you decide this?' he asked.

'The other night. Night before last.'

He nodded slowly, looking away from me. 'Timing's good, then,' he said. 'Might have been awkward.'

As if to prove this was true, an agonising silence fell on us.

'I'd still like to see you,' I said. 'You know, as friends. I had an amazing time the other evening.'

'So did I,' he said, 'but it's probably better we don't see each other for a while.' He started climbing the stairs.

'James, wait,' I said, following him.

'Sorry, Eoin.' He turned on the step and looked back down at me. 'I told you, when I fall, I fall hard. And I don't need to fall for you.'

And then he was gone. I sat on the bottom step and closed my eyes, focusing on the steady beat of pain in my nose, until it blocked out everything else.

Chapter Twenty-six

'Wake Trevor up, would you?' I said to Billy, as I swallowed a pair of ibuprofen tablets. The café was almost empty. 'I'll close the coffee machine.'

I pulled out the cleaning products and the brush for scrubbing the group heads, while Billy hovered around Trevor, clearly unsure of how to rouse him. Eventually he gave him a light tap on the shoulder, then jumped back as Trevor started awake.

'Time to go,' Trevor announced, to the empty room.

'Yeah,' said Billy, creeping forward to clear the table. 'Oh,' he added, 'I haven't seen you since the epic comeback on Wednesday.'

I listened to the pair discuss the agony and ecstasy of losing a three–nil lead, arguing the merits of a player whose name I just about recognised.

Trevor stood and dusted off his yellow corduroy jacket. 'Your friend's been in the wars, hasn't he?' he said to Billy, nodding in my direction. 'I remember getting a cricket ball to the nose once,' he continued, as he left, 'and I was wearing glasses at the time. Last I saw of those. Or anything for the next few days.'

I watched Trevor through the window as he wandered off.

'Are you a Spurs fan?' I asked Billy.

'Yeah,' he said. 'Why?'

'No reason,' I said, 'though I think I have an old programme at home you might like.'

'Oh, nice one. I collect those.'

I measured out a tiny hill of detergent, twisted the portafilter into the group head and started the flow of water.

'You can head home, Billy,' I said. 'It shouldn't take me
long to close.'

'Nah, I'll stick around.'

'Really, go on.'

Billy blushed and scrunched his nose. 'I … Hugo said …'
He crossed and uncrossed his arms, clearly nervous.

'What did Hugo say?'

Having silently run his own orders for the day, the chef
had shuffled off around three, assuring us as usual that it had
been a crazy lunchtime, while shrugging off my attempt to
thank him for his earlier heroics.

'He just said to stick around until you're done,' said Billy.
'In case that guy comes back.'

The idea of the waif-like Billy taking on that morning's
assailant was touching and hilarious in equal parts. 'Fine,' I
said. 'Well, you can at least sit down. Do you want a sandwich?' I threw him a bag containing a leftover toastie.

'Oh, wow! Thanks, Eoin.'

'You're welcome,' I said, as he tore open the bag. 'It fell on
the floor.'

Billy didn't even blink before taking a gigantic bite.

I was restocking the milk fridge when I heard a loud banging on the door. I poked my head above the counter, fully
expecting the giant to be back for more. I was barely any happier to see that it was Uncle Al. I was surprised it had taken
him this long to get wind of the morning's incident.

'What happened to his set of keys?' I asked.

'I'd better let him in,' Billy said, scrunching up the brown
bag.

I sighed, gave the fridge a quick wipe with a cloth, and stood. Al marched past Billy, walked up to the counter and silently scrutinised me for a moment. He seemed unsurprised by my appearance. 'What did he look like?' he asked.

'He was … big,' I told him. Jax was right: I was no good at descriptions.

'Yeah,' Al said. 'I know the guy.'

He sighed, and ran his hand over the strands of hair plastered to his scalp. He looked tired, and I found myself wondering just how old he was. After a moment he opened his eyes and slapped his hand on the counter. 'Right,' he said, 'time to close.'

'We were just finishing,' I said.

'Nah, nah, I've had enough of this shit. Bill, go and pull down the shutter. You,' he said, pointing a thick finger at me, 'get the money out of the safe.'

When I came back upstairs with the contents of the safe in a bag, Al was laying out the day's takings and card receipts across the counter. Billy stood beside him.

'Al,' I said, 'I was actually just about to do the cash-up.'

He ignored this and said, 'What's your rent?'

'My rent in my house?'

Al nodded, and when I told him, he grabbed the bag off me and counted out the figure in twenty-pound notes. He stopped, holding a fifty up to the light. 'Shouldn't be taking these,' he said. 'Lotta fakes floating around.'

'That was me,' said Billy, who was hovering near the counter. 'I didn't know.'

Al grunted, and tossed the fifty in Billy's direction. 'Right,' he said to me. 'Count that. Month's rent, gives you plenty of time to find a new place to work. Can't say fairer than that.'

Was I being fired for getting punched? I'd been planning on leaving, but not like this.

'Al,' I said, feeling thoroughly fed up, 'I don't want to find another job and, anyway, isn't it up to Rebecca—'

'Rebecca's a fucking junkie,' said Al, his voice breaking.

'Al,' said Billy, with a sharpness I had never heard him use before. 'Don't say that word.'

Al waved him away, but took a breath and said, 'Rebecca has a problem.'

I looked at Billy, not quite believing that I was seeking clarity from him. Billy nodded. 'She does,' he said.

I looked at the stack of notes in my hand and wondered what I'd been missing. Every now and then Rebecca would refer to wild times she'd had in the past, but usually it was with the distance of an ageing rocker looking back at the nineties, shaking their head with fond nostalgia. It had never crossed my mind that she might have struggled with addiction, or be struggling with it still.

Al was chewing his top lip, his face contorted in what looked like a mixture of anger and sorrow. I found myself reframing the arguments between him and Rebecca, who always painted him as an interfering old codger.

'So, where has she been?' I asked, but the answer came to me immediately.

The missing money. Jax and I hadn't thought to put Rebecca on the list of suspects. Had we learned nothing from Jessica Fletcher? This explained why cash-ups had become much more accurate after we changed the hiding place for the key to the safe: Rebecca must have been sneaking notes out of the float while the café was closed. I pictured her creeping down the stairs the night I was out with James, searching for the key or maybe something to sell, and instead coming across the bag of cash, just sitting there on the desk, like a miracle, left for her by the useful idiot she'd put in charge. I felt, not for the first time that day, stupid and found out and cheated all at once.

'She was doing well,' said Al, 'really well with the café, and you kept it going okay for a while, but this is getting dangerous, fucking dealers hanging around and punching staff. I mean look at your fucking face.'

I raised a hand to my busted nose and tapped it lightly. The skin was stretched tight, as if my swelling was wrapped in cling-film.

'Here,' Al said, and counted out another five twenty-pound notes. 'You're a good chap, consider it a bonus.'

'James,' I said, 'he hasn't been paid. And Hugo.' None of this was making sense.

'I'll deal with Hugo,' Al said. 'What do we owe that James?'

I looked around the café. Other than my house, I had spent more time here than anywhere else in the past couple of years. I couldn't wrap my head around the idea that I wouldn't be coming back, that the coffee zombies would bang on a door that wouldn't open. And Trevor, where would he go? I didn't even know his second name.

'Come on, fella,' said Al, as my eyes began to water. 'We haven't got all day.'

I assured Billy that I'd be fine unlocking my bike on my own. He patted my shoulder as Al locked the door of the Quarter Turn. 'See you soon, yeah?' he said.

'Sure,' I replied, though if there was one thing I'd learned since moving to London, it was that people you met, whether it was in a job or a house share, tended to disappear whenever that context was removed. Then again, maybe that was just me. I wondered if other people put the effort into keeping up with former colleagues and flatmates, or if everyone here was essentially a loner.

'Tell James I said hi,' added Billy. 'Maybe the three of us could hang out.'

For various reasons, I doubted very much that this would happen. If it did, it would probably consist of Billy prattling on merrily while James glowered across the table at me. I nodded all the same.

Billy and Al wandered off while I made my way back to the lamp-post where my bike was locked. I pulled out my phone as I reached the bike and considered who I wanted to message. Cars rolled slowly towards the traffic lights, drivers tapping steering wheels as they endured the rush hour. A tall man in pastel pink shorts walked past with his three dogs, seemingly impervious to the autumn breeze.

I wrote a draft of a message to Jax, then deleted it. I felt she deserved to know the answer to the café mystery, but I still wasn't sure she wanted to hear from me.

I put the phone away, unlocked the bike and clipped on my helmet. I hesitated, then took out the phone again. After a few minutes, and several drafts, I messaged James.

So the QT is closing. That really was good timing on your part. I have some wages for you. Let me know if there's a day/time that suits to drop them round.

I wanted him to suggest I bring them over now. I wanted to talk to him, even if I didn't know what to say. I shivered in the evening air, and looked around me for a few more minutes, phone in hand, waiting for the buzz of an incoming message. It was something I didn't know about James yet: how long did he usually take to reply to messages? I would hear back from Jax within two minutes or three days later, with very little middle ground. Rich left long gaps in work hours, and was consistently prompt in the evenings. Ciara was alarmingly quick to reply at all hours of the day and night. I imagined myself asking James his opinion on this, and what he might have to say about slow repliers.

I searched my jacket pocket for my bike lights. If he hasn't replied by the time I have these on and flashing, I thought, I'll just head home. I fiddled around with the lights for as long as I could, taking out the batteries and popping them back in, until I accepted that James wasn't going to reply, and got on the bike.

This was just a crush, I told myself as I cycled. James was completely charming, and I'd met him at a very specific moment, when Rich and I were experimenting with our relationship and I was feeling vulnerable, as well as stressed out by work and maybe a bit giddy at the prospect of being with other men. This feeling would pass.

And yet I wasn't sure when my memory of the night we'd had together would fade. I couldn't help thinking even now of how good James had felt, how soft yet firm he was when I held him. He had laughed when I described him afterwards as dense, and with good reason: it didn't sound like much of a compliment, but that was the best word I could come up with.

I stopped at a corner where one residential street crossed another, and caught my breath. The exertion was making my nose bleed again. I held a tissue to it and checked my phone. Still no reply from James, but a message from Rich.

Hey, how was your day?

Only okay, I replied. *Can I come over?*

Everything okay? x

Yeah, I just really want to see you. x

Then I wrote: *I got punched in the nose at the cafe. Feeling pretty awful.*

What?! Do you want me to come and meet you?

No, I'm okay, I'm on the bike, I just think I want to see you.

My phone finally buzzed as I stepped off the bike outside Rich's house. It had taken James about twenty-five minutes to reply. No Ciara, I thought, but not bad.

Sure, he wrote. *Would bank transfer be okay? Can send you the details.*

Well, I thought, that made things clear at least. James definitely didn't want to see me. I'd lost him, along with my job and maybe my best friend as well. Better hold on to what I had.

I knocked on the door, and laughed at the look of horror on Rich's face when he opened it.

'Who did it?' he asked. 'Was it a customer?'

I laughed again, this time at the image of Trevor socking me in the face. I kept laughing as Rich led me inside, and I only stopped when he held a smashed-up bag of ice to my nose. Then I just stood still and waited for him to take care of me.

Chapter Twenty-seven

Just after midday I had a second shower, in the hope that by doing so, I could kick-start my first Monday of unemployment. Standing in it just made my eyelids droop, though, so I turned down the heat until I was gasping in the cold water and a little more awake.

The weekend had felt a bit of a blur. I had slept for about ten hours at Rich's house on Friday night, waking up briefly to swallow some painkillers. I found myself yawning again by mid-afternoon the next day as Rich and I followed the Parkland Walk from Alexandra Palace over to Highgate Wood. Rich was going to a gig with Andrew in the evening, and offered to find me a ticket, but the very idea of loud noise and crowds was enough to make my nose start bleeding again, so I insisted that he went without me. At Rich's suggestion, we went to Margate for the day on Sunday, and at one point, he disappeared from the pub we were in and came back with a copy of *Orlando*, saying he'd noticed I hadn't had a book in my hand for days. I wasn't in the mood to read it, but I found it comforting just to hold.

On the train back from Margate, I told Rich I'd go to mine and try to get a good run at the week. He had been very kind all weekend, but somehow this was making me feel worse. Several times he had reassured me that the Quarter Turn closing was for the best, when my mind had really been on James and how I'd messed things up.

On Sunday evening, I resolved to be up and looking for a job by 8 a.m. I actually overslept and ended up opening my laptop around ten thirty. I then spent half an hour watching James's appearance on *Doctors*, pausing it whenever I spotted a familiar smile or frown cross his face, before telling myself to snap out of it. By midday I had finished half an application, and the weight of the rest of the day began to press down on my head so hard that I couldn't concentrate.

I returned to my room after the second shower and picked up my phone, hoping that by some miracle I would find an email with a job offer in my inbox, preferably one that included an attachment telling me what to do with the rest of my life. No such email had arrived, and I flopped down on the bed, still in my towel, idly swiping through news sites. Maybe, I thought, a nap would be the real kick-start to the day that I was looking for.

But then I noticed the Grindr icon. I had forgotten to delete it when Rich and I agreed to be exclusive again. I knew I should do so now, but instead of dragging the icon to the trash can, I gave it a tap. Just to say goodbye, I told myself.

There was something comforting about the faces, the muscles, the memes and the landscapes that filled the screen, the profile names uncomplicated and to the point. I eyed the green dots hungrily, suddenly feeling wide awake and eager to meet someone else with nothing to do on a Monday lunchtime. As I scrolled up and down the grid, a message came through.

Hey

Hey, I replied.

Up 2 much?

I stared at it and thought about going on. This was probably wrong, I thought, but how wrong? If I didn't meet the guy, how much worse was it than looking up porn, or flirting with someone at a bus stop? And maybe this guy would just be looking for a friend, even if his 'Looking For' preference was set to 'Right Now'. It could be fun just to chat.

Clearly I spent too long thinking about it though, because eventually I got another message.

Asshole.

And with that my correspondent gave up and went offline, taking his green dot with him.

I deleted the app, dropped the phone and turned over into the pillow. This was bad stuff, I thought. I needed something else to get me through the day. I wanted a job, but I also wanted to find someone to talk to without relying completely on either my boyfriend or a hook-up app. I hoisted myself off the bed and started towelling off, wondering how on earth I could find that.

In their brightly coloured Lycra, stretched tight across six-packs and beer bellies alike, the cyclists resembled a flock of exotic birds gathering beneath a grey sky and preparing to fly south for the winter. Dressed as I was in a grey hoody and a pair of O'Neills tracksuit bottoms I had acquired around the age of sixteen, I worried I might be the pigeon that was about to be rejected by the flock.

I had spent an hour or so searching online for a cycling club I could join, but most of the ones I found seemed to go on massive expeditions into Hertfordshire. Attracted by the more achievable prospect of a few laps around Regent's Park, I had signed up for a trial evening with the High Rollers, whose website included a banner notice clarifying that the use of the word 'High' should not be taken as an endorsement of drug-taking in amateur cycling, which they strongly opposed. Watching the Rollers taking swigs of cloudy drinks and gulping the odd pill, I wondered if the disclaimer had been protesting too much.

Between the gear and the supplements, I was feeling intimidated before I got within twenty metres of the group and slowed down so much that my bike started to wobble. I finally merged with the flock in an awkward shuffle, my feet either side of the crossbar. A few members were inspecting someone's new toy, and the clip-clop of their cleats on the footpath was a further reminder that, despite cycling everywhere and every day, I still wasn't much of a cyclist. I felt much as I had on my night out with James and his friends in the club, before I got too drunk to notice: that I should be feeling a sense of belonging, but that somehow I was still an outsider, unfamiliar with my own tribe's language and uniform.

'You look lost,' said one man, as I climbed off my bike and looked around for some sign of a leader.

'I usually do,' I said, and smiled. When he stared back at me, I asked, 'Is this the High Rollers?'

'We are,' he said, removing his goggles and polishing them on his jersey, which, I read, he had earned by scaling La Marmotte. I assumed this was a very steep mountain, or possibly a range of very steep mountains.

'Have you ridden before?' he asked, fiddling with the strap of the goggles.

'No, I just pushed this all the way here,' I said, indicating my bike. 'But I'm sure I'll get the hang of it.'

'On Monday evenings, we do laps of the park,' he went on, as if I hadn't answered. 'It's interval training, and some of us do reach very high speeds, so just be careful on bends.'

'How many laps?' I asked.

'Listen, mate, just do what you can,' he said, clearly bored of this conversation. He turned away from me, tugged his shorts down his bulging thighs and yelled, 'Okay, guys, saddle up!'

I clambered back onto my bike as the flock took off, the snap of cleats into pedals echoing like gunfire. A car beeped at the group as they fanned out across the road, and five or six of the cyclists near the back raised their middle fingers in response.

I started pedalling, and as I caught up with the back of the peloton, I experienced a brief moment of hope: perhaps, on my trusty old bike, I would not only keep up with these preening, Lycra-clad imposters, but outstrip them all, so that afterwards, in the pub (I assumed there would be a drink to celebrate my performance), I would be surrounded by new friends and admirers, who would ask how on earth I had reached such mighty speeds.

Fantasies like this one had always been how I spent my time on the bike. Cycling home from a party would be the occasion to replay and extensively rewrite an argument I'd lost. The ride back from a disastrous exam would allow me to compose the perfect answer to the perfect essay question, which I would have handed in, if it weren't for that pesky Department of Education. My bike was where I played out the version of my life which was filled with triumph, smiles and simplicity.

So it was particularly sickening when, after a few minutes, I saw my fantasy literally vanish before my eyes, as the group stretched out, picked up speed and disappeared around a bend in the road. Even when they came into sight again, I could see that I was never going to catch up with them. In fact, it seemed very possible that I would actually be overtaken by the cyclists at the front of the group while I was still on my first lap. Rather than watch my nemesis glide past me, I resolved to take the next exit I came to, pedal slowly home and pretend that my pathetic attempt at finding a group had never happened.

'Fast, aren't they?' I heard someone say over my shoulder.

I looked around. The not-quite-Liverpudlian had shaved off the Freddie Mercury moustache I had nicknamed him for, and looked about five years younger as a consequence. He was dressed more appropriately than I was, in a long-sleeved black-and-white jersey and regular sports shorts, but his bike looked more suited to a hillside scramble than the Olympic-speed training session we had apparently signed up for.

'You joined a sports club,' I said, dropping back so we were level.

The Cyclist-Formerly-Known-As-Freddie-Mercury nodded, breathing heavily. I heard an unhealthy crunch as he switched gears.

'I joined … three,' he panted. 'Hurt my ankle … frisbee.'

'Ouch,' I said. 'But otherwise, fun?'

He nodded and tried to pick up speed, calf muscles straining as he willed the heavy bike forward. I dropped behind him to show my support and pretended I couldn't hear his gasps.

'Listen,' I called, after another minute of this, 'I could do with a breather. Do you feel like a break?'

We pulled over and wheeled our bikes to a bench. While Freddie put his head between his legs, lifting it occasionally to slug on a bottle of purple energy drink, I watched the first wave of High Rollers pass, happy that we had saved ourselves the humiliation of being lapped. The guy in the finisher's jersey didn't even notice us: his eyes were fixed on the road ahead while he bellowed something about air miles to the cyclist just behind him.

'I'll bet you a tenner they break red lights,' I said to Freddie. 'And yell at pedestrians using zebra crossings.'

He nodded and took another gulp of his drink.

'I see you shaved off the 'tache,' I added.

He nodded again. 'I just thought better safe than sorry, you know,' he said. 'After your message.'

It took me a moment to catch up with him.

'Well,' I said, 'you stopped short of shaving your head, at least.'

Freddie gave a short laugh at this, but no more. He had got his breath back, so I guessed there was more to his silence than a simple lack of oxygen.

'I'm sorry again, by the way,' I said. 'About the crabs, I mean.'

Freddie flinched at the word, but shook his head and said, 'Nah, you're all right. It happens, doesn't it? Just a bit … embarrassing all round, isn't it?'

'It shouldn't be,' I said. 'But, yeah, it is. I hope you didn't have to send any awkward texts because of it.'

He shook his head again, eyes on his trainers, his mouth bunched tight, looking like the striker who's missed an open goal. 'No danger there, mate,' he said. 'Between one thing and another, I've not been back on that particular horse.'

Oh, Christ, I thought, I've broken him. However good or bad the open relationship might have felt to me and Rich, it had apparently wreaked havoc on anyone who came into contact with it.

'Only a matter of time, though,' I said, returning to the bland, bright tone I'd used in his room. 'The baby-faced look suits you.'

Freddie glanced at me sceptically. 'You like it?' he asked.

'Sure,' I said, and gave what I hoped was an encouraging smile. 'You look great like that.'

I smiled again, and then he came for me with the sudden movement of a monster in a horror movie, mouth open and tongue leading the way like a prehensile limb. 'Woah!' I said, leaning back and out of his reach. 'Fuck's sake, Freddie.'

He looked at me in utter confusion. I'd never actually asked for his real name, and if I had, I'd forgotten it.

'I mean, sorry,' I went on quickly. 'Sorry, my fault, I think I was giving off mixed signals. I just … Actually, my boyfriend and are exclusive again, so …' I held up my hands, fingers spread, in a gesture suggesting this was something non-negotiable and out of my control.

'Oh, right,' he said, still looking confused and defeated. 'I did think I hadn't seen you online recently.'

How often had he been checking? 'Yeah,' I said. 'We thought we'd be happier just the two of us.'

'Well, no wonder, after the time you'd had with me,' Freddie said.

This self-pity was getting a bit much, so I said, 'Should we get back on the bikes and have another go?'

Just then, another flurry of cyclists passed by, reminding me of how little I wanted to join them again.

'Or,' I went on, 'we're actually not that far from the canal. We could walk the bikes along there and get a drink in Camden?'

I was surprised to hear myself suggest this, but I didn't want to part from Freddie a second time with both of us feeling sad and a bit pathetic.

'I didn't realise there even was a canal,' Freddie said. 'Sounds nice.'

'It's great,' I said. 'It's actually one of my favourite parts of London. I found it by accident when I first moved here. I got lost, and then I was just in the middle of all this green and water, and it was such a relief. I always feel a lot calmer when I'm walking along the canal.'

'Do you do it often, then?' Freddie asked.

'No,' I said. 'Barely ever.'

I could feel him looking at me while I thought about what I'd just said. What else did I neglect to do in London, choosing instead to approach the city as a never-ending obstacle course I just had to survive?

'You're in your head a lot,' he said.

I opened my mouth to tell him he hardly knew me, then thought again. 'Yeah,' I said instead.

'Me too. And I've this theory, right, that London's no good if you're in your head. Like, there's too much of it, and too many people, and then they end up in your head, and you start to worry that you can't manage them all, you know?'

I stayed silent.

'Anyway, I'd be up for having a look at this canal,' Freddie said. 'And I promise I won't jump you again.'

'You'd better not,' I said, as I stood up, 'or you and that bike are going in the water.'

We were drinking pints out of plastic cups at Camden Lock when Freddie asked me how I knew his name. It wasn't anywhere on his profile, and he didn't think he'd ever told me.

I said it must have been a lucky guess.

Chapter Twenty-eight

I took a sip of the latte I'd been offered while I waited for my interview, and winced. I'd never been one of those people who talked about coffee like wine, sniffing for notes of sandalwood and freshly mown hay in their Americano, but I knew burned espresso, and this tasted like something that had been brewed in a fire pit.

I looked round the café, which was about twice the size of the Quarter Turn, low-ceilinged and gloomy even mid-afternoon, the kind of place suited to dark, rainy days when the gloom would become cosy and the steamed-up windows would hide the outside world. Various lampshades and ornaments hung from the ceiling, and I noticed a shelf in one corner, stacked with what looked like a fairly ancient selection of magazines. The coffee machine looked new, and I wondered how my latte had gone so wrong with such impressive equipment.

'All right,' the owner said, as she sank into the seat opposite me and shoved on a crooked pair of glasses. 'So it's …' She squinted at my CV. 'Ee-oh-een?'

'Eoin,' I said, 'like a throw-in.'

She looked up so sharply that her glasses flew off her head and onto the floor. From behind the coffee machine came the screams of overstretched milk.

'A throw-in,' I repeated, over the wailing, as the owner stooped to pick up her glasses, 'like in football, you know?'

The owner sighed as the milk's screams subsided. 'Okay, Eoin-like-a-throw-in-like-in-football,' she said, leaving her glasses on the table between us, 'I'm Inès, like Inès, and I'm looking for a new manager. Reckon you can do it?'

'Well,' I said, 'that's basically what I've just been doing.'

'Basically?'

I nodded and reached for my cup, then reconsidered. I didn't want Inès to see me grimacing at the taste of her coffee.

'I was managing a café while the owner was absent due to ill health,' I said, hoping this wouldn't prompt too many questions, 'and that involved doing rotas, stock-taking, managing relationships with other staff members ' – poorly, I added in my head – 'so I suppose that would put me in a pretty good position to ... to work somewhere new in a ... in that capacity,' I finished, annoyed that I'd let myself run out of steam. This had happened in every interview I'd ever sat in my life.

'Okay,' Inès said, 'any particular achievements in your time there?'

I had foiled an attempted burglary by getting punched in the face, I thought, but out loud I said, 'I created a cleaning rota.'

This was both unimpressive and a lie, but I reasoned that the day I'd asked James to clean the high shelves might qualify as the start of a rota. It had certainly been the start of something: that was the day I'd realised he didn't hate me, the first time he'd made me laugh. I wondered, for the hundredth time this week, if he'd texted me, and felt myself itching to look at my phone.

'So what would you bring to the job?' Inès asked.

Oh, God, the one question I should have anticipated, and I had nothing. I looked over Inès's shoulder, hoping that inspiration might be written on the wall, but all I could see was a brown-and-cream-coloured canvas with different varieties of coffee printed on it. *Mocha* was stamped in bold capitals, while *Cappuccino* was scrawled in loopy cursive, a love heart dotting the *i*. It was so hideous that I felt my eyes widen in horror. I turned back to Inès. 'I want to run a café,' I said.

Inès laughed. 'Oh, I don't know if you do, my love.'

'I do,' I said, 'so I suppose what I'd bring is the desire to learn, and figure out how you actually turn a profit – like, I wouldn't just be going through the motions, because if I know how to manage this place well, I'll know how to manage my place well.'

Inès picked up her glasses and started tapping them on the table. 'I wouldn't like any of my staff to be going through the motions, as you say,' she said.

'No, but plenty of people do.'

'Okay. Anything more tangible you'd be bringing, though?'

I could see she was unconvinced. Feck it, I thought.

'How new is your machine?' I asked.

'Couple of months,' she said, looking over at it. A faint smile played on her lips.

'Well, the coffee out of it isn't as good as it could be.'

'No?' she asked, her smile gone.

'I think this café is great,' I said. 'I love the fact that it doesn't have exposed bulbs and brickwork.'

Inès gave an affirmative grunt, clearly proud of not having such pretensions.

'But,' I went on, 'I don't see the point in spending the price of a car on a new machine if you're going to serve terrible coffee. I trained people in my last job, and they picked it up really fast.'

I thought again of James, the gentle flick of his wrist as he finished pouring the milk, and felt a small pulse of sadness pass through me. When would that stop happening?

'Anything else?' Inès asked.

'Yes,' I said. 'I'd get rid of that.'

I pointed at the canvas. Inès looked over her shoulder and turned back to me, her glasses askew. 'I have never had a decent coffee in a place with word-art on the wall,' I said.

'What would you replace it with?' Inès asked.

'Anything,' I said. 'Just get rid of it.'

I waited for her to tell me to piss off, but after a moment she threw back her head and laughed in a way that reminded me of Hugo's self-generated and inexhaustible mirth.

'All right, Mr Eoin-like-a-throw-in,' she said, 'I'm going to give your last employer a call and see what they say ... Al, is it?'

I nodded, unsure how that call would go. I hadn't told Al I was putting him on my CV as a referee, but Rebecca was hardly an option, and who else was I going to put there?

'And what do you reckon? Think you can make a few coffees while you're here?'

'Sure,' I said, 'I'd be happy to.'

Inès looked back at the canvas and started laughing again. 'My ex bought that. She said it made the place look dead classy.'

'Well, I respectfully disagree,' I said, grabbing my coffee as I stood up, looking forward to pouring it down the sink.

Chapter Twenty-nine

I stood in front of the drinks fridge and tried to decide which sparkling wine would be best. Actual Champagne seemed a bit excessive, but I didn't want to celebrate with a reduced bottle of own-brand fizz either. I finally settled on one around the fifteen-pound mark. It had a medal on the label, which I thought I might peel off and stick to my chest later in the evening. At the checkout, I wanted the cashier to ask what the occasion was, just so I could explain that at the end of my afternoon in the café, Inès had offered me the job, and had even permitted me to snap the word-art canvas over my knee in my first act as manager. Rich was coming to my house anyway, and this seemed like the perfect way to mark a fresh start and even a deferred celebration of our sort-of anniversary.

As I unlocked the bike and pedalled off, I began to practise how I would tell Rich about the perfect trial shift, in which I'd picked up the order system Inès was running, got on well with the other staff members, and had a moment of good luck when one of the pregnancy-yoga ladies happened to come in, saying how pleased she was to see me in another café. And, according to Inès, Uncle Al had described me on the phone as a stand-up lad, not like some of the Irish he'd known in his time. It was about as good a reference as I could have asked for, and went some way to justifying the hours and the headaches, not to mention the punch in the nose, that I'd endured over the past month at the Quarter Turn.

This would be a great winter, I told myself, as I wheeled around the corner of my road. As manager, I'd be in charge of rotas, and once I was settled into it, I could make sure I had time off to spend with Rich, do the things he wanted, see his friends more often and be on time when I did. With a salary, I could actually plan holidays and even think about savings, or a house. Well, maybe a house was a stretch, but at least we could talk about the idea without making Rich laugh.

I'd only just closed the front door behind me when Rich knocked.

'I was waving from down the road,' he said, as I opened it, 'but you were in a world of your own.'

'I have good news,' I said, almost knocking him off his feet as I pulled him inside and closed the door.

'Oh, yeah?'

'Basically, the trial shift went well, and I've been offered the job!'

With a flourish, I produced the bottle from my bag, holding it up for him as a kind of proof.

'Oh,' Rich said, and turned to shut the door behind him. 'Is this another café?'

'Yeah,' I said. 'I told you about it during the week. It's the management position.'

Rich frowned and shook his head slightly. Hadn't I told him?

'Sorry,' I said, 'I didn't even say hello just now, I was pretty excited.' I felt ashamed of my exuberance now. The highlights of my shift floated out of my head, and I became self-conscious, standing there with the bottle. I put it down on the couch and wiped the condensation off my hand.

'That's cool,' Rich said, dropping his bag and sitting down. 'It's just, it sounded like you might be looking to do something a bit more ambitious, now that you're clear of the other place.'

'This is ambitious,' I said. 'I've never managed anywhere before.'

'Yeah, sure,' he said, and picked up the bottle of sparkling wine, worrying the edge of the label with his thumbnail. 'Why do you want to manage a café, though? You're capable of doing more.'

'Well,' I said slowly, 'this is what I like.'

'Really? All you ever did was complain about the Quarter Turn.'

I wondered if this was true. Sure, I often vented about the Quarter Turn, but that was because I wanted to make him laugh. If I talked about the details of it, or about the fun it could be, Rich always seemed to glaze over, so naturally I had focused on the contrarians, the complainers, the nightmare moments.

'And honestly,' he went on, 'I was looking forward to not having to hear about coffee and customers for a while. I mean …' He gave me the sympathetic but piercing look I imagined he usually reserved for misbehaving students. 'Is this what you moved to London for?' he asked.

I took a step back. I felt as if someone had shoved me hard in the chest, knocking the air out of my lungs. The room felt tipped off balance. Rich must have spotted this because, after watching me for a moment, he dropped the disappoint-ed-teacher look. 'You're a bit pale,' he said. 'Are you okay?'

'I moved to London for you,' I whispered. The sheer confusion that spread across his face was frightening. I knew I had concealed the fact when we were first seeing each other, worried that it would scare him off, but hadn't he realised in the years since? 'Why else would I be here?' I asked.

Rich gave a nervous laugh. 'You were moving here any-way,' he said, 'I wasn't even in London when you came over.'

He held eye contact with me as he spoke. Either he was committing to a bald-faced lie, or he really believed what he was saying. I turned and walked away as Rich stood up from the couch. I could feel that my breath was shallow and catching in my throat. I circled the room, gripped by the terrifying thought that, for six years now, I'd been making every choice in my life based on one person, who didn't even realise what I was doing. I'd left the friends I had in Dublin, and once I was here I'd stepped away from almost every offer of friendship and community because I wanted to leave what time I had outside work for Rich. And why? Clearly other men were attracted to me, and one was maybe more than just attracted, so why had I changed my life for this one?

Rich was beside me now, rubbing my back. 'What's the matter, Eoin?'

I waited until I was breathing more steadily before I answered. 'I met someone,' I said at last.

Rich dropped his hand and leaned against the wall beside me. How odd, I thought, how awkward it felt, the two of us huddled in the corner of the living room while we spoke.

'Was it someone you met while we were open?' Rich asked.

'Yeah,' I said. Then, deciding I'd had enough of half-truths and omissions, I added, 'It was James, the guy who was working in the café.'

Rich shut his eyes tight and groaned in frustration. 'Do you want to be with him instead?' he asked, after a moment.

I was tempted to say that I didn't, or that it was over now anyway, but I stopped myself. Say what you really mean, I thought. 'I don't know,' I said. 'But I feel different.'

'What do you mean?'

'I feel like he saw me in a different way. Or maybe,' I went on, 'when I was with him, I saw myself in a different way. I didn't feel like I was in the wrong job, or not good enough, or not sorted enough. I didn't feel odd or quiet. I didn't feel like

I was pretending. I just felt like me. I felt more like me with him than I do with you.'

This, I realised, was an awful thing to say, but as soon as the words were out of my mouth, I felt far calmer. I took a deep breath, stood up straight and lifted my T-shirt to wipe my eyes.

Rich looked winded. 'I never meant to make you feel like you weren't good enough,' he said. 'How did I...?'

But as I watched him search for the words, I realised that it was over. I was breaking up with Rich. This was the last time I'd be in the same room with him as a boyfriend. I had the strange sensation of floating on the ceiling and looking down at us both, the way survivors of near-death experiences describe watching doctors trying to resuscitate them when their heart has stopped. And, much like in a near-death experience, I felt somewhat serene as I looked down. There was no need to debate or recriminate any more. 'It's not your fault,' I said. 'I just think I gave up a bit of me by being with you. And I sort of want it back.'

'Want what back?'

I shrugged. 'Just ... my own life, I guess. Thinking for myself, and about myself, and what I really want.'

'We can change,' said Rich. He sounded panicked now. 'I can give you more space ...'

'Would you ever move to Dublin?' I asked. 'If that was what I wanted?'

I expected him to answer as he usually did, by asking me if I wanted to move to Dublin, but instead, he simply thought for a minute, his eyes drifting by the books on my shelf, as if looking for an answer on their spines. 'No,' he said in the end.

We stood there in silence for another few minutes, and I tried to think if I had anything else to say. Curiously, though, my thoughts began to drift, and I found myself thinking of the new café, running through the names of the colleagues

I'd met earlier. A song lyric passed through my head, and then the question of whether Champagne had always been sparkling, and if not, when had they come up with that? And then my thoughts alighted on James, and I began to wonder what would have happened if I had realised before now that he didn't just make me happy, he made me feel like me.

I looked at Rich, who had clearly just said something. 'I'm sorry,' I said, and was about to go on, when I realised I had nothing to go on to. 'I'm sorry,' I said again.

After Rich had gone, I sank into the couch and closed my eyes, feeling again as if I was floating in space, but with a more pronounced sense of vertigo than before.

I heard the creak of a floorboard, and looked up to see Polly, frozen in the kitchen doorway. She had one foot raised, and was clearly midway through tiptoeing past me.

'Oh, God,' she whispered, and I could see that she was pale and panicked-looking. 'I really didn't mean for that to happen. I was in there and I heard you come in and I didn't move and then it sounded fractious and so I stayed put and I'm so sorry.'

'Polly,' I said, 'I need a drink.'

I looked at the bottle of cheap sparkling wine wedged into the back of the cushion next to me. 'Would you share this with me?' I asked.

Polly nodded, went back into the kitchen and re-emerged with two jam jars we used as tumblers.

'Congratulations on your new job,' she said, and patted me gently on the back when I bent forward and rested my head in my hands. Then, as if reading my mind, she began tearing open the foil around the cork.

Polly had gone to the corner shop for a second bottle when I pulled out my phone and rang Jax.

She answered after one ring. 'Eoin.'

'I'm sorry,' I began.

'Shut up,' she said. 'What I said to you the other night was awful, and of course it's not true. You have all sorts of other friends – I mean you literally brought another friend to the event. I was just feeling … I don't know, I was embarrassed and maybe a bit jealous and I took it out on you, I think.'

The thought of Jax, confident, gregarious, creative Jax, feeling envy towards me was bizarre. Anyway, I thought, there wasn't much to be jealous of now.

'Well, to be honest,' I said, 'you're right. I don't have many friends. And that's why it hurt.'

I heard Jax sniff at the other end of the line.

'But that's not your fault,' I went on. 'I think I've maybe been a bit lost, or a bit scared, and I sort of need to put myself out there a bit more.'

'Maybe you could join a club,' said Jax, and then, when I started to laugh, 'What's so funny about that? I'm in the Weavers Society.'

'I'll consider it. But listen,' I said, 'dare I ask if anything has happened with Aaron?'

'He's engaged.'

'Oh, for fuck's sake.'

'Yeah.' Jax's voice drooped downwards as she spoke.

'When did you find out?' I asked.

'Couple of days ago. It was their anniversary, or someone's birthday, or something. Sheri in the office told me.'

I took the empty bottle to the kitchen, shook the dregs into the sink and dropped it into the recycling bin.

'I think I'm going to ask him for a talk,' Jax was saying. 'If I bump into him at lunch, I'm going to see if he wants to go for a drink.'

'Right,' I said cautiously. 'Is … is that definitely your plan, or would you like a second opinion?'

'Go on,' she said, though her tone suggested she was by no means sure she did.

'Don't look for him, don't suggest a drink, and if he approaches you, pretend you don't know him. He doesn't deserve you, or the time you're giving him.'

'But I need to know what he's thinking.'

'Why?'

'Because otherwise it's incomplete. I don't know whether he actually likes me or not, whether it means something.'

'But he can't tell you whether it means something or not.'

'He might.'

He won't, I thought. And you can't hang around waiting for someone else to give things meaning. To give you meaning.

'Well, it doesn't sound like it means much to him,' I said. 'It sounds more like someone having eleventh-hour nerves ahead of his proposal. I can't say it bodes well for his marriage, but it's sort of ...'

'Sort of not my business?' Jax suggested, sounding defeated.

'Maybe, yeah.'

'You're probably right,' she said. 'It just hurts a bit.'

I sighed and looked at my reflection in the kitchen window. 'I know what you mean,' I said.

'Is everything okay with you?' Jax asked.

'Not really, if I'm honest.'

'Oh, God, what can I do?'

I heard the sound of Polly's key in the front door. 'Come over,' I said to Jax, 'and bring booze.'

Chapter Thirty

'I had no idea you were gay,' Billy said. 'Fair play.'

He gave me a pat on the shoulder and smiled. Now that I had gone a month without having to make sure he didn't set fire to anything, I could appreciate how endearing Billy's good nature was.

'I'm not sure how you missed it,' I said. 'Didn't you ever hear me comment on attractive men in the café?'

'Yeah, probably I did,' Billy said, 'though I have a terrible memory. Anyway, commenting on people doesn't mean anything.' He looked around the pub, which was filling with people waiting for the play to start in the small theatre upstairs. 'That guy's good-looking,' he said, nodding towards the barman, 'and so is she,' he added, pointing at a nearby woman. She turned in our direction, frowning. Billy waved and the woman, caught off guard, waved back. Billy turned to me, smiling triumphantly. 'Does that make me bi?' he asked.

I turned to the bar, choosing not to pull on that particular thread. I had been weighing up whether I would drink tonight, but decided it wouldn't hurt.

I had asked Jax if she was free to come to James's play, but she had a date organised, her third in as many weeks. She was no longer paying attention to Aaron, who was apparently still smiling at her whenever he got the chance. I hadn't been sure if Billy would be interested in attending a fringe play about the Brothers Grimm, but when I got in touch he was delighted at the prospect of seeing James perform.

'So do you have a boyfriend?' Billy asked, as I tried to catch the handsome bartender's eye.

'I don't,' I said. I was still getting used to this idea, and saying it out loud felt surreal. 'We broke up about a month ago.'

'Oh, sorry, man. Had you been going out long?'

'Oh, five or six years,' I said, trying to shrug off a fifth of my life. It would become a smaller fraction as time went on, after all.

'What happened?' Billy asked.

I grinned at his guileless directness, and toyed with the idea of going into it all. 'We just drifted apart,' I said.

Billy nodded solemnly as I ordered a drink. 'You know,' he said, leaning into me conspiratorially, 'James is gay.'

'I do know that, Billy,' I said. 'Do you want a drink?'

'Oh, yeah, I'll have whatever you're having.'

A bell rang, and the crowd started shuffling towards the theatre entrance.

'Might be a bit soon, though,' Billy went on, 'for you to be thinking about other guys.'

'That's true,' I said, and handed him his pint. 'Shall we go in?'

The theatre was tiny, with two rows of chairs running the whole way round the stage. It smelt of warmed-up dust and herbal cigarettes. James was sitting in the middle of the stage, smoking and scribbling on a yellowed piece of paper. Seeing him, I felt a gentle jolt of adrenalin, and prayed that he wouldn't look up and see me before I'd had time to compose myself. When I booked the tickets for the show, I had imagined watching him from a safe distance, but I realised as I looked around that there would be nowhere to hide. I just prayed there wouldn't be any audience interaction.

'Oh, shoot,' Billy said, as some of his beer slopped out of the glass and onto the floor. A harried stage manager appeared with some blue roll and mopped it up.

'Ha, that blue roll takes me back,' Billy said, elbowing me so that some of my pint joined his on the floor. 'We needed a fair bit of that in the café, didn't we?'

He was speaking as if our days in the Quarter Turn had been a decade ago, rather than the previous month. I steered us towards a pair of seats in the second row, near the door we had come in. I wanted to be as far from the stage as possible, and close enough to the exit to flee if I really needed to.

'Speaking of the café, how's Rebecca getting on?' I asked Billy.

'She's okay,' Billy said. 'She's actually in rehab now.'

'Have you seen her?'

'No, no. Everything I hear is from my mum talking to Uncle Al. He sees her as often as he can.'

I was going to ask just what kind of relation Uncle Al was when the audience lights dimmed and James rose from where he had been writing.

The play was a two-hander, in which one of the Brothers Grimm is haunted by the ghost of his late brother, who makes him rewrite all the stories they collected together. James played the dead brother, and throughout the performance transformed himself into various characters from the fairytales. I didn't really see the point of the play, but it was worth it just to see James on stage, where that expansive, chaotic movement he showed in everyday life grounded an otherworldly character like the ghost. Mercifully, none of the show involved the audience, though at various points James looked in our direction, and I felt my face burn under his gaze. I kept thinking of the last time I'd seen him, and the night we'd spent together. Watching him now, illuminated and in his element, James seemed like a different person, unrelated to the one I'd felt laughing beneath me as I kissed his neck.

At the curtain call, Billy gave an appreciative whoop that drew James's attention. He briefly squinted and smiled in our direction as he bowed.

'That was amazing!' said Billy, as we filed out of the theatre. 'James is such a good actor. Do you think we'll be able to see him if we hang around?'

'I'd imagine so,' I said. 'It doesn't look like the kind of place with a separate exit for actors.' We lingered near the bar until James emerged from the theatre, smiling modestly at the huddle of people who surrounded him.

'Looks like he has a lot of fans,' said Billy. From the middle of his circle, James looked our way and waved. He started to move in our direction, but someone grabbed his arm, and he turned to greet them.

'Do you want another drink?' I asked Billy, steeling myself for my first interaction with James since I'd transferred him his wages.

'Nah, man, I'll have to go soon,' he said. 'I'm up early tomorrow.'

'Where are you working?'

'I got a job with the UN,' he said. I stared at him. 'It's a kind of graduate thing,' he added.

'Oh. Congratulations.'

'Yeah, it's crazy stuff,' he said, shaking his head. 'Can you imagine me at the UN?'

I couldn't, but then again, I had no idea what kind of person worked at the United Nations. Maybe Billy would fit right in. Maybe the world needed more cheerful daydreamers in positions of power and influence. Still, I was about to ask him if he was telling the truth when James broke from his group and came our way, smiling broadly. 'Thanks so much for coming,' he said.

'You were great,' said Billy, 'I can't believe all the voices you can do.'

'Yeah, it really is the funny-voice show,' said James, and turned to me. 'Thank God I didn't do an Irish one. I wouldn't be able to look you in the eye, Eoin.'

'I've heard your Irish accent,' I said. 'It really wasn't that bad.'

We chatted for another minute about the show, and then Billy gave James an update on the café, which was now being converted into a CBD retailer.

'Hugo's going to run it,' he said.

James laughed loudly, the sound of which, I realised, I'd missed more than anything.

'And how are you doing, Eoin?' he asked, throwing a quick glance over his shoulder. 'Sorry,' he added, 'that's my agent. She brought a casting director tonight so I've got to go and do some boring chat in a minute. How are you, though?'

'Grand,' I said, then figured I might as well be brazen. 'I was only saying to Billy, it's all change. I've a new job, newly single, everything's … yeah, different.'

I watched James's face as he nodded, trying to guess what he was thinking.

'What's the job?' he asked, after a moment.

'I got that manager job at the café in Crouch End,' I said. 'The one you suggested I apply for.'

'I knew you would,' James said. 'Considering you ran the Quarter Turn pretty much single-handedly, managing must be easy for you.'

Billy laughed. 'Single-handedly,' he repeated, amused by the absurdity of the idea.

'Ah, yeah,' I said, 'it's not so bad. And I've started this arrangement with the bookshop down the road, we're going to host book clubs for them, stock local-interest titles, that sort of thing.'

I shook my head and looked at the floor, conscious of how small this sounded, given that I'd just watched James on stage, doing the one thing he most wanted to do.

But James shook my shoulder and said, 'That's amazing. Sounds like you're making your mark.'

'Ah, yeah,' I muttered, struggling to find anything else to say. 'Sure, listen.'

James held my gaze for another moment, before saying, 'I'd better head back to these guys. But thanks again for coming.'

It was over. I had spent most of the past week deciding whether or not to come and then, once I had booked, wondering how it would be to see James again. And now it was barely an event, it was just a series of polite exchanges.

'See you guys soon,' James said. He gave my shoulder a squeeze. 'Keep in touch.'

He strode back to his agent, and as we made for the exit, I heard his laughter drifting across the pub.

Outside, I said goodbye to Billy, who was taking the Tube, and crossed to the bike rack opposite the pub. I wrapped up for the cycle home, thinking about James's parting words. 'Keep in touch.' That was the sound of being fobbed off. I had thought going to his show would be a chance to reconnect, maybe to start again. And he had just volleyed the ball back into my court.

'Fuck it,' I said out loud, and pushed off.

As I pedalled past Angel station, I cringed at how keen I must have seemed to James, showing up to his play after weeks of silence. But by the time I was on Upper Street, I found my thoughts had turned to the rest of the week. Tomorrow was another knitting evening at Jax's, where I was forcing myself to concentrate on my dropped stitches rather than my conversation skills. At the weekend, Freddie and I would be going for a slow cycle around some park or other, probably stopping for a coffee after ten minutes of exercise. Maybe, I thought, I would give Polly's door a knock when I got back to the house, which was feeling a lot less like a hostel since the two of us had got drunk on cheap Prosecco with Jax.

Breaking up with Rich had tipped my universe off balance. Most mornings, I woke up to find myself confronted by a wasted half-decade of my life, and at night, I would imagine the comforting shape of him next to me as I fell asleep. But more and more often, when I walked Sláinte with Ciara, or sat making plans for the café with Inès, I felt as if the world was finding a new axis, and I got a sense of what my life could be like with no one but myself to blame or thank for what it was.

But still, at the traffic lights at Highbury and Islington, I pulled out my phone to check. And still, when I saw that James had sent me a message, my heart leaped.

See you soon? x

I imagined him firing it off mid-conversation, barely looking at the screen as he nodded along with whatever his agent was saying.

The light turned green and I started pedalling again. I passed into Highbury Fields and dropped a gear as I climbed the gentle slope. The harder I pedalled, I thought, the sooner I'd be home, and then I could compose just the right reply. I'd suggest James come by the new café, and promise him a coffee on the house.

At the top of the hill I paused, one foot on the ground, watching my breath dissolve in the air. I stayed there for a few minutes, calculating how long it would take to get home, and how long it would take to get back to the pub. I considered how it might feel to arrive and find that James was gone. Disappointing, I reckoned, but nothing I couldn't handle. Then I thought of how James's face might look as he turned to see me, the way he'd tilt his head to one side, ready to hear what I had to say. I thought of how much I wanted to ask him, how much I wanted to tell.

Then I turned around, and started cycling back down the hill.

Acknowledgements

I'm deeply grateful to:

Melissa Nolan and Michael Peers, who offered such essential encouragement and insight on the earliest drafts of this book.

The Irish Writers Centre, particularly the team behind The Novel Fair.

Laura Williams, for believing in the book, and for being such a brilliant source of advice and perspective.

Lily Cooper, for invaluable guidance, creativity and enthusiasm.

The team at Hodder & Stoughton for all the work that went into this book.

RB Kelly, Nessa Matthews, Ruth Murphy, Katherine Jack, Guy Warren Thomas, Shazia Khawaja, Ana Kinsella and Jane Bradley, for the time and suggestions you gave me along the way.

My wonderful friends, especially Gareth Balai, Ben Cullen, Nick Murphy, Sarah Madigan, Jenny Walters, James Corrigan, Tom Syms, Sara Joyce, my amazing book club(s), and the gang at IML, for all your support while I was working on this.

My family, for all your love.